Par

Pandora's Box 3

An Anthology of
Erotic Writing by Women

edited by
KERRI SHARP

BLACK
lace

Black Lace novels are sexual fantasies.
In real life, make sure you practise safe sex.

First published in 1998 by
Black Lace
Thames Wharf Studios,
Rainville Road, London W6 9HT

Extracts from the following works:

Ménage	© Emma Holly
Unhallowed Rites	© Martine Marquand
Bonded	© Fleur Reynolds
The Hand of Amun	© Juliet Hastings
The Name of an Angel	© Laura Thornton
The Stranger	© Portia Da Costa
The Succubus	© Zoe le Verdier
Dangerous Consequences	© Pamela Rochford
Jasmine Blossoms	© Sylvie Ouellette

Short Stories:

Fetish Love	© Novella Foster
Fresh Meat	© Miranda Stephens
Flight of Fantasy	© Miranda Stephens
The Meeting	© Alice Rowan
Circles	© Gillian Martin

Illustrations © Insa Heiss 1998

Typeset by SetSystems Ltd, Saffron Walden, Essex
Printed and bound by Mackays of Chatham PLC

ISBN 0 352 33274 3

*All characters in this publication are fictitious and any resemblance
to real persons, living or dead, is purely coincidental.*

Contents

Introduction

*B*lack Lace books keep getting better. Five years into this revolutionary imprint and there's no shortage of great stories and new authors. The past year has brought a wealth of new talent to my attention. Expanding the list has meant that authors based in the US, and those who prefer to write short stories, have found an outlet for their work through us, and have provided some outstanding, fresh and innovative erotica. Due to the success of our anthologies and the *Sugar and Spice* collection of short stories, I'm looking to publish more books in this format. The short stories in this collection demonstrate how powerful and arousing concentrated fantasies can be.

We are also excited about our first non-fiction Black Lace book – *Women, Sex and Astrology*, published in June 1988 – which contains a unique erotic profile chart and allows you to discover how Venus and the asteroid Eros can work their sexual magic for you. It's like no other astrology book and is explicitly about sexual relationships. Next year we are publishing the long-awaited collection of our readers' sexual fantasies. I assure you they're hot!

I hope you enjoy reading *Pandora's Box 3*. As ever, it

was a difficult but delightful task selecting the extracts from the vast backlist we can now boast. Remember: others may have imitated us, but none can equal the diversity or the perversity!

Kerri Sharp
Black Lace Editor
February 1998

Ménage

Emma Holly

Ménage is a stunning debut erotic novel from talented American author Emma Holly. The writing is fresh and witty and the setting is contemporary. This extract is from the first chapter of the book, where Kate Winthrop discovers that her flatmates Sean and Joe are not all they seem. The three friends embark on a complex relationship: a kinky *ménage à trois* which pushes the boundaries of anything they've tried before. It's a warm and touching story of unconventional love in modern America.

Emma's other book for Black Lace is *Cooking Up a Storm*, which is set in a Cape Cod restaurant. Abby, the restaurant's owner, needs something to give her business a lift. The answer comes in the form of playboy-chef Storm, whose aphrodisiac menu brings people flocking to Abby's place. As in *Ménage*, Emma's characters feel like friends and, while the sex action is as hot as it can get, there is an underlying sense of warmth and humanity to the story. Emma lives in Massachusetts and has been nominated as erotic writer of the year.

Ménage

On the night it began, I bounded up the stairs to my two-hundred-year-old colonial town house in the heart of Philadelphia. The shiny green shutters gleamed against the brick as if winking in welcome. Despite the tree-lined seclusion of Society Hill, the cacophony of rush hour sang in my ears. I loved this reminder of the city's vitality. My body hummed with its energy. My heart pounded, strong and free. My skin tingled in the brisk autumn air and under it all, like a fruit ripening for harvest, my cunt warmed at the thought of the half-read erotic novel waiting by my bed.

Masturbation first, I thought, then dinner, then TV, then to bed with my smutty book.

Back then, nothing made me happier, or hornier, than a productive day at work – preferably a long one. Not only did it prove that, at thirty-three, I still had plenty of go in me; it proved I was as good a breadwinner as Tom – better, in fact, because I didn't have to be a lawyer to do it.

'First thing we do, let's get rid of all the lawyers.' Kicking off my Adidas, I tossed my keys on to the Queen Anne side table in the hall. My hair clip followed.

With a sigh of relief, I dug my fingers through my

sheep-thick curls and massaged my scalp. Heaven. I flicked on the lights. Apart from its usual creaks and groans, the old house was quiet. My lodgers must be out cruising the bars on South Street.

A thrill ran through me as I imagined the picture they'd make: one dark, one fair, both gorgeous and young, both fairly reeking with erotic possibilities. The connection between Sean and Joe was palpable. I could almost smell the sex on them, like animals in heat. Could some of that heat be for me, I wondered, or would they keep it all to themselves?

Pondering that very question, I smoothed my black riding jacket over the swell of my breasts. I loved the way the black velvet hugged my generous curves before nipping in at my waist. Paired with a snug pair of Levis, I knew the jacket bordered on obvious, but I wasn't one to hide my figure – not when I worked so hard to stay in fighting trim.

In any case, having two scrumptious young studs in the house tended to make me clothes-conscious. And body-conscious, I thought, peering up the narrow spindle-banister stairs to make certain I was alone.

No shadows moved on the landing. No Robert Cray Band growled seductively through the hall. I'd never heard Robert Cray before Sean and Joe moved in, but once I had I was hooked. That man really knew how to sing about love. I could have eaten him up just listening.

My sex melted like butter at the thought. I loved giving head, which probably kept my marriage together longer than anything else. Seventeen-year-olds simply don't do that sort of thing well.

Smirking to myself, I took the stairs two at a time.

Maybe I'd slip into Joe's room and borrow the CD. He wouldn't mind. Despite Sean's attempts to make me – and Joe, for that matter – believe he was one hundred per cent boy's boy-toy, I knew Joe was sweet on me. Sean had an early accountancy class, so every morning Joe and I ate breakfast alone. Lately I'd been coming down in my embroidered silk kimono. How he blushed if I bumped his leg under the table or bent to drag the frying pan out of the cabinet.

Of course, my derrière is one of my best features. Power walking will do that.

Anyway, most days Joe finished breakfast with a boner too big to let him stand. There he'd sit, a napkin draping his humped-up dick, a prisoner of my erotic torment – and his own shyness. Sometimes I'd press a goodbye kiss to his clean-shaven cheek for the sheer pleasure of watching that napkin jump.

Joe made me enjoy being a woman again.

Reaching the landing, I saw he'd left his door open. I caught a whiff of soap and Aramis, the purest aphrodisiac I knew. My palms tingled with excitement. I didn't intend to snoop, merely grab the music and go. Even so, my heart skipped at the prospect of having his private space all to myself. Who knew what I might stumble across?

As though it divined my thoughts, Joe's *Phantom of the Opera* poster glowered as I sauntered to the CD player. Robert Cray's *Strong Persuader* lay on top of the stack. Joe knew I liked the album, and knew I might wander in if he played it. I suspected he played it as often as he dared. I tossed the plastic case into the air, caught it neatly, then stopped in my tracks.

Joe's jockstrap hung from his bedpost. The white pouch sagged with the memory of its burden. I knew from our breakfast sessions that he was well-hung. Oh, yes, Joe was a six-foot, hard-as-a-board, twenty-three-year-old stud.

I fingered the sweat-dampened cotton. The mouth of my sex gave a little gasp and a trickle of warmth ran out.

This was too kinky. What the hell, though. Men liked women's lingerie. Why shouldn't I be aroused by a jockstrap? I brought the cotton to my nose and sniffed the combination of good clean sweat and young man's musk. Immediately, I felt an urge to keep the thing, to sleep with it under my pillow or press it between my thighs while I stroked myself to climax.

I told myself the urge was juvenile, not to mention thievish, but I shoved the underwear in my pocket and ignored my twinge of guilt. Worse, I continued my survey of his room. I touched the military crease at the bottom of his mattress, evidence of Joe's self-disciplined nature. It was a young man's bed, narrow, the sort a man could carry from his parents' house because he couldn't afford to buy something bigger. That bed made me think of raging, unrequited hormones, of jacking off with his big brother's *Playboy*, or waking up to sticky sheets.

God, I was crazy to even consider messing around with someone that young.

Annoyed with myself for more reasons than I could name, I turned to gaze at my reflection in the small, square mirror on the back of his door. At five foot five, I could see myself from the neck up.

Trying to be both fair and honest, I faced a smooth-skinned woman with wide blue eyes and a mop of unruly auburn curls. My fitness walking, in addition to keeping my curves where they belonged, lent me a flattering outdoor blush. My lips were generous, softly pink, and my cheekbones owed a debt to some forgotten Scandinavian ancestor. All in all, my face appeared a good deal more open than I really was. People would never guess at my reserve from looking at me. Only when I smiled would the twinkle in my eyes lead anyone to suspect I harboured secrets.

My lips curved upward. In my opinion, that grin and the mischief in it were my best features. I shouldn't have let my sense of fun become a stranger to me. I'd been burnt by my divorce, it was true, but that was no excuse for failing to take advantage of the opportunity Fate had so kindly set in my path. Joe was twenty-three, an adult.

If I had any nerve at all, I'd let him know – in no uncertain terms – that I was more than ready to play.

Unfortunately, that was easier said than done. Losing my smile, I sighed and shut Joe's door behind me. The third floor called: my bedroom, my big grown-up bed, my two hundred pages of masturbation aid.

A sound halted me at the door to my room: a rhythmic rattle, like a blind flapping against the window – except the sound was too fast for that; too fast and getting faster.

'Slow down,' hissed a voice: Joe's voice. 'I think I heard someone.'

Another voice groaned something coaxing. The rattling slowed but did not stop.

My hand flattened over my pounding heart. Joe and Sean were fucking in my room. A wave of heat swept me from scalp to ankle – instant, intense arousal. I didn't even have time to take offence. Awash in cream, my clit beat a frantic tattoo against the seam of my jeans.

My knees gave way. My hand brushed the door. The latch clicked. The door swung open an inch. Wincing, I grabbed the frame for support.

I could see them through the gap in the door. Oh, could I see them. Both men were stark naked. Joe was bent forward at the waist, his arms propped straight on my footboard. His legs were straddled wide; every muscle in his thighs and calves stood out with tension. There was no mistaking what that tension was, either – Sean was sodomising him. The force of his thrusts made the bed rattle. His tight pink buttocks clenched as he forged in and out.

What a cute rump Sean had. I'd been so distracted by Joe's crush on me, I'd never noticed. Now I longed to kiss it, to bite it. My knuckles whitened on the door. With an effort, I forced myself to remain still.

Sean was shorter than Joe, but he looked at home on top. He caressed Joe's hair-shadowed torso with a handful of yellow silk. Its trailing edge brushed Joe's upthrust cock, which bobbed like a spring at the contact. Sean chuckled and repeated the tease.

Apparently, he enjoyed tormenting Joe as much as I did.

But what of it? Sean wasn't my concern. Joe was. I turned my attention to my favourite tormentee.

Sweat spiked Joe's straight dark hair. His face red, he grimaced – but not, I thought, with pain. As I watched, he arched his back and tipped his buttocks higher.

Accepting the offer of access, Sean gripped his shoulders and levered deeper. 'Gotta have it, don't you? Can't hardly go a day without it. Hell, if I did you every hour, you'd still want more.'

'Fuck you,' Joe responded, even as he pushed whole-heartedly into the next thrust.

Sean laughed. He nipped the apple of Joe's shoulder and rubbed his cheek across the smooth olive skin. The gesture made my insides turn over. I hadn't thought Sean capable of tenderness – or that his relationship with Joe was more than a power trip.

'Would she do this for you?' he asked. 'Would she lay you over the end of my bed and bugger you till you begged?'

She? I wondered. She as in me?

Joe choked out a laugh. 'That would take some doing, considering her equipment.'

Sean laughed, too, and then I really felt like an intruder.

But it was my room! Taking a quick breath for courage, I shoved the door open. The lovers froze, mid-stroke.

'Shit,' said Sean.

'Oh, my God,' said Joe.

Young Joe's face was a canvas for his emotions. I read contrition in the compression of his lips, embarrassment in his flaming cheeks. 'Kate. We didn't expect you back so early.'

'I guess not,' I said.

At the dryness of my tone, he tried to disengage. Sean wouldn't have it. His muscular arms formed a vice around Joe's waist. With a short grunt, he slung himself deeper. Joe couldn't stifle a groan of pleasure.

That groan was all the impetus I needed to step inside.

Joe's head came up. His cognac-coloured eyes darkened. That's when I knew my lodgers were here, in my room, because the chance I might walk in lent a thrill to the proceedings. But I could live with that – considering the thrill they'd given me.

Hiding a smile, I shrugged out of my jacket and hung it over a chair. One pocket bulged with Joe's stolen jockstrap. What a bad girl I was, and getting badder by the minute. Beneath my apple-red turtleneck the tips of my breasts felt cold, as if they'd been capped in steel.

Sean was the first to notice. His thrusting stuttered to a halt.

'Well, well, well. Looks like our landlady isn't miffed, after all.' He circled one finger around Joe's nipple, a tiny mirror of my own. 'Why don't you ask her if she wants to join us?' Clearly, Sean expected me to run from this challenge.

'Yes, why don't you?' I said, my voice as sultry as I could make it.

Joe's gasp sounded loud in the hush of my attic bedroom. His prick bobbed up another inch – and stayed there. Had I ever seen anyone swing so high? I stepped closer. The tip of his penis was shiny and full, plum-red, plum-shaped. I licked my lips. Joe moaned.

Behind him, Sean eyed me like a snake eyes a mongoose. He didn't pull free, though. Maybe he didn't realise I wanted him right where he was.

I circled the locked pair, savouring the sheen of sweat and the ripple of lean male muscle. They made a pretty picture, what with Sean so fair and Joe so dark. Sean's buttocks tightened as though he could feel my eyes on them. Then I reached the other side.

No one could miss how my perusal had energised Joe.

His erection grazed the skin beneath his navel. I suspected it was painful. It looked good enough to eat.

He looked at me and bit his smooth lower lip. 'Do you – do you want to join us?'

'That depends on your partner,' I said. 'Were you serious about the invitation, Sean? Or testing whether I'd bite?'

'Try it and I'll bite back.' He bared his teeth. 'And I do like women – in case that's what you really want to know.'

Smug, sexy bastard. I'd deal with him later. In fact, I was looking forward to it. For now, though, Joe and his beautiful boner were my primary concern.

I gestured towards my shirt, capturing his eyes. The soft cotton clung to my tautened nipples. He stared at the little nubs. 'Would you like me to take this off?' I asked.

'W-would I?' He shook his head to clear it. 'Of course I would.'

Sean snorted. I ignored him. Grasping the hem in both hands, I pulled the shirt over my head, then shook out my auburn curls. Now I wore nothing but jeans and a lacy black push-up bra. Both men's eyes widened, visibly impressed.

See, I mentally told my ex. Some men appreciate what I've got to offer. Some men wouldn't trade me for a raft of flat-chested teenagers.

Emboldened, I ran my hands up my sides and cupped my breasts. I lifted their weight the way a man might; my nipples crested the edge of the lace. A low cry broke in Joe's throat.

'Amen,' Sean seconded. His gaze roved my chest as he used the bundled silk to draw a slow figure-of-eight on Joe's belly. I had the oddest feeling he imagined he was touching me.

Curious, I tugged the yellow cloth from his hand. When I shook it out, it turned out to be a skimpy silk teddy. It did not belong to me, but someone had sprayed my Chanel No. 19 all over it. I did not know what to make of this, or of Joe's cringe of horror.

'Whose is this?' I asked.

Joe's eyes flew open. 'I thought it was yours.'

Sean cleared his throat. He looked embarrassed. 'Um, that's what I told him. I thought he'd – well, I didn't want him to mess up your nice underwear. I have sisters. I know how women get about that stuff.'

I pressed my lips together against a laugh. 'Very considerate, Sean.'

Joe frowned – not a reaction I wanted to encourage, so I tossed the lingerie aside and shimmied out of my jeans. That got his attention, especially when I dropped to my knees and scooted under his arms between him and the footboard. I considered his rigid penis. It was long as well as thick. This was going to be a challenge, but a nice one. Knowing he watched, I circled my tongue suggestively round my lips.

'Oh, God,' Joe moaned.

Sean's hands were all that held him back, all that held himself firmly lodged. Both men were panting now, caught on the hook of my suspense. A sense of incredible power sang through my veins. I let my breath wash Joe's groin. His hips bucked forward.

'Please, Kate, I can't stand it. Please touch me.'

I touched him. I rubbed my face like a cat along the 'V' of his inner thighs. I kneaded his calves until the knots softened under my palms. I kissed the smooth thrust of his hip-bone. I speared my fingers through his lush pubic hair and then, when his breath was coming in sobs and Sean's hands had clenched into white-knuckled fists, I opened wide and took one drawn-up testicle into my mouth.

'Kate.' Joe stroked my curls with a trembling hand. 'Kate.'

I knew then that, no matter how good Sean made him feel, no one existed for Joe but me. I mouthed my way around both sides of his sac, testing his weight and

11

fullness, smoothing the dark wire-silk hair with my tongue.

'Ready?' I asked, treating the root to one tiny, teasing lick.

Too breathless to answer, he yanked his other hand off the footboard and buried it in my hair. I'd almost licked my way to the head when his fingers tightened and jerked me back.

'Wait,' he said in a high, thin voice. 'I need a condom.'

Sean cursed. Obviously, he'd had enough delay. 'Don't be such a prude. Just pull out before you come.'

'But I'm dripping.'

He was indeed. Tiny droplets of preorgasmic fluid seeped from the eye of his prick.

'I'll take care of it,' I said, and did the honours with the stash I kept in my bedside table.

When I took Joe's cock in my mouth again, he sighed, long and liquid. I felt as if I were the kindest woman alive. This time I swallowed all I could reach, bearing down and up in a steady rhythm that had nothing to do with teasing and everything to do with relief. Sean began to thrust in time to my sucking, bumping Joe forward. Ever the gentleman, Joe braced his legs to prevent being pushed too far down my throat. He couldn't know I loved the added pressure; loved the sensation of witnessing and doing at the same time.

Too turned on to resist, I moved Sean's hands on to Joe's balls. Sean gave them a squeeze.

'Oh, yeah,' he said. 'Buddy, you are primed.'

That taken care of, I was free to see to my own pleasure. I slid my hand into my lacy panties.

Joe's cock abruptly changed angles in my mouth. He was craning around to see. Had he watched a woman masturbate before? The thought that he might not have tightened the coil of heat in my belly. Maybe he'd enjoy seeing more.

I brought my hand back to the lacy waistband. 'Would you like me to take this off?'

'Yes.' He was so breathless I could barely hear him. 'Please.'

I released him long enough to twist out of my panties, then slid two fingers between the slippery petals of my sex. Joe's tongue curled out to wet his upper lip. He swallowed. I promised myself I'd let him taste what he was hankering for before the night was out.

Then Sean broke the heated moment. 'Think we could hurry this up? I can't hold out much longer.'

'So come,' Joe said.

'I want to come with you.'

'So grit your teeth. Ah, yes.' Joe hummed with delight as I bore down towards his root. The sound drove me wild. I frigged myself faster and spread my knees as far as I could so Joe could see. He could hear, too. My fingers made a rapid, squelching sound in all that juice. Joe's shaft thrummed its approval against my palate. Under his velvety skin, he was hard enough to hammer nails. I tongued the sweet spot beneath the head. His knees threatened to buckle.

'Do that again,' he said. 'Oh, yeah. You're going to have to hold on, Sean, because I intend to make this last.' His hands stilled on my head. 'Unless you're tired?'

I laughed and sucked harder. Years of practice had given me jaws of steel. I'd last as long as he could, which – from the feel of things – wouldn't be much longer. No one could get that stiff and not be close to blasting off.

'Oh, man,' Sean complained.

'Oh, yes,' Joe praised.

Their reactions were too much for me. I had to come. With one hand gripping Joe's knee for support, I rubbed my rosy bud faster, chasing the pleasure.

Caught up in his own chase, Sean lost the last shreds of his control. 'Come on.' His belly slapped Joe's back as he went into overdrive. 'Do it, do it, I can't – I'm coming, damn you.'

My fingers slid through my excitement. I thrust the

longest into my wet, summery heat, felt the muscles flutter and clutch, felt the achy sweetness spread.

But Joe beat us both. His cock jerked an instant before Sean moaned like a foghorn, an instant before my body spasmed in ecstasy. Lost to everything then, the orgasm shook me like a rag doll, jerking me from the inside out until my legs collapsed and my head thunked against the bed.

Joe immediately slipped from Sean's hold to kneel beside me.

'Kate. Sweetheart.' He gathered me against his body. 'Did you hurt your head?'

'I'm all right.' I rubbed the sore spot, more dazed by his concern than by the thump I'd taken.

'Poor thing,' he murmured, rocking me.

Left without his partner, Sean stepped towards the window and turned away. The setting sun gilded the curve of his spine. He raked back his short blond hair. His shoulders sagged. A little worry tightened my throat. What if he really cared for Joe? Then a truly horrible thought brought my hand flying to my mouth. 'Oh, God, Joe, I didn't bite you, did I?'

He kissed the tip of my nose. 'No, sweetheart, you let go just in time.'

With a flattering lack of effort, he scooped me off the floor and set me on my king-sized bed. Sleepy and warm, I let him remove my bra – which was the only clothing I had left. His hands passed over my breasts in gentle exploration, a strangely comforting gesture. Then he pulled the chenille coverlet up to my neck.

To my surprise, considering Sean's possessive streak, both men settled on either side of me. Sean snuggled against my back and sighed with exhaustion. I patted the arm he draped around my waist. In all my fantasies, I'd never dreamed of seducing him.

Of course, I hadn't really seduced him tonight. He'd just gone along. Well, more than gone along – he'd enjoyed himself. So why did I feel as if I'd stolen something from him? Why did I feel protective? Most of all, why did I wish we could do it again – not just Joe and I, but the three of us together?

Divorce rebound, I thought. You figure if one man will prop up your self-esteem, two should send it through the roof. I didn't believe that, though. I'd caught a glimpse of the real Sean tonight, and it had struck a chord.

We had more than our lust for Joe in common.

The question was, what did I intend to do about it? Keep it light, I thought. Treat it like a game and no one will get hurt.

The object of our affections lifted the erotic novel I'd left by my bed a lifetime ago. 'Hm,' he said. One finger stroked the naked clinch on the cover. 'I'm sure you sleepyheads don't need it, but I think I'll read you a bedtime story.'

The sound of furious whispers woke me, that and the circling caress of a hand on my hip: Joe's hand. Already I recognised the long fingers, the gentleness all out of proportion to his years. Or perhaps his gentleness depended on youth. Perhaps life would roughen his soft edges.

The thought disturbed me. In fact, being disturbed disturbed me.

I feigned sleep, which was not an easy task. Sean's naked front spooned my naked back and his erection nuzzled the crease of my buttocks. Lust told me to squirm closer. Curiosity told me to be quiet and listen. Curiosity won.

'What is your problem?' Sean hissed.

'She's asleep.'

'Don't worry. She'll like it.' Sean's chest was damp with excitement, his nipples pebbled and hot. Whatever 'it' was, I suspected he'd like it, too.

'But I've never done it before.'

Sean reached over me to ruffle Joe's hair. 'It's not hard. Hell of a lot easier than going down on a man.'

'What if I can't find it – and how do you know?'

'I had a life before I met you, you know. Just because I like men better doesn't mean I can't appreciate a good-looking woman.'

'But I thought – You never said –'

This was getting too private for me. 'I'm awake,' I said and laid my hand on Joe's belly. His stomach muscles jumped.

'Oh,' he said, and, 'Oh, man,' when my fingers ventured lower.

Grasping the root of his erection, I pulled slowly until the flare of his glans crossed my palm. He caught my hand before I could stroke him again.

'Behave yourself,' he said. He threw the covers off the three of us and stared at me in the moonlight. His hand trailed down the curve of my side. 'You are so beautiful.'

My skin heated under the compliment. Had anyone said those words so convincingly before?

The mattress creaked as he scooted lower on the bed. I heard the coverlet fall to the faded Turkish carpet; heard the rush of Joe's breath. Did those hastened exhalations signify anxiety or arousal? I prayed he wasn't doing something he didn't want to do. He kissed the tender skin beneath my navel, then rubbed his face across my fleece. Aside from the endearing gesture, which he repeated, he didn't seem to know where to start. My concern intensified.

'Here,' said Sean. He lifted my upper thigh and arranged it over Joe's shoulder. The scent of male sweat and female musk perfumed the air.

Joe kissed one plump lip.

When he went no further, Sean said, 'Watch.' His hand, callused from the construction work he did every summer, slid down my belly. He combed through my curls to part my labia.

He did indeed know what he was doing. His first and

second fingers slid into the slick valley either side of my clitoris. Up and down he rubbed, the smooth pressure tugging skin and nerves and spreading my gathering moisture until my whole sex felt oiled. Finally he squeezed the tenderest morsel between two fingers. The tip bulged towards Joe's waiting mouth.

'See,' Sean said with a hint of triumph. 'No trouble finding that.'

'No trouble at all,' Joe agreed, and his tongue curled out to lap the delicate offering.

His touch spurred a delicious throb of sensation. I fought not to squirm. Joe licked me again through Sean's tight fingers, more firmly this time. Oh, he had a good mouth; a natural-born, pussy-loving mouth – soft, but not too soft; curious and flexible. Every nerve-jangling contact called a sound from my throat. Helpless to stop myself, I clasped his silky head and pulled him closer.

'Let go,' Joe rasped.

I stiffened but, to my relief, he meant Sean. Pushing his friend's hand aside, Joe surrounded the apex of my sex with his mouth. His lips tugged my clit while his tongue massaged it. I began to struggle, my orgasm just out of reach. He stroked the inside of my wrist with his thumb. 'Hush,' he said.

But I couldn't hush. It felt so good. I wanted to come so badly. My hips rocked into each suckling pull. Sean pushed forward, helping me, branding my backside with his cock.

Then Joe let go. 'Switch on the light,' he said.

Surprisingly obedient, Sean yanked the chain on the Tiffany lamp. Red-amber light bathed our tangled bodies. Like neon, the glow highlighted muscled arms and thighs, wide chests and soft breasts – three healthy animals rubbing against the boundaries of love.

Joe backed away to view his handiwork. His thumbs spread me wide. The sight of my glistening sex seemed to mesmerise him.

'Don't stop now,' I said, caught between laughter and frustration.

'Just a sec,' he assured me.

His head came up at something Sean was doing behind my back. 'No, man. You're too big. You'll hurt her.'

Well. That made me turn.

Sean was twisting the top off a tube of lubricant.

'I wasn't going to,' he said, all innocence. 'Besides, she's not that much smaller than you.'

He looked to me for permission, hope kindling in his face. Rather than give in at once, I measured his cock with my eyes. What he lacked in length, he more than made up for in girth. Sean cringed. If he could have made it smaller, I think he would have.

'He's too thick,' Joe said.

'But not too long,' Sean wheedled, then sighed. 'I suppose you're an arse virgin.'

'I'm afraid so,' I admitted. 'Nothing bigger than a finger.'

He looked so crestfallen that I assured him I wasn't saying never. Sean had made sacrifices tonight, and had been a sport about it. He deserved to be able to play his favourite game – and who could say I wouldn't enjoy it? Joe obviously did.

'That's settled then.' Joe planted his hands on his hips. 'Fingers only.'

'One or two?' Sean teased.

Joe shook his head at him, but the corners of his mouth twitched. He settled back between my legs, not so nervous this time. 'Now.' He parted me again and licked me once to say hello. 'Where were we?'

Sean waited until I was squirming against Joe's mouth to begin his probing entrance. Despite my resolve, I couldn't help tensing. My ex had done little more than rub me there, and that only when he thought I was taking too long to come.

'Relax.' Sean pressed the edge of his teeth into my nape. 'Easy now, easy.'

Joe hummed the echo of this croon while Sean pushed two lubricated fingers past the furled rosebud of my anus. Goose bumps prickled along my arms. In his fingers slid, to the first knuckle, then the second. When they hilted, he massaged me from the inside in slow, firm strokes.

The surprising burst of pleasure made me groan. He scissored his fingers apart, widening me, no doubt preparing me for the day when he would storm that fortress with his cock. I groaned again. His unfamiliar intrusion woke a hidden set of nerves. They lit up like sparklers under his expert touch. Suddenly Joe's suckling seemed not too gentle, but almost too intense to bear.

'Good girl,' Sean praised, his voice shaky with arousal. His hips rocked mine forward, the demands of his sex too urgent to ignore.

He shifted behind me and rearranged himself. His shaft moved, practically scalding the crease of my inner thigh. With his free hand, he pressed it up against my pussy. The shape of him, the smoothness of his skin, the frantic pulsing of his veins, called down a gush of cream.

'Oh, yeah,' he said, anointing himself with the thoroughness of a connoisseur. 'Baby, you are hot.'

Joe nuzzled lower, taking a taste for himself. From the way Sean whimpered, I knew he'd received a lick, too.

'I'll get to you,' Joe promised him.

But first they got to me.

'Faster?' Sean said, increasing the stretch of his fingers.

I could only gasp.

Joe took that as a 'yes' and increased his efforts. In seconds, the first climax hit me. My neck arched, my legs stiffened. Joe reached up to squeeze my nipples between his fingers and a second drum-roll shuddered through my sex.

Feeling it, he laughed and flicked my clit with his tongue in a lightning-quick rhythm I thought Sean must

19

have taught him. Crying out loudly enough to wake the neighbours, I ground my pussy into his face and came again.

'Cool,' said Joe, when I finally floated back to earth.

'Come here,' I said with the ragged remains of my breath.

He slid up my body and we kissed, our first kiss – hungry on his part, languorous on mine. He tasted of me and himself, a combination of sharp and sweet. To my surprise and pleasure, he kissed without coyness or hesitation. His tongue delved into my mouth as if he couldn't get enough of me, as if he wanted to pass his fever for me through the kiss. It was catching, all right. In minutes, I was ready to take him.

Too overwhelmed to speak, I took his sex in my hand and guided him towards my gate.

He stopped me with a tiny shake of his head.

For one awful moment, I feared I'd mistaken the extent of his interest. If he didn't want vaginal sex, maybe he wasn't as bi as I'd thought.

'No,' he breathed a millimetre from my ear. 'When we're alone.'

Our eyes locked, just for a second, but long enough to shock me with the intensity of emotion that passed between us. I couldn't define the feeling. Longing was part of it, and fear, and hope. Hope was the scariest, I think.

Sean stirred behind me, breaking the spell. He reached for Joe, took his cock from my grasp and smeared it with lubricant until it glistened in the lamplight, cherry-wet, cherry-red. I felt Joe's body tremble. His eyes lifted and searched mine. Focused on his own goals, Sean tugged until their shafts nestled side-by-side between my thighs.

'Press tightly,' he said, and pushed my leg down with his hand.

The pressure jammed their pricks together. Joe's slipped on my skin, on Sean's skin. Joe hesitated. His lips moved with words I never heard – an apology, I believe. Then they embraced each other around my body, kissed each other wetly beside my ear, and buffeted me with the fervour of their grease-slicked thrusts. Sean gripped Joe's buttocks so hard the indentations turned white. Joe flattened my breasts with his chest. Their grunts and gasps aroused me all over again. I could have listened all night, but neither man was in a mood to dawdle. Watching me take my pleasure had cranked them up. Now they wanted theirs, right away, and no monkey business.

They came simultaneously and so quietly I felt embarrassed for crying out.

Sean rolled away from me first, then Joe. Snuggling up to my favourite pillow, Joe promptly fell asleep.

'Thanks,' Sean mumbled from the other side of the bed. 'That was fun.' Then he was out, too.

Some things never change, I thought. Still, there was a spring in my step as I padded into the shower to wash off the night's adventure.

The water streamed over me, soothing my tired muscles. My soapy hand drifted between my legs. I'd have one last firework before sleep. As my fingers pursued the little explosion, a single refrain beat through my head: *When we're alone. When we're alone.*

Fetish Love

Novella Foster

Fetish Love is the first of our short stories. Set in that most liberated of cities, Amsterdam, it explores the fun that a girl can have with a young and pretty transvestite.

Fetish Love

Jane leant back from her PC and rested her eyes by scanning the view from the floor-to-ceiling windows of her new Amsterdam office. It was a bright and sunny day; strong light swept the canals. The water, broken up by choppy breezes, lapped the canal walls as ducks and seagulls vied for scraps thrown by tourists.

Jane felt invigorated. It was a splendid location; not an anonymous office block on the outskirts of the city but an elegant eighteenth-century building on the Kaisergracht. She leant back further, her long legs shapely in sheer stockings and high-heeled shoes, her body flattered by the smart pin-striped suit she favoured for the office.

Jane was tall, five foot nine, her build athletic rather than curvaceous. Her hair was auburn, cut in a geometric bob, her features expressive, especially her grey-green eyes. She was not pretty, but she was certainly attractive. She held an air of authority and confidence that belied her comparative youth. She knew certain men found this incredibly sexy. She loved it and used it to her advantage, at work and at leisure.

'Good morning. My name is Peter Van Heek.' The voice sounded mellow, almost treacly. Jane startled out of her reverie and turned and looked into the most startling blue eyes. God, she mused, some of these Dutch men are just too gorgeous.

Jane always liked her men tall, and Peter was tall: six foot two at least, with a muscular yet rather light build. He seemed boyish really: snub-nosed, wide-mouthed, topped with a mass of blond, curly locks. I wonder if his pubes are just as golden, she fantasised. I suppose I could ask, she thought.

Peter Van Heek was the new pre-sales consultant. He worked closely with Jan Stad, the big, bombastic head of sales Jane had met a week earlier. Jane thought Peter stunning in his well-cut suit and expensive shoes. She guessed his age at twenty-three, maybe -four. She sub-consciously pressed her thighs closer together, feeling intently the arousal of her sex, the dampness staining the latex thong she wore tightly pressed into her crotch. It was so much sexier than wearing no underwear at all and so erotic to be able to indulge her fetish at work. Come on, Jane, she told herself. You are his manager. Behave!

Peter flashed a brilliant smile and spoke, his English perfect yet retaining the slight, earthy Dutch accent that was so attractive. 'I hope you approve of the office?' he said.

She did. A new office and a new job in a fantastic new city. She had long needed a change from London and now found herself running the Amsterdam office of a fast-expanding software company. She answered Peter with enthusiasm.

'It's wonderful, Peter. And the flowers?'

'Yes, we Dutch have a special way with flowers; we breed excellent bulbs.'

I'm sure, winced Jane to herself as she mentally undressed him. Such supple young limbs; such energy; such a questioning look in those ice-blue eyes; such longing in her own.

'I see you admire the Amaryllis.' Peter delicately

touched the tip of one deep-red petal. 'They are so sensuous are they not?'

Jane nodded, her thighs trembling. She ran her fingers lightly down one long thick blade of the giant crimson plant. It was in full flower. Five exotic blooms on one head, each as large as a man's open hand. Others were less advanced, their fat silken buds poised ready to burst open, like giant vulvas. Jane composed herself.

'Peter, the tulips by the window. They are so colourful.'

'Yes, our early tulips are the best in the world, I think,' he said proudly. He walked over to the massive display of colour beneath each window, his movements fluid and effortless like a young tawny lion.

'You are too warm? I shall open a window.' Peter spoke softly and stooped to unfasten the lock. His beautifully moulded bottom filled his trousers perfectly. Jane could not take her eyes off his stunning contours, but then, what was this? Could it be? The tailored outline of his suit seemed broken. As Peter straightened up it was plainer to see; he was surely wearing a suspender belt and stockings underneath his suit.

Oh God, Jane sighed to herself, touching her own sheer hosiery through her skirt. Are all Dutch men so open about their sexuality? Never before had she experienced such immediate lust for a man and for a cross-dresser. She loved imaginative sex, especially games of domination and submission, but a transvestite – and such a pretty one – seemed a pure gift, a luscious opportunity. Six words drilled into her brain: I want to play with you. They formed on her lips, barely audible save to her own reeling senses. It was unlikely Peter had heard such muted whispers, yet he half turned, ran a hand through his tousled hair in a flighty gesture, and smiled provocatively.

Jane glanced quickly around the large open-plan office. It was still early; only two consultants were at their consoles. They seemed engrossed in their screens and took no notice of Jane and Peter by the window.

Jane decided immediately, her professionalism taking over. There were three ways she could play this. She could ignore his fetish enjoyment of female underwear. Hardly, she mused. She could summon Peter into her private office and challenge him on his dress code. Possible. Or she could ask him out for a drink. She knew only too well what she'd really like to do: To take Peter, pretty blond Peter, and bend him over her knee. To spank his luscious bottom. To ride his cock. To feel his masculine hardness sheathed in satin and lace. Oh, bliss!

Peter had opened a window. Cool spring air wafted in. He looked her straight in the eye. 'You are alone here in Amsterdam?'

Jane, robbed of the initiative, answered quickly. 'Yes, for the time being.'

Peter smiled wickedly.

'Then let me show you around. There is much to do in Amsterdam, yes?' he continued animatedly. 'There is a grand event soon, a ball at the zoo. It is the place to be seen. Please come as my guest.' He was so straight-forward, Jane acquiesced immediately.

'I'd love to, Peter. Thank you.'

Inadvertently, she glanced again at Peter's thighs and his secret pleasure. Yes, undoubtedly, stockings. She could just make out the little round indentations of the suspender buttons pressed against the wool of his trousers. Perhaps he was also wearing little panties? Her mouth watered as she pictured Peter's manhood, barely covered in satin or lace, tantalisingly gift-wrapped especially for her. He was taking a risk, thought Jane. But then risk-taking to some was a pure erotic charge; Jane knew this only too well.

Peter caught her glance and his pupils dilated. He was really turned on by the situation. He wants me to know; he wants me to know he's a cross-dresser, realised Jane. She took a decision.

'Peter, shall we continue in my office? I have a meeting at ten but it gives us enough time to sort through some diary dates.' Oh, God, she sighed to herself. What has happened to my judgement? It seemed to Jane that moving abroad – and particularly to Amsterdam – had given her licence to behave outrageously.

Jane led the way to her private office, her heart thumping. She had always admired transvestites; they seemed to epitomise sensuality and promised a more diffused sexuality: a greater awareness of female pleasure. The ambiguity and sheer compulsion of cross-dressing excited her, and flirtatious Peter seemed the perfect match to her own fetishistic preferences.

Jane, walking quickly ahead of Peter, felt that flutter of delicious anticipation between her legs as she savoured the opportunity awaiting her. Her imagination raced and she visualised Peter in a tight satin corset and high heels, his glorious manhood erect and eager to pleasure her.

'Sit down, Peter.' Jane swallowed hard. The room was hot and she removed her suit jacket. God, was she really doing this? Had she gone mad? She pressed her thighs together and the resultant surge of desire made her wince with growing pleasure and a hint of trepidation. Peter was exotic; forbidden. He was offering himself to her. She could not refuse him.

Peter sat as ordered on the chair facing Jane's desk. He looked sheepish and defiant at the same time. Jane guessed it was a challenge. She took up the gauntlet.

'Peter, as your manager I must discuss dress codes with you,' Jane said feebly, sitting down on her desk directly facing him. 'I have noticed a certain flamboyance in your style, a certain unorthodox approach to office protocol.' Peter's eyes shone. Bastard, thought Jane, he's enjoying this too much. He's controlling me!

The transvestite moved his thighs slightly apart and slowly traced the outline of the suspender down the inside of his thigh, just brushing the telling bulge between his legs. He leant back, his hot pink tongue salaciously moistening his lips, signalling his intention and desire.

Jane stood up and moved towards him, her natural inclination to dominate rescuing her from embarrassment. 'Peter, I need to discuss dress codes with you,' Jane repeated, this time softly and decisively as she removed the wet latex thong from under her business skirt. Peter shifted again on the chair. Looking far too relaxed, he placed his arms behind his head and stretched out his fine body on the chair. A naughty smile played around his expressive lips. His legs opened wide in invitation and he waited.

Jane was astounded. Cheeky little cross-dresser, she thought, slightly annoyed. She leant over him without breaking eye contact and stuffed her rubber thong deep into his beautiful mouth. She smelt the sweet freshness of his breath, corrupted with latex and the musky secretions from her sex. She slapped him suddenly across the face, once on each cheek, calling him a hopeless little pervert, a sissy, a slut. A she-male not worthy of any sort of sexual liaison, save self-abuse.

She removed the gag and bent to kiss those trembling lips. Peter's face was flushed, his eyes moist with tears from the suddenness of his punishment. He murmured something. Jane just caught what he said: beautiful soft words which inspired feelings of lust and tenderness in her.

'Yes, mistress, yes, mistress Jane. Please humiliate me. Please dominate me!'

Jane needed no encouragement, she was enjoying herself so much.

'Peter, show me your body, take off your clothes.'

Peter willingly stood up, unsmiling now, totally immersed in the role play. He removed his suit and shirt to reveal his smooth hairless body. His legs were finely shaped and well defined in their sheer stockings, the shiny tip of his erect cock peeping out of its useless covering of scanty lace.

'Take them off.' The command was short and urgent. 'Let me see you. Turn around.'

The cross-dresser obeyed while Jane moistened two fingers in her wet pussy and ran them across his old-fashioned suspender belt; the sort with six thick straps, such as those worn with fully fashioned stockings.

She ran her fingers down the golden contours of his buttocks to rest provocatively between his well-defined cheeks. She moulded and massaged that perfect flesh, then took him by the shoulders and turned him around to face her again.

She picked up her discarded thong, then flicked it suddenly across Peter's engorged cock and swollen balls. He gasped in suprise as his penis kicked and bounced in protest at this new indignity. She held him firmly by his shoulders as she delivered such sweet punishment to his scrotum and upper thighs. She slapped those tender parts with infinite care and tenderness.

Peter threw back his head in a submissive gesture, moaning with the excitement and wincing with the pain. With each slap, Jane experienced minuscule flutters of orgasm. She was tempted to strike him really hard and bring herself to climax but she knew the resonant sound of flesh on flesh would reverberate far into the open office space and, besides, she sensed a submissive she-male like Peter could only tolerate a certain level of punishment.

Instead she spoke slowly, weighting her words with authority and sexual excitement.

'Peter,' she said, taking his hand and leading him to the centre of the small room. 'Peter, go down on your knees with your back to me. I don't want you to look while I'm spanking you. And you're not to make a noise. If you do, I'll repeat the process all over again, understood!'

'Oh! Jane, mistress Jane. Yes, please! I deserve it!'

'Enough. I didn't ask for comment. Just do it!' Jane showed her impatience with her new slave by gripping his golden hair and roughly pulling back his head. She kissed him hard on the mouth, her needy tongue penetrating that sweet-tasting opening. She held him stretched backwards for a few moments, delighting in the awkwardness of his posture, the beauty of his taut limbs, the surrender of his will to hers.

Deep in her sex, Jane could feel the tension rising like little bubbles bursting inside her; she licked her lips greedily in anticipation of Peter's humiliation. She placed the high heel of her leather shoe firmly between his buttocks, neatly dividing those firm cheeks, the suspender straps framing his delicious bottom. She placed a condom on the point of the heel, and gently probed the entrance to his tight puckered orifice.

'So, Peter, you like that too much, I think. You know, sometimes, I've heard your presentations are not quite up to scratch. Would you not agree? Answer me!' Peter was only able to nod in reply.

Jane picked up a long thin ruler lying on her desk and struck him hard on one smooth bottom cheek. In quick succession she delivered six blows; three lovingly placed on each orb. Jane's hand shook, so overwhelmed was she from the excitement of her task, and her desire for Peter's shame and pain. She felt the wetness between her thighs as Peter's bottom took on a bruised, rosy glow. She repeated the action, this time with her hand, alternately spanking and caressing, caressing and spanking. She moaned as the transvestite wriggled and arched his back each time Jane's hand struck home.

Jane reached for a small vinyl vibrator she kept specially for business trips. It was discreet enough to slip into her handbag or the side pocket of her laptop. She seated herself on the small of Peter's back, facing his punished cheeks. She placed the whirring tip directly on her clitoral hood with one hand, while reaching underneath for the erection she knew Peter was attempting to conceal. She grasped the long thin phallus and firmly worked it with her other hand for a few minutes. She milked him, and tiny drops of pre-come stained the satin of his suspender belt. She brought him near to climax, then stopped.

Jane was serious now; the mounting tension between her legs was far too insistent.

'Peter, get up. Come to me now,' she ordered. She repositioned herself on the desk, pulled the dishevelled cross-dresser towards her, and encircled her long thighs around his slender waist, at the same time pushing his face into her dark, soft bush.

'Show some initiative, Peter. Use your lovely mouth,' Jane said tersely.

Peter, looking flushed and confused, took her stiff, pink clitoris between his wet lips and ran his pointed tongue into the pulsing entrance of her sex so skilfully that Jane felt her climax mounting. She tamed her impatience, stroked his hair and whispered sweet words in his ear: words she knew only Peter would understand. She let go, control vanished, and her astounding orgasm was upon her.

Peter sat back on the chair, eagerly awaiting his turn at pleasure, his penis red and distended, the long shaft twitching in anticipation. His abused body was tense with desire as he awaited the next command. But Jane had other plans.

'Peter, I'm leaving now. I'm running late. This is what I want you to do. You are to relieve yourself manually as soon as I go through the door. Then, you are to wear my latex thong as well as your suspenders, instead of those useless bits of material that pass for knickers. You are to wear them for the rest of the day, and every day, until I instruct you to stop, understood?'

Peter looked crestfallen and Jane's heart went out to him.

'It's for your own good,' she said smiling, then kissed him lightly on the cheek, turned and left for the refuge of the ladies' loo, leaving Peter to his shameful lonely pleasure.

Ten minutes later, Jane was back in the open office space. It was nearly time for the weekly briefing to be chaired by Jan as head of sales. Jane felt his larger-than-life presence immediately he entered the room. He addressed Jane first: a pleasant booming greeting as he shook her hand. His penetrating gaze, huge physical size and sheer confidence intrigued her. She knew Jan was top of the league. He always achieved target and seemed popular with everyone. God, he is big, Jane wickedly thought to herself.

He stood, all six foot four of him, looking down at her. His thick legs resembled tree trunks. His arms showed sinewy and muscular under his thin shirt. Must work out a lot, thought Jane, a flash of lust upsetting her equilibrium.

Jan spoke, as Peter, looking flushed and slightly crumpled, hastened to join them.

'I see you've met Peter,' said Jan. His dark eyes flashed, and a look, a combination of amusement and inquiry, swept his striking features as he turned to the younger man. For a split second Jane sensed embarrassment from Peter. An idea took hold, and Jane, with a shudder of disbelief and excitement, realised that Jan had somehow witnessed their intimacy.

Peter turned to the big salesman, his body language almost coy, an edge of rebelliousness to his voice. 'Yes, Jan, and she has agreed to partner me at the Europerve ball.'

Jane was stunned.

'The what?' She felt foolish. 'Is that what it's called?'

Jan came closer, his large bulk intimidating. 'So, Europerve,' he teased. 'Yes, Dutch decadence. You will enjoy it. Peter is the perfect partner. I, too, am attending. It is Europe's favourite fetish event. The place to be seen. Bad taste, amoral, yet supremely sophisticated. We must dress to impress. Is that not so, Peter?'

Jan touched Peter gently on the arm. Surely an intimate gesture, thought Jane. She shivered and imagined the big man thrusting his cock into Peter's gentle backside and then into her own eager flesh. Enough, thought Jane. She gathered up her notes, picked up her laptop and led the way into the meeting room.

Jane made sure Peter followed her instructions to the letter. For three days, she knew he was wearing her rubber thong. She knew, because she carried out spot checks on him. It was plainly evident, however, that Peter was continually aroused. He sat, legs crossed, bent over his computer, desperately attempting to hide his shameful secret.

Jane delighted in his predicament; she was training him up well. She stood and watched as he walked about the office, the telling bulge between his legs restricting his movements. She knew he dare not adjust his clothing for fear of exposure and discovery.

She would approach him at his console and converse seriously about the latest project management schedule, all the while examining those impenetrable blue eyes. Her hand would slip from the broad contours of his shoulder, then make its way down his back and into the gap between flesh and material, and Peter would moan: a soft, muted sound, hardly uttered. Jane would feel the moist hot rubber pulled tightly into his crotch and bum hole. She would brush her hand against his jerking cock and finger his balls, lying so sweetly framed between the suspender belt. Then, with a little pat on his arm, she would speak:

'Peter, how's the project on that new supermarket coming on? Do we have a timescale on it yet?' And Peter would answer, averting his gaze, head bowed over his console, legs together, motionless.

On the last day of his test, Jane called him into her office.

'Peter, come, we have some planning to do.' But,

instead of leading him into the office, she led him to a door marked FIRE ESCAPE. The wrought-iron staircase wound its way along one entire side of the old building. She pushed it open and they stood together in cool spring air, three floors up. The canals and landmarks of Amsterdam sparkled in the morning sunshine.

Peter shivered, and Jane put her arm around his waist, speaking to him slowly.

'This is your final day of obedience training in the office, Peter. Just do what I say quickly and without fuss and you'll have your reward at the fetish party tomorrow night.'

Peter darted a glance at Jane, his eyes wide open in astonishment at the imaginative setting she had chosen for his final humiliation.

Without preamble she undid his fly and felt inside, probing the warm masculine softness of dormant desire. She knew Peter was far too frightened to be aroused; at least for the time being.

'Take them off, Peter; the shirt as well.'

Peter mouthed incredulously, 'But, mistress –'

'No excuses. The sooner you comply, the sooner we can return to the nice warm office. Do you think I'm enjoying this?' she added playfully. Peter stripped quickly, looking around him anxiously. Down below, the people of Amsterdam hurried past, oblivious to the tiny drama unfolding above their heads.

The transvestite stood naked but for his feminine embellishments: the latex thong; his sturdy suspender belt; the fishnet stockings and, what was this? Jane was obviously annoyed.

'Peter, I'm very disappointed in you,' she said. 'Did someone give you this to wear? Was it Jan?'

'No, no Jane, it just felt so right, I couldn't resist it. Please don't be angry!'

Jane touched the short black satin slip scornfully. 'Take it off. It's poor quality anyway. I'll keep it as a memento of your pitiful attempts at manipulative play.'

Poor Peter was utterly shamefaced. He knelt down of his own accord and begged for forgiveness.

'Please, mistress Jane, another chance,' he pleaded.

'Later, Peter. For now, I want you to bend over and submit yourself to a dozen slaps on your rump in full view of Amsterdam.'

Jane delivered them quickly to a whining Peter as he gripped the iron handrail with both hands. She heard a delicate sob escape his clenched lips and pity welled up in her. She raised him up and clasped him to her, his almost naked body deliciously pressed into hers.

'Dear Peter, I forgive you. Come now, dry your tears.' She felt his cock stir against her and gently she cupped his balls in both hands, bent her head, and kissed them briefly.

It was time to return to the office, for they would be missed, Jane thought anxiously. She could lose her job for this but the thrill of exhibitionism was so special, she was willing to take the risk. However, for Peter it was different; he was her responsibility.

It was the night of the ball and Jane was excited. She had special plans for Peter.

'Be glamorous,' he suggested in the office when questioned on dress codes. 'Stand out: rubber, leather. PVC, futuristic. The more outrageous the better. I shall go as Petra.'

'Naturally,' said Jane, 'and I shall wear my skin-tight rubber catsuit.'

'Perfect. I shall pick you up at your apartment at ten o'clock tonight. Maybe we'll have time for some play before the party. It carries on until the small hours.' Peter smiled suggestively and Jane nodded in agreement.

To be honest, she could not wait.

Jane, sitting by the window, saw the taxi draw up and park by her apartment. It was situated on the top floor of an old merchant house on the Prinsengracht Centrale

– one of the four main canals of the city of Amsterdam, known as the Grachtengordel: the girdle of canals. The houses here were tall, elegant, and extremely spacious. The huge open-plan living room was flooded with light from six large windows set in original seventeenth-century brickwork. Three overlooked the canal at the front, and three the back. The view was essentially cityscape. The grand façade of the Rijksmuseum sprawled to the left. In front was an array of rooftops, windows and decorated gables. To the right was the Leidesplein and the architectural intricacies of the Art Deco American Hotel, in which Jane had often stayed on earlier business trips to Holland.

She was ready, dressed in her black latex catsuit and thigh-length leather boots. She wore her auburn hair in a sleek geometric bob, highlighted with red and silver shimmer.

'Oh, Peter, you look amazing,' she said. 'You were quite correct when you thought I would never recognise you at the ball.'

Peter kissed her on the mouth tentatively. 'Jane, dear, I am Petra for the evening. Do you like my costume? I made it myself.' Blond Peter had, with the help of a glossy black wig, metamorphosed into a glamorous alter-ego. His make-up was so much more expertly applied than her own, thought Jane. Not brash or drag queen, but beautifully shaded in soft shimmering colours. His lips were pencilled in fully with a rich plum stain, his moody blue eyes accentuated with deep sensuous kohl.

Jane longed to kiss her pretty Petra but first she touched his silver corset top and felt the static run through her hand.

'Petra, you look like a tall dark Madonna,' she said. He did. His false breasts were squeezed into a pointed bra that could have been designed by Jean Paul Gaultier. They seemed to point at Jane and she could not resist the urge to touch them lightly as she looked appreciatively at his transparent tight plastic skirt.

His long lean masculine body was accentuated by the feminine lines. Silver panties only just managed to cover his manhood. His fine strong legs were adorned in tiny fishnet hold-ups. The suspender belt he'd worn in the office had been discarded and his feet were now encased in five-inch-heeled red vinyl ankle boots.

'Petra, dressing must have taken you ages, especially shaving and waxing. I'm really impressed.'

'Dear Jane, thanks. You look wonderful yourself; dominant woman personified. Look, I've brought you a gift.'

It was a handsome whip, the handle impregnated with studs culminating in a dozen long leather thongs. She fastened it to her belt: the finishing touch.

Jane looked Petra up and down critically. He was already showing signs of arousal, the plastic skirt hiding nothing. Jane took his hand and led him carefully on his icicle heels through into the small conservatory which divided her penthouse from the apartment opposite. It was dark, save for the streams of silvery moonlight that shone through the glass roof.

Petra looked around in astonishment. 'Jane, I see you love plants and flowers, too; especially the Amaryllis.'

The conservatory was like a temperate jungle, packed to bursting with foliage and unusual blooms. In the centre of the terracotta floor, a tiny water feature bubbled and trickled, its magical sounds complimenting the luscious aroma of the strange flowers.

'Petra, you know I love the exotic,' she said. She sat on the leather sofa, her rubber suit tight and restraining, like a second skin. She spoke, an edge of command to her voice. 'Petra, come and sit next to me, but first take off your plastic skirt. I want to see your erection.'

Petra lowered his eyes in humility. 'Please, mistress, I cannot. It's too shaming.' Jane showed her irritation by flicking the thongs of her new untainted whip across his bulging manhood.

'Petra, this is a command.'

The TV gasped with surprise and pleasure. He immediately removed the skirt and seated himself in an upright position next to Jane, not daring to look her in the eye.

'Now, Petra, take this bottle of Perv-o-shine and polish up my rubber suit; you are to pleasure me.' The crossdresser unscrewed the top, poured some clear liquid into the palm of his hand and proceeded with strong, energetic and knowing hands to apply a polished sheen to Jane's soft catsuit.

She lay on her stomach and pulled open the zip which revealed her aching sex and firm round bottom. Petra sat astride her and set about his task with great enthusiasm. He polished and rubbed, rubbed and polished, until Jane in her catsuit seemed to shine and sparkle. The rubber was hot by now, and seemed part of her: the smell, the heat, the feel.

Now and then, Petra intentionally let his fingers slip into her opening. The sudden hoped-for touch sent her into near-climax, so hot was she from this perverted encounter.

'Petra,' she whispered. 'I didn't give you permission to touch me there.'

Petra mumbled an apology then continued his ministrations. Jane turned on to her back and lay open to him, her latex-clad body primed and tuned by this fantastic she-male. Jane spoke:

'I want you now, Petra.' The transvestite stood up in all his glory. 'Remove just your panties and enter me,' she said.

Petra obeyed. He stood above her, wobbling slightly on those five-inch heels, his long golden body alive with desire for this demanding mistress. Jane knew he felt unworthy of her, and to fuck her somehow seemed too much too soon, but she no longer cared. She must have him.

She watched, as, with infinite care, he neatly placed a condom on his naked cock and entered her body with a great sigh of lust, tempered with resignation.

'Oh, Jane,' he whispered. 'Let me be your maid, your servant, your slave.' He thrust into her, each movement pleading with her: pleading for more punishment, more humiliation.

Jane was not listening. She was lost in rapture. She felt his body, hard and unyielding. She gripped his buttocks and felt the sharpness of his pointed breasts scratching the softness of her latex suit. She ran her hand through that glossy black wig and marvelled at the beauty of Petra, her own TV.

Petra gasped as he drove into her harder and faster, his climax mounting.

'Now,' Jane cried. The cross-dresser lightly crushed the erect button of her clitoris between two fingers, and Jane erupted with her orgasm. Her vaginal spasms gripped Petra's cock so tightly that he immediately spurted his come deep inside her.

They sat together on the sofa eating grapes and drinking black coffee, expertly brewed by Petra. It was one o'clock in the morning. Jane felt insatiable, so sweet were the intimacies with her cross-dresser. Still hot in her latex, she touched Petra on the thigh and stroked the warm skin between stocking top and silver corset. He relaxed, breathing deeply, leaning into her warmth, his breasts pointing at the dark sky visible through the glass roof of the conservatory. Jane reached from behind and placed a hand on each pinnacle. She squeezed them and spoke in a conspiratorial whisper:

'Petra, there is another game I want to play.' She walked across the terracotta floor, opened a drawer, and pulled out a long thick roll of sturdy cling-film and a coil of soft white rope. 'Take all your clothes off this time, Petra; hands by your sides. I'm going to wrap you up, restrain you, and restrict your beautiful body.'

Petra stood up and eagerly disrobed. Eyes closed, he

awaited the touch of his mistress. Jane faced him, and to her delight his cock awoke. Naked now, his manhood was the centre of her universe. She spread the film, beginning at his neck. Tightly, so tightly, she wound the stuff in a criss-cross action around his upper body, occasionally patting his bottom and stroking his heavy balls with encouragement.

She broke it off at the waist then continued on his lower body, firmly binding his straining cock and balls. His strong thighs she covered; his legs tightly knit together.

Petra tottered on his heels.

'Don't worry, Petra, I'll catch you if you lose your balance. I'm pretty strong.'

She bound the coil of rope around his ankles, just above the red vinyl boots, and his wrists she tied together in front, just above his packaged manhood. She kissed his slightly parted lips, then spoke in an excited whisper.

'Petra, open your mouth wide. I want you to wear this.' She then pushed a rubber ball-gag between his perfect teeth, tying the leather straps around the back of his glossy black wig. He was complete.

Jane, trembling with excitement, stood back and admired her handiwork. She stepped out of her latex suit, her body naked and sweaty with the rubber contact, her breasts full, the nipples erect. She rubbed them against the transvestite's taut, cling-filmed loins. Jane looked into his eyes and she knew this was so right. The perfect match.

Jane moved behind Petra. 'Lean back into me, I'll take your weight. I'm going to lie you on the terracotta tiles, by the Amaryllis.'

The cross-dresser relaxed and obeyed his mistress. It was impossible for him to move otherwise, so strong was the tensile grip of the film; such firm bondage, so easily applied.

She lay him carefully on his back, her precious TV,

and sat astride his bulging loins. She touched herself, prising apart her swollen labia for him to see. She used her vibrator on her clitoris and moaned with pleasure as she watched his eyes fill with desire.

She lay upon him, outstretched, and just held him for a while. Then, with her long sharp nails, she tore apart the film around his genitals. His hard cock, released suddenly, bounced into her fingers, and she played with it awhile, delaying further the orgasm which was almost upon her.

Jane released the gag: she needed his tongue now; she needed his mouth.

She sat on his face, her wet sex smeared across his lovely features. She rubbed herself, her clitoris finding his tongue. She licked her index finger, pushed her hand beneath his buttocks, and edged into his rear passage. She slid her digit in and out, feeling the muscles of his anus relax. She massaged the rim of his bottom whilst he groaned and writhed in his restraints. She came suddenly, gloriously, and cried aloud as Petra lay beneath her, still on the edge of sexual release.

'Oh, Petra, soon, I promise you,' she said.

Jane quickly cut through the film and helped the transvestite to his shaky feet. She walked again to the drawer by the Amaryllis, this time returning with a tape measure. Petra stood still, his urgent penis stiff, purple with need.

'Oh, mistress, please, please!'

Jane spoke. 'Petra, I want you to masturbate as I measure you.'

'Measure me for what?' Petra said incredulously. It was a mild transgression of the rules, but he just had to ask.

'Your chastity belt, of course. You'll wear it for me in the office, as part of your training schedule. Only I will hold the key: the key to pleasure.'

Petra smiled. 'Yes, Jane.' He looked pleased.

Jane measured his erect penis, her touch light and

accurate. She traced the tape around his balls and up through his legs towards his waist.

'You have a choice, Petra – leather, or stainless steel?'

Petra gasped his answer as he gripped his penis in one hand and, with a practised motion, brought himself to climax, his creamy come spilling on to Jane's fingers.

'Steel, please.' He moaned in his passion and sank into the soft settee, exhausted.

Jane wrote down his perfect measurements. How appropriate, she thought. Her lovely Petra in a girdle of steel. He was hers, and hers alone.

She joined him on the sofa, all thoughts of the fetish ball erased from her mind.

Unhallowed Rites

Martine Marquand

Each day in the Convent of Santa Agnetha brings Allegra new challenges. She has already been awakened to forbidden pleasures by looking at her guardian's collection of depraved illustrations. She has tried to deny her true passions by submitting to life as a nun. But the twenty-year-old beauty can find no hiding place, as all who encounter her succumb to her erotic allure. Firstly, fellow novice nun Celina shows Allegra how she can enjoy the most wanton pleasures without the presence of a man. Then the spiteful and dominating Sister Ino wishes to exact strange punishments on Allegra's flesh. In the following extract, Sister Ino has discovered Allegra's taste for depravity and wishes to submit her to further indignities. This time, the young priest Brother Guillam is invited to the proceedings and Allegra is initiated into an unholy union.

Martine Marquand mixes elements of sexual ritual with religious practice and succeeds in creating a potent blend of perversity. This is one of my favourite books in the series and a must for anyone who understands the appeal of sin as excitement. She is writing another book with an historical setting for Black Lace entitled *A Feast for the Senses*, which will be available in January 1999. Martine takes a psychoanalytical approach to sexuality and believes the modern woman is still haunted by taboos which are no longer appropriate. However, her writing shows that we can have a lot of fun with those taboos.

Unhallowed Rites

Allegra set about finding her companions. However, they had long since left the refectory, and soon she realised that there was no food left to break her fast. Wandering into the kitchen, she found one of the servants, who supplied her with some bread and cheese which she bundled up and carried outside to enjoy in the sunshine. Unable to hear or see any sign of the other novices, she wandered for a while through the gardens, looking for a pleasant, shady spot where she might picnic and also collect her fractured thoughts. At last, arranging her skirts, she set herself down beneath a large tree overlooking the small field where the chicken coop and outhouses lay.

With a new appetite, she tore at the crusty bread and salty cheese, feeling glad to be alive on this luxuriously warm day. The other novices must be at work somewhere but it was hard to imagine chasing after them, when the glimmer of sunshine through leaves and the happy trilling of the birds made this such an idyllic spot. Leaning with her back against the trunk of the tree, she let herself doze a little, enjoying at last the new calm which had suffused through her body since the previous night. If only, she allowed herself to think privately, such acts were not a very great wickedness. The girl was so lovely – and so ferociously responsive. Allegra was secretly pleased that just once in her life she had experienced such a passionate coupling. It was a pity, really, that she would never have the experience again. And a pity too, that Celina must suffer for it.

The sound of whistling suddenly disturbed her reverie. Looking about, Allegra noticed for the first time that one of the workmen was hard at work on the small farm. He at least seemed happy at this work, she observed. He was a young, strong-looking youth, with black curling hair, and broad shoulders beneath his ragged shirt. He whistled a pretty tune as he threw corn to the poultry and collected eggs from their perches. Next he fed the old donkey and then, seating himself on an old crate, began to comb his hair.

Allegra could not help but laugh to herself to see the youth take such care with his appearance. Maybe he guessed a little about the effect of his manly presence on a community of secluded women. It would not be hard to imagine how a youth such as this could take hold of a woman's desperate daydreams, even though he was clearly of a lower, rougher order. To her secret delight, he next began to fill a tub of water from the pump; in a few seconds he had pulled off his shirt and stood naked to the waist in the sunshine, like a graceful god from the days of the pagans.

She could not help but admire the strong muscles rippling beneath his copper-sheened skin; as he ran a wet rag across his body the sunshine outlined every masculine curve. His shoulders were broad and strong and his torso revealed the powerful effects of good, honest labour. Showing every signs of enjoying his private bath, the young fellow next set to washing his hair. Though lacking the luxury of soap, he went at it like a puppy-dog, dousing his head in the tub and then shaking his dark curls until they hung in damp tendrils down his back. Finally, he looked around himself, clearly checking to see if he was being watched. Allegra's heart skipped a beat as he seemed for a second to look directly at her where she sat above him masked by trees. But undoubtedly he could not see her, sitting down low as she was, in her dark-brown dress.

With a quick, almost furtive movement, he loosed his breeches. Then, with a rapid sliding movement, they were off and he stood completely naked for her to inspect at her leisure. His legs were as stout and well formed as the rest of him, covered in a fuzz of dark hair. Giggling to herself, Allegra considered the rest of his anatomy. At first he stood with his back to her, and her eye followed the long flank of his back and the paler skin of his neat, curved buttocks. As he turned, her giggles stopped. Indeed, beyond Leon's timid attempt to despoil her, she had never actually seen a male member in all its glory. Now, the youth's long phallus hung swinging down between his thighs, pink and fleshy, with the heavy scrotum bulging behind in a mass of curly hair.

Allegra's mouth fell open; peering between narrowed eyes, she clambered forward on all fours, striving all the time to get a better view of the mysteriously attractive organ. Soon she was crouched on the grass, staring round-eyed at the young fellow as he began to douse his stomach with handfuls of refreshing water. Next he grasped his long member and lifted it to scrub its length.

Once again, as she leant on her elbows with her rear end pushed back, she felt a wave of delicious sensation stir in her body. What would it be like to help the young fellow with his ablutions – to touch the very thing he touched? As he washed it, she could see it grow a little wider and ever so slightly stiffer in response to his own touch. So what if a young woman were to touch it, to rub it, to squeeze it?

In response, she felt her own inner muscles squeeze with delight. She thought of playing with it gently, maybe stroking it and watching it rise – as a throng of images rushed into her mind, she found herself squeezing her thighs together in anticipation. If only he knew about her, kneeling here, ready for him – what could she fancy them doing together, what tasks could she find for such a glorious piece of flesh?

It was difficult not to be horribly aware of the growing dampness between her legs, of the tight bonds of her corsets pressing hard against her hanging breasts. Sighing, she wondered idly if there might be any opportunity to befriend the young workman and let events follow the course of nature. But then she recalled his station in life – he was only a rough and lowborn menial. She must not forget herself. She was a member of the nobility, and sworn to be a nun as well.

The next thing Allegra heard was a loud whistling sound very close to her ears. Then she felt a blow, a sharp, agonising blow on her prominent rump. In a moment she struggled to get up. It was Sister Ino, switch in hand, with a face of purple fury. The terrifying nun stared at her with eyes rolling white in her crimson face. Then with a vicious gesture, she raised her arm.

'How dare you!' Allegra cried, raising her hand to stop her. 'Creeping up on me like that. Why do you people think you can do that? I am only here minding my own business. Now, let me find the others. I have work to do.' At this, Allegra abruptly pushed past the older woman, running at a smart pace back to the convent. Only faintly, she could hear Sister Ino murmur, as if repeating a litany to herself: 'Through discipline is purity. Humility by pain.'

That evening Allegra was surprised to find Celina at her door again. The girl stood meekly outside with her candle, her face a picture of tearful humility.

'What is it?' Allegra asked.

'Allegra, please may I come in? I have nowhere to sleep.'

'You can sleep wherever it was you slept last night, can't you? I will not bother with you again.'

The girl's face twitched, fighting back tears. 'I only need – if nothing else – I beg you, let me get a change of linen. Sister Ino has . . .'

'Has what? Oh, no. Has she punished you?' The realisation that her complaint about Celina's behaviour the previous night might have already led to such a consequence both horrified and excited Allegra. Without comment, she let Celina into the room, watching her with fascination. 'What happened?' Allegra was all ears as she led the girl over to the bed. But, on reaching it, Celina winced. It was clear she could not sit comfortably.

'You remember she told me to report to her room. I did so and received fit punishment for taking you wandering in the garden. But it is obviously of no matter to you. Please just let me change my linen.' Suddenly Celina's face grimaced as a sob rose from her heart. 'Oh, Allegra, do take pity on me. I cannot sleep out there on the hard benches in the chapel. Please let me share your room. I will only lie here quietly and not disturb your peace at all.'

Allegra's mind was working quickly as the girl spoke. So the punishment she had received from Sister Ino had only been that already threatened on their walk yesterday. It seemed Celina had no idea as yet of her complaint and the second punishment she would inevitably receive that evening. Poor girl. It almost melted Allegra's heart to think of Celina receiving a second, undoubtedly more severe punishment from the sisters later that night.

'Here, let me help you,' she offered. But Celina could not sit, only shuffle on to the bed lying frontwards, so that she might relieve her sore buttocks of any pressure. There was nothing to be done but help her unlace her skirts and petticoat, carefully holding them back so nothing touched the sensitive skin. As her petticoat fell to the ground, Allegra was shocked to see the red weals Sister Ino's switch had left on the girl's peachy flesh. A

51

dozen or so stripes marked the skin of her rounded cheeks, rising in ridges of crimson. The skin was not broken, however, only stinging mercilessly as the girl wriggled this way and that on her stomach, trying to find a position in which the pain would lessen.

Allegra sat on her bed and contemplated the unfortunate girl. It would be a surprise to Celina to be summoned for a second time, but nevertheless it would be most embarrassing to actually warn her. No, she would have to be surprised, for otherwise she might accuse Allegra of betrayal. And, indeed, although the two girls had studiously avoided each other all the wearisome day, now they were back in each other's company it was hard not to feel the glimmers of friendship revive once again.

'Allegra, is there nothing you can do to help me?' Celina moaned, shifting from one side to the other.

'There is nothing I can do, as you well know,' she replied. 'Just tell me, will you, what exactly happened when you went to Sister Ino's room?' For Allegra had cast her mind back to the afternoon, and realised she too might have to face the terrible nun herself at some future date.

'I cannot,' she moaned. 'For it is a terrible secret. I know it is meant to make me pure, but in truth it only heats my humours even more.'

'Celina, you are truly disgusting. I do not wish to know about your perversities.'

At this, a long silence ensued. But Allegra was intrigued. Her friend looked quite fetching now, with her bare bottom raised on a pillow and her thighs a little parted to ease the pain. The series of weals, too, looked oddly arousing on the twin spheres of flesh which rose in such a pronounced fashion from the narrow curve of Celina's waist. 'Maybe I could ease your wounds.' Her voice, when it came out, was rather thick and breathless.

'Yes, that would be nice. We have no ointment, only a little oil.'

'Very well.' Like a sleepwalker, Allegra fetched the oil and warmed a little in her palms. Even when she shook herself to recollect her virtue, she reassured her conscience that she owed her friend a little relief from discomfort in readiness for the next assault.

Sitting on the edge of Celina's bed, she let a little oil trickle down on to the reddened flesh. The girl flinched, but sighed when Allegra rubbed it in with the gentlest touch. Allegra's fingers slid sensuously across the soft skin, feeling the flesh give way to her probing caresses. Soon the whole of Celina's rear was slippery with the oily emollient and still Allegra let her fingers idly wander. Some of the oil had collected in the cleft between Celina's cheeks, and, scarcely knowing what she was doing, Allegra began to probe the girl's secret parts. The oil meant there was no resistance as her index finger found an orifice she had not expected to find. Feeling her friend stiffen, Allegra halted.

'No, go on,' Celina gasped.

Ever so gently, Allegra penetrated the little hole, feeling herself grow powerfully excited at this surprising conquest. The effect on Celina was electrifying. Her thighs drifted ever wider and now Allegra could see the reddish hair and swollen lips of her vulva as the girl uncontrollably lifted her rear to get ever more pleasure from that single stiff digit. With her other hand, Allegra reached out to explore the more familiar slit which opened below. It was no surprise that the whole area shuddered and gaped.

Allegra barely knew what it was she wanted to do; just the sight and scent of the girl overwhelmed her senses. Still teasing the little orifice with one finger, she began to probe gently to find another. The lips were hot to the touch and sensitive to the slightest brush of her fingers. A wail of gratification erupted from Celina. At last she found it, and, stiffening her fingers, began to thrust them in unison with the other. The girl was in ecstasy now, meeting her thrusts with her grinding hips, soaking her fingers with the unctuous honey released by her body.

'Yes, please don't stop – oh, faster, faster.'

Allegra obeyed, driving her fingers like short, sharp pistons into the girl's twin entrances. The result came quickly. With a series of panting breaths, Celina pushed herself down on the two sources of pleasure, faster and faster, until Allegra felt a great muscular grip squeeze her fingers again and again. In her spasm of bliss Celina cried out hoarsely, groaning with the violence of her release.

With a great sigh, the girl relaxed, trembling slightly from the force of her deliverance. 'Please,' she sighed, 'let me kiss your very centre. I want to drive my tongue to your very soul.'

Turning over, she reached up to help Allegra undress. Too dazed by lust, too swollen herself by the blood pounding through her veins, Allegra could no longer resist. She too ardently needed release. She too craved the probings of the girl's sensitive fingers and tongue. Sitting on the bed as the naked girl pulled off her kerchief, Allegra had only one thought in her head: physical satisfaction. Rabidly, the pair both pulled at her unwieldy clothing, dragging at her laces, uncovering her hungry flesh.

So when the knock rapped out loudly on the door, Allegra was too dazed to hear it. It was Celina who whipped on her shift and struggled over to open it. At the door stood Sister Ino. With a shock of recollection, Allegra heard her speak of the time having arrived for punishment. Guiltily, she watched Celina. But Celina crossed back to the bed and took her hand.

'I am sorry,' Allegra whispered to her dear friend, almost choking with regret.

'What do you mean? You must go at once. It is I who am sorry for you.'

'Why?' Allegra felt she might be waking from a dream to find herself living in a nightmare.

'It is you who must go with Sister Ino. She has come to fetch you for your punishment.'

Almost fainting with fear, Allegra followed Sister Ino down to the convent chapel. At times, she wondered if her legs would carry her any further as she leant against the walls of the corridor for strength. Terror gripped her as fiercely as a fever, leaving her dazed and breathless. She longed to escape, but did not even have the strength to try.

'Get along, now,' the terrifying nun ordered, reaching to grasp her wrist and drag her onwards. Flinching, she struggled to be free of the woman's touch.

'No,' she whispered hoarsely. 'I will walk alone.' As much staggering as walking, she reached the ornate room behind the novices' chapel. At the far end, Sister Ino pulled a second curtain to one side, revealing a steep flight of stone steps leading downwards into the depths of the earth.

'Down there?' breathed Allegra. 'I do not think I can.'

'Stupid girl,' the nun snapped. 'Get down there.'

With a shove to her back, Allegra began the long descent, feeling as if she were dropping down into a dark well. After a few terrified moments, she saw that after every score of steps a flame burnt low in a wall sconce, but, between these, she had to feel her way down from each step with her toes. With her fingers spread wide along the surface of the cold wall, she did her best to steady herself in the gloom. Behind her, the stout sister grew impatient and jabbed her back and shoulders to make her hurry.

After what seemed almost half the night, Allegra reached the flat solidity of a dead end. With a sudden shove, the stout nun reached past her and pushed a heavy door. Beyond lay the glimmer of candlelight and the sensation of people moving in a large room.

It took some while for Allegra to adjust her eyes. What she saw did not calm her nerves at all. She was in a large and high chamber, painted in the rough, colourful manner of a pagan temple or ancient cave. Where there might have been a figure of Christ on the altar wall there was instead a vast figure of a woman dressed in a thin, revealing toga. In her outstretched hands was what appeared to be a bundle of twigs. Beside her was a life-sized crucifix, oddly striking in that it appeared to be standing upside down. Allegra did not recognise the cold, disdainful gaze of the icon from any book of saints she knew.

The large fresco was illuminated with a mass of waxen candles, so the sharp features and fair hair of the holy woman, if that was what she was, flickered and shifted in an oddly lifelike fashion. Below her sat the Prioress and most of her order, all shrouded in black and obviously expectant of their arrival. With a final harsh shove, Sister Ino propelled her to the centre of the room.

'So, Sister Almoro. We meet again.' There was the slightest lilt of laughter in the old woman's voice. The rest of her company appeared also to watch her with a measure of amused detachment. Again, there were males as well as females in the group, of various ages and ranks. The handsome Abbot could also be seen, observing her wryly, among younger, fresh-faced priests.

'Let me recall,' the Prioress announced exultantly. 'Was it not you, our new sister, who begged to be judged? Who claimed she was better than her companions? Who wished to be tested? Well,' and here the old crone's eyes shone with twinkling venom, 'tonight we will test your resolve.'

The flesh around Allegra's heart constricted so tightly, she felt she could hardly breathe. She spun around to escape, but the formidable Sister Ino stood guard by the only door.

'Come forward. Let us see you.'

Quaking, Allegra shuffled forward.

'Your dress is in some disarray, is it not? Now why, pray, is that?'

It was true, for half of Allegra's laces hung open and

her shoulders and chest were bare where the kerchief had gone astray.

'I was preparing for bed,' Allegra mumbled.

'I cannot hear. You must indulge an old woman. We have an aid to make you speak a little clearer. Step on to the birching block if you please.'

Wild-eyed, the girl looked about her. Between herself and the gathered assembly stood a carved block of solid wood. In the centre of the surface was a pointed promontory, like the sloping back of a settle. She had no idea what it was.

'I don't understand,' she whimpered.

With a loud sigh, the Prioress turned to a figure waiting quietly at the side of the room. 'Domica, help the girl.'

At this, the figure approached Allegra. Although dressed in the dark habit of the order, the figure wore a mask of black velvet, such as the Venetians wear at carnival time. This made Allegra yet more fearful. Suddenly, she realised what it was that the block of wood reminded her of – the grim blood-blackened wood of an executioner's block. And this figure, although garbed like a sanctified nun, also wore a mask like one of the State's official executioners. As the figure grasped her arm, Allegra screamed.

'Do not fear,' the figure whispered secretly into her ear. 'You will bear it.'

Only slightly less alarmed, Allegra allowed herself to be led to the block. Flinching, she noticed a pail of liquid by the side of the block wherein stood several bundles of birch twigs. Terror of the pain to come gripped her. It was only with the mysterious Domica's help that she was placed in a kneeling posture, with her upper body bent over the promontory of wood.

'Now that you are a little more comfortable, perhaps you can tell your sisters how your dress came to be disarrayed?'

Allegra was closer to the Prioress now, and recognised

from her easy tone that this was to be some kind of preamble to an habitual, ritual punishment. Desperately, she wondered for how long she might be able to spin out the time. 'I was preparing for bed,' she announced in a stronger voice.

'For whose bed?' At this, there was the sound of gentle tittering from the rest of the group.

'For my own,' Allegra asserted.

'You lie. Domica, inspect the subject.'

At this, the girl felt the masked figure reach behind her and try to lift her skirts. Twisting around, Allegra struggled to shake her off.

'Domica. Brother Guillam. The restraints.'

The next moment Allegra found herself held in two sets of strong arms and pushed forward across the little hill of wood. First her wrists and then her ankles were seized, and bound in leather straps which neatly slid through metal rings attached to the birching block for that purpose. Frantically, Allegra pulled on the restraints, but they held her as tightly as a dog in harness. She was kneeling on the block, with her upper half held bent across the stepped back of the block. Her head hung down, facing the company of clerics, with her wrists closest to them in the bands of leathers. Her ankles were held slightly apart in similar straps. She was completely helpless, at the mercy of this strange sisterhood whose violent rites of gratification she could barely imagine. The two figures moved back behind her as she stared at the Prioress with heartfelt fury.

'I ask again, inspect the subject.'

This time, as her skirts were lifted, Allegra could do nothing but pull despondently on the restraints and look with eyes like daggers at the loathsome perpetrator of this indignity. She could feel the woman Domica carefully pin her skirts up above her waist. The effect upon the victim was to produce a burning paroxysm of shame.

'What do you find?'

In a gesture of supreme humiliation, Allegra felt the

nun known as Domica slide her fingers between Allegra's bare cheeks. With a rapid gesture she found the girl's secret entrance and slipped a finger in and out. 'She is damp.'

'And what is your opinion, Brother Guillam?'

Allegra almost exploded with anger as the young priest now pried into her flesh as well. 'How dare you!' she screamed. 'This is defilement; may you all be witness to my violation!'

But again, it was no use. The restraints allowed her virtually no movement. Although they did not hurt at all, they were effective in keeping her tightly bound in only one undignified position. As the priest's more stubby hand slipped into the warm liquid at her centre, she felt him spread his fingers in seeming delight, probing her sex with a sensuous, caressing touch.

'She is indeed damp and ready,' the priest reported in a surprisingly cool, detached voice.

'Very well,' the Prioress continued. 'Let the charges be stated.'

It was Sister Ino who read the charges, and read them with delight.

'The sister known as Almoro is charged with the following offences. That she did, on her first night in this institution, take carnal pleasure with the sister known as Celina or rightly as Dorico. That she was herself lewd and lascivious is proved against her. On the second day of her habitation here, she was found, by myself, to be spying upon the youth Luca as he stripped to a state of complete undress. That her intentions were again of a lewd nature was made clear by the abandoned posture I discovered her in. Later that night she did again inflict carnal pleasure of a most unrefined manner upon the novice Celina known as Dorico. Only my own interruption at their room prevented her from further indulging in her craving for lustful satisfaction.

'Finally, the above offences are greatly magnified by one single fact. She does not accept her own nature. She is in a state of rebellion against every instinct of her body. So, to the charge of lewdness, I add the far greater offence of hypocrisy. In complaining to us of the wickedness of Sister Dorico, she intentionally acted as a hypocrite and liar. In accusing others she tries to make herself appear good. Her soul is at war with her flesh. This is the charge I make.'

Throughout this speech Allegra's jaw dropped with astonishment. How did they know these things? Furious as she was, a glimmer of recognition twinkled in her mind as she listened to Sister Ino's description of herself. And yet, and yet – she tried so hard to be good. There was still within her the capacity to withstand all of this; she knew it.

'What do you say to the charges?' The Prioress eyed her with disdain.

'I deny them,' she shouted.

'You what?' The Prioress was truly enraged. 'It will be the worse for you if you do not confess.'

'I do not care,' Allegra spluttered. 'You are all wicked, too. I have tried to be good, I know in my heart. If you punish me, it is you who do wrong.'

The company appeared to mutter reproachfully. Clutching the arms of her chair, the old woman leant forward, with eyes blazing like live coals. 'So, you deny your offences? I warn you, it will be the worse for you.'

'I do,' Allegra cried, holding on to the last vestige of her pride.

'Domica. Prepare.'

For some time, Allegra lay across the block, panting with extreme fear and anger. For a while she closed her eyes, wishing with all her heart she might wake up in her narrow bed, or even back in the green luxury of her chamber in the Palazzo di Rivero. But when she opened her eyes again, she was still in the gloomy, underground chamber with the vast fresco of the enigmatic woman staring down upon her. In time, a hush fell on the room.

'Aphrodite Philomastrix, Our Lady of the Scourge,'

intoned the Prioress, 'we bring before you our rebellious sister, Almoro. She has lost her way in the byways and labyrinths of untruth and hypocrisy. She is misled by pride and self-glorification. We ask that you help her to find her true nature.'

It seemed to Allegra from her position on the block that the great painted image of the Aphrodite nodded benignly.

'Sister Almoro. Do you repent?'

Again, it was anger rather than fear which flooded through her veins. She would show them her strength, for sure. 'I do not.'

'Sister Almoro. You know why you are here. I warn you, take this opportunity to repent.'

'No!'

'This is your final chance. In a moment I will instruct Domica to thrash you with the birch upon your naked flesh. I have calculated the punishment to represent each of your offences, multiplied by the further offences of mutiny and pride. The total number of lashes you will receive is twelve.'

The company around the Prioress muttered at this. The victim herself could hear Domica gasp at the decreed total of lashes. Suddenly fear raised its worm-like head again, but Allegra swore to herself she would prevail.

'Do you, for the very last time, repent of your offences? Do you beg Our Lady of the Scourge to be spared the gift of chastisement?'

'No!'

'Very well. It will be the worse for you. You will receive twelve good lashes on your bare buttocks. They will leave a mark by which you may remember this foolhardy act of pride. Head down! Lie still! Domica, the birch!'

In a frenzy of fearful expectation, Allegra did as she was bid. Holding her breath, she waited. A loud swish filled the air, and she tensed her muscles for the impact.

Then a loud crack split the air. Pain engulfed her, almost forcing a howl from her throat. But she withstood it. Again, the high-pitched hiss rose in the air. Again, there was the burning agony of contact. By the third stroke, her eyes were running with water, her face screwed up against the hard wood. How could she bear any more? Now she could feel the stripes rising in ridges on her flesh. The thought entered her mind that she might do anything to save herself from more pain. Then she gritted her teeth with hatred for the Prioress and told herself to be stronger.

The fourth and fifth strokes fell like molten rods. At the sixth, a cry mixed of pain and affront rose to her lips which only the greatest self-control succeeded in stifling. At last there was a pause. To her surprise, Allegra found that, once the birch ceased, much of the pain ceased too. It smarted well enough, but in a more diffused, tingling fashion.

'Well,' said the old woman. 'Now you have tasted the pleasures of the birch, do you repent?'

Could she take any more? After half the allotted strokes she had been close to begging for mercy. And yet – only half were now left. Perhaps she could leave the chamber still with her head held high.

'Very well. I interpret your silence as continued mutiny. Brother Guillam. Administer six lashes at once.'

This time as Allegra tensed, it was not the thrash of the birch she felt first. Instead, the young priest reached forward and gently centred her buttocks to achieve a better aim. There was something about his caressing manner which again reminded her of his indelicate exploration of her sex. She judged the young priest was not averse to his role – indeed, quite the opposite. He had not hurt her, only brushed across the reddened surface of her flesh like a harmless flame.

When his first blow fell, Allegra realised that the woman Domica had indeed spared her the worst. With a crash the bundles of birch twigs fell and this time only the leather restraints held her in place. Without them, Allegra would have instinctively fled like a scalded cat. But again those softly intrusive fingers guided her throbbing rear back into place. Only this time, as he departed, he could not resist a sensual flicker downwards to the readily parted lips below.

In spite of the pain, Allegra flushed yet more at this casual transgression. The thrashing by the woman Domica had been light and oddly neutral. Now, as Brother Guillam lifted his arm to chastise her, she heard a deep groan emerge from his chest. Secretly, she knew it was not a response to physical effort, but to deep, choking lust. Almost playfully, she wriggled her bottom, so he had to break off his duty and grasp her flesh between his hands. His breath was fast and uneven; he seemed to knead her cheeks as he pushed them down into place. Again, as the birch fell, a tortured groan escaped from his lungs.

Three strokes remained. Her skin burnt now, like molten flame. But the worst of the agony was countered by her overwhelming awareness of the young priest's appetite. Now she wanted him to want her, indeed wished she could command him to kiss and lick the painful results of his labours. Secretly, she guessed he must be wildly throbbing beneath his robe, struggling in a private agony of violent lust. Again, she wiggled the fleshy target of his rod, feeling the power of her sex smiting him down.

Unnerved, he put the rod down and reached out with both his hands to hold her still. She could hear him panting as he grasped her thighs, pushing his thumbs into the warm flesh, leaning against her as if he desperately wanted to throw himself on to the block too and summarily mount her fiery rump.

'What is it?' the Prioress barked impatiently. 'Why do you delay?'

'She will not stay still,' Brother Guillam protested, his

voice cracked and hoarse. 'I believe she is playing the wanton.'

'Ah,' the old woman cried. 'Then finish your task, for I have another idea for our spirited Sister Almoro. Get along now, administer the twelve.'

With some trouble still, the young priest administered a further lash. As the last one was about to fall, again Allegra moved, jutting her rear towards him, so she guessed he might be once again smitten by desire. Unable to control himself this last time, he grasped her by the parting at her thighs and pushed her back towards the block. In doing so, unseen by the others, his broad fingers pushed hard inside her, penetrating her most secret entrance. So it was with a shiver of excitement that she felt the last blow fall and the pain seemed to mingle with her pleasure in a seething cauldron of arousal.

'Now, let her kiss the rod,' the old woman commanded.

As she still knelt in bondage, the young priest stood before her, with the harsh birch rod in his hands. 'Kiss it,' he murmured.

Stretching forward, Allegra raised her heavy, lust-filled eyes. 'I should rather it was your rod I kissed,' she whispered. And as her lips met the brittle collection of birch twigs, she looked at his face and saw there, too, the flush of stifled carnality and eagerly parted, gasping lips.

'Brother Guillam, stand before us now.' Reluctantly, it seemed, the young priest left his victim's side and presented himself to the gathered company. 'I have a fancy,' the voice continued, 'that you are not of such a continent nature as your priesthood would suggest.' Again, there seemed to be the suggestion of a snigger from some of those who listened. 'Would I be correct in saying you took pleasure in this grave duty?'

The young man shook his head, but did not speak.

'It is proved easily enough. Lift your robe.'

Shaking his head again, the young priest backed away, horrified at the Prioress's command.

'In the name of Our Lady Philomastrix, lift your robe.'

Slowly and with great reluctance, Brother Guillam raised the hem of his robe. Straining her neck, Allegra tried to watch the scene. Unmistakably, she saw the silhouette of a stiff and ready phallus rising from the pit of Brother Guillam's stomach. A collective murmur of reproach and excitement spread through the watching group. The young priest emitted a sigh of despair.

'Do not be dejected, our beloved brother. For Our Lady has suggested to me a test, by which we might examine your control of the flesh. Do you beg to be forgiven?'

Throwing himself on his knees, Brother Guillam groaned that he would do anything to prove himself worthy again.

'Very well. Domica. In a few moments I will ask you to administer twelve loving strokes to the buttocks of this, our beloved brother. Guillam, meanwhile you must prove your mastery of the lust which this young girl has aroused within you. For the duration of the beating, you must copulate with this girl, but at all times demonstrate your complete control. At the end of the beating, you must not have spilt a drop of semen. Do you understand?'

'Yes, I do.'

'Only if you can exhibit such complete self-denial will I allow you to wear again your priestly garb. If you should spill yourself, you will be defrocked this night.'

'Thank you. I will not fail.'

'Very well. You may prepare.'

As Allegra listened, she could scarcely believe the words she heard. Again, anger fuelled her to struggle against her bonds. This was outrageous; she was being used as no more than a receptacle to test the youth's self-mastery. It was the ultimate height of mortification.

'How dare you,' she began, but before her haranguing could continue, the Prioress had interrupted her.

'Domica, the gag.'

Before she could do any more than wail in indignation, a thick leather strap had been wound about her mouth and quickly fastened at the back. Not a sound could emerge from her stifled mouth. The feeling of helpless vulnerability was complete. As the priest moved behind her, she felt like a trussed animal, held rigid on the block. The indignity of her position, with her rear exposed by the pinned-up petticoat, seemed to her complete.

But next she found that the priest and nun were adjusting the straps which held her ankles. With two sharp movements her legs were pulled wider apart, exposing the soft, vulnerable inside of her lips. Unable to protest, Allegra could only whimper at the shame of it, knowing the priest must be eyeing her stretched labia with lust-engorged senses. At last it seemed all was ready. Domica lifted the birch and Brother Guillam swung on to the block, kneeling behind her.

With a sudden tender gesture, he stroked Allegra's hair. 'Forgive me,' he murmured. 'For I would not choose to despoil you.' Then, turning to the Prioress, he asked, 'Is she not virgin?'

'In flesh she may be, but not in spirit.' The old woman sounded bored. 'And for certain if you do not climax, she will still be untainted. But if you cannot restrain yourself, then you must bear that as well on your conscience.'

'I understand.'

Allegra was aware of the heat of his body pressing against her. With a sudden movement he lifted his arms and pulled off the priestly robe. Now she could feel his firm flesh, warm and sensual against her burning skin. Gasping for breath now, he edged forward.

'I shall try not to hurt you,' he whispered. At this she felt for the first time the rounded head of his cock nudge against her gaping thighs. It felt large and heavy and stickily damp. Uncontrollably, she rolled her head to one side, gasping with delight. It was bumping against the soft skin of her thigh, teasing her with its promise of complete gratification. With a suppressed moan, he grasped his own pendulous flesh in his hand and aimed it at the girl's entrance. He pushed as gently as he could; the sweet wetness of her cleft guided him until he found what he sought. Meanwhile Allegra felt her heartbeat race as if she were reaching the end of a long and arduous race. Instinctively, she tilted herself backwards to receive him, but still his girth held him back from an easy entrance. The sensation of the smooth, round end of his flesh pressing only a finger's breadth inside her made her swoon with pleasure.

'To enter, I must anoint myself at your fountain,' he murmured, and began to rock slightly back and forth, so the swollen head became wet and slippery. Gagged as she was, and held helpless, Allegra could barely tolerate the waves of rapture engulfing her sex. If he had set out to tease her to the edges of ecstasy, he could not have done better. The head of his weapon was slowly working across her swollen lips, her throbbing bead of pleasure, and back again to the rim of her entrance. Very, very slowly, he eased the blood-engorged member deeper inside her, stretching her passage around it in a deliciously satisfying manner. Soon she could feel the swollen head inching its way inside her, nudging and tormenting her until she whimpered into the leather gag with frustration.

'Are you not ready yet?' the Prioress barked impatiently.

'Almost,' the priest grunted. 'She is unused to penetration.'

'Then push and be done with it.'

Gasping for breath, that was all the priest could do. Getting a firm hold of Allegra's waist, he leant forward and thrust the wide swelling of his phallus hard inside her. The effect was like spark to tinder. Suddenly Allegra felt herself pushed hard against the immovable force of the birching block. Then she could travel no further. The stiff rod drove its bulky way hard into her being, further and faster than she had ever imagined anything ever could. Closing her eyes, she felt herself hang there, with her sex upended, almost lifted aloft by the length of the priest's stiffened member.

'Domica. Begin.'

As she heard the first of Domica's harsh lashes against the priest's bare buttocks, he began to ride her with cool assurance. As his long rod thrust back and forth, Allegra tumbled into a fiery dreamworld behind her closed eyes. She could feel the full engorged girth of the thing, rubbing back and forth, torturing her senses to the limit. One second she could feel the bulky head ramming against the very depths of her stomach, the next it silkily withdrew, almost to the tip, before see-sawing back, again and again. She was only vaguely aware of the sound of the birch, although each time on its impact he dug deeper and deeper into her rapidly pliant flesh. Now, as he filled her, she became aware of the complete length of his flesh, titillating the very gates to her womb with the hard pressure of his tip. Each time this happened, she heard him stifle his breath, desperate not to climax inside her.

Now that her entire passage was slippery and yielding, Allegra felt the urgency spread through her loins to climax. The thing inside her was turning her most delicate nerves to fire, stoking her muscles to squeeze every drop of satisfaction from his bulging rod. With an instinctive loss of control, she began to thrust backwards on to it, driving herself back and forth on to his cock like a wild harlot.

'No,' he whispered wretchedly, 'keep still! You make me wild. Any second I'll shoot my seed.'

Hardly able to control herself, Allegra froze. She was shivering on the edge of climax, her nerves tormented by his ceaseless pounding, back and forth. Like a raging poker, he stoked on and on, slapping into her dripping entrance. Suddenly it was too late – she felt her inner muscles begin to tighten, gripping the vein-ribbed length of his member. With a desperate gasp of abandonment, her pelvis began to spasm around him. But it was too late. At that moment the last blow from the birch fell and with heartfelt relief he pulled his agonised member out of its honeyed nest.

Allegra wanted to scream. She had been only a second away from full womanly satisfaction. If they had been alone, she knew that he, too, would have been unable to resist the powerful spasm and would have emptied his flood inside her aching womb. If they had been alone, she would have thrown herself at him, licking and rubbing him until he begged her on his knees to let him continue. Miserably, she buried her head against the hard wood and cursed.

Around her, she was aware of Brother Guillam's feat being applauded. Glancing up, she could see through tear-filled eyes his crimson posterior and the even redder bulge of his stiffened wand, dancing above his hairy stomach. In time, he was allowed to dress once more in his priest's garb and slowly it seemed that the throng dispersed.

Soon, only Domica remained, and she set to loosing Allegra's bonds.

'You poor creature,' she soothed. As Allegra stiffly rose from the block, she felt her body ache with both ill-treatment and unsatisfied passion. 'Would you like me to soothe you?' the masked nun asked, holding out her arms. 'I will soon help you feel better.'

Allegra guessed what she meant. No. She had experienced enough of their games and their violent rites of satisfaction. She felt weak and very tired. 'If you please,' she said humbly, 'I only wish to be shown to my bed.'

Bonded

Fleur Reynolds

Bonded, Fleur Reynold's fifth Black Lace novel, is set in a decadent and jet-setting world where Sapphire Western is a beautiful young investment banker. Within this environment, Sapphire becomes involved in dark, heightened games of sexual intrigue and revenge. It is difficult to know which people she can trust. Even as she denies her attraction to handsome banker Everett, passions rise and the stakes climb even higher. In this extract, Sapphire gives in fully to her libidinous desires, within the very circle of people she knows are morally and dangerously seductive.

Other Black Lace novels Fleur Reynolds has written are: *Odalisque*, a rich tale of family wealth, intrigue and depravity; *Handmaiden of Palmyra*, set in third-century Palmyra, an oasis in the Syrian desert; *The House in New Orleans*, in which Ottilie Duvier, upon inheriting her family home, is forced to lease it to a decadent German count famed for his excesses; and *Conquered*, a story of sixteenth-century Peru, where Inca princess Inez, after escaping from the conquistadors, is initiated into the sensual ways of an Amazonian tribe.

Bonded

Sapphire was sitting drinking iced coffee in the cool, chrome and marble air-conditioned café-bar.

When she'd first arrived, expecting Auralie to be there, Sapphire had been bursting with her incredible news. She hadn't been able to take in everything that had happened in the lawyer's office. She was in deep shock, and thought that repeating it, telling what had occurred to someone, especially an old friend, might make the whole episode feel more real.

But, as time ticked by, the impact mellowed and gradually Sapphire began to change her mind. When Auralie eventually appeared, Sapphire had definitely decided to keep her information to herself. She was not going to tell anyone what she'd learnt and that, apart from some minor bequests to her brother and various family retainers, she was her father's sole beneficiary and an incredibly rich woman.

'So sorry I'm late,' said Auralie. 'Gerry phoned me.'

'Gerry? Your ex-husband Gerry?'

'Yes; he wants me to have lunch with him and his father, for some reason. Can't think what for, so that's why I'm going, but I made it later so we can have time together. Now tell me, Sapphy, how was your business?'

'Fine,' replied Sapphire.

'*Trés bien*,' said Auralie. 'In that case, *chérie*, stop the coffee and let's drink cocktails. I'll need some Dutch courage for my meeting. I'll have a Kir Royale – and you?'

'A Bellini,' replied Sapphire.

Sipping their drinks, the two young women talked and chatted; gradually, Sapphire opened up her heart to Auralie, telling her how she'd fallen for a man and how beautifully he had seduced her. She hadn't got as far as telling her friend how Carola Finestein was in his office before Auralie interrupted.

'Does this paragon have a name?' asked Auralie.

'Yes; Everett de Bouys,' replied Sapphire shyly.

'Everett de Bouys?' exploded Auralie. 'Oh, *mon Dieu*! Forget him, *chérie*. Forget the bastard.'

'Why?' asked Sapphire, quite taken aback by the vehemence in Auralie's voice.

'I've just heard he's going to marry my bitch cousin, Jeanine.'

'Jeanine?' exclaimed Sapphire. 'Everett's going to marry Jeanine?'

'That's what I heard.'

'Oh no,' said Sapphire and burst into tears.

'Oh, I'm sorry,' said Auralie, putting an arm around Sapphire. 'Now you must forget him.'

'It's not that easy,' said Sapphire tearfully.

'Yes it is; you fuck someone else,' said Auralie defiantly.

'Auralie!' said Sapphire, her old-fashioned primness returning. Then she thought, well, perhaps Auralie had the right idea. 'Who?'

'I don't know who,' said Auralie, her eyes wandering over her friend's chest. 'Have you ever had a woman?'

'No; don't be ridiculous,' said Sapphire, quite shocked, but less shocked than she would have been had she not drunk three Bellinis. 'Why, have you?'

'Yes.'

'Oh!' said Sapphire, leaning across the table. 'What's it like?'

'Exciting, *chérie*,' said Auralie. 'Soft, and – ' Auralie licked her lips '– and juicy.'

'What do you do?' asked Sapphire.

'Kiss, and stroke and suck,' said Auralie, lingering on the word suck.

'Suck?'

'Yes. Another one?' asked Auralie, indicating the empty cocktail glass.

'Yes,' said Sapphire, throwing all caution to the wind. 'What do you suck?'

'Pussy,' said Auralie, hailing the waiter.

'Pussy! You mean, down there?'

'Yes, that's right; between your legs,' said Auralie; then as the waiter came up, added, 'two more please.'

'Oh Auralie, how naughty you are. I'm sure you're just teasing me,' said Sapphire.

'You could say that,' said Auralie.

'You'll be telling me soon you've had a man and woman together,' said Sapphire.

'I have,' said Auralie.

'No!' said Sapphire. 'Oh, Auralie!'

The waiter brought their drinks and Sapphire quickly sipped hers. She was fascinated and appalled.

'Are you wet?' asked Auralie, not drinking her cocktail.

'What?'

'Are you wet? I mean can you feel yourself opening?' asked Auralie again.

Sapphire didn't want to answer straight away. She was ashamed of the tingling in her belly, the sudden feeling of excitement that was flooding through her lips into her belly and then down to her sex.

'You are wet, aren't you, Sapphy?'

Sapphire, not trusting herself to say anything, looked around the room, as if that would help her with her answer. 'Yes, I am,' she admitted, nodding her head.

'Have your nipples gone stiff?'

'Yes,' said Sapphire; then, in a whisper added, 'tell me about it, Auralie. Tell me.'

'You've never done it?'

'No!'

'You've never been laid by a woman?'

'No.'

'You've never been screwed by two people?'

'No,' said Sapphire, draining her cocktail down in one.

'*Chérie*, what have you been doing with your life?'

'Making money,' said Sapphire honestly.

'Oh, *chérie*,' said Auralie, 'fucking is much more fun.'

'Yes, I agree,' said Sapphire, lisping drunkenly and remembering her night spent with Everett. 'But who can I fuck here?'

'Somebody'll turn up,' said Auralie. 'I have great faith in what you're wanting and needing suddenly arriving.'

'Well, I need my bed,' said Sapphire standing, then leaning on the table as the room started to go around.

'I'll get you there,' said Auralie, taking her arm and guiding her out of the café.

The sticky heat hit Sapphire. She was suddenly much more drunk than she had been in the cool restaurant and nearly collapsed.

'It's not far,' said Auralie, as she looked up and down in vain for a passing taxi. 'Lean on me, *chérie*.'

Auralie took a small side turning on their way to the Staples Hotel. The narrow walkway turned into a street full of beautiful old colonial houses: leftovers from the British Empire. Hidden from the main drag, leafy from the many trees overhanging the high walls, and without the relentless sun burning down, it was cooler. It was there they met Jethro.

Sapphire saw him first, which surprised her; she thought she was past seeing anything.

'Auralie, there's Zinnia's husband, Jethro Clarke,' slurred Sapphire.

'*Mon Dieu!* So it is,' said Auralie, endeavouring to hold Sapphire upright.

He was closing the high gates set into the equally high wall of a large private house before entering his waiting chauffeur-driven limousine.

'He wanted to fuck me,' said Sapphire blatantly.

'I'm sure he did,' said Auralie.

'I suppose this is where you're keeping Ana Tai?' Auralie shouted. 'But I know where Zinnia is.' Sapphire began to slip from Auralie's grasp. 'Sapphy, stay here a moment,' she said, and propped her up against the limo. 'No, don't slide down. Hold on to the car if you feel yourself going.'

'Yes,' said Sapphire, who was quite happy to hold on to anything as the street came up and met her eyes and the palm trees floated off to greet the sun.

Auralie grabbed Jethro by the sleeve. 'Jethro,' she said, 'you're a dealer; and dealers deal. Now, I've got something you'd like, and you've got something I want. So, let's swap for the information that you need. You have Ana Tai. I want Ana Tai. You want Sapphire. I have Sapphire. And – and this is the big one, *chérie* – I know where Zinnia is.'

'Fine,' he said. 'Where?'

'Is Ana Tai here?' asked Auralie, pointing to the house behind them.

'Sure is,' he replied.

'Let's go there; then we're both certain of achieving our objective,' said Auralie.

Jethro hesitated.

'What's the matter, Jethro?' asked Auralie. 'Oh, you've chained her up, have you?'

Sapphire was vaguely aware of their conversation and then, as she slowly slipped down, noticed Jethro looking at her. The next moment she was high on his shoulders, being carried through the gates and into the garden of a luxurious modern house. Hazily, Sapphire noticed that the garden was well-established but the house was very new. Somebody had obviously pulled down the previous edifice and built this one in its stead.

The roof had a Far Eastern, Chinese feel to its shape; the huge picture windows were surrounded by stained black wood. Inside there was a sparse but vast open-plan reception room, which was decorated in a theme of shades of white, grey and black. The walls were a milky grey, the marble floor tiles black and white, and the chairs and settees covered in black silk. There were a few strategically placed paintings, chosen for their designer quality and suitability for the décor rather than for any artistic merit. Large black ceiling fans whirred against the humidity of the atmosphere. It was anonymous, well designed, expensive and completely impersonal.

'Whose house is it?' asked Auralie: the question Sapphire also wanted to know the answer to.

'Petrov's,' replied Jethro, carrying on walking through the open-plan reception rooms and up the glass staircase to the bedrooms.

Jethro opened a door on to a cell-like room with narrow uncurtained windows set close to the ceiling. The floor was a dark grey marble, covered in thick black and white Chinese silk rugs. In the centre of the room was a queen-sized bed.

Jethro put Sapphire down on the large bed occupied by Ana Tai, who was lying asleep on its grey silk coverlet. Sapphire gave a sudden intake of breath and tried to get up, but Jethro pushed her down again. Sapphire tried once more but her legs had turned to jelly. She was too drunk to stand.

She lay there and looked at the girl, who was blindfolded and wore a neck-iron with chains leading to a padlocked hook on the wall. Her wrists were handcuffed together and were locked above her head. She was clothed only in a sparkling white shift, which showed off the beauty of her brown body. The rings in her labia were clearly visible and were attached to chains which ran down her legs and ended at padlocked anklets. Her buttocks were bare and there were deep welts across her rump. Somebody had given her a good whipping. The whips were arranged around her but just out of her reach. On a table beside the bed was a selection of dildoes and a tray full of various sweet-smelling oils.

'Ana Tai,' Jethro called softly, and stroked her bare buttocks.

'You want me again?' asked Ana Tai, spreading her legs wide.

'No,' said Jethro, letting Sapphire slither on to the bed. 'I've brought a friend for you to play with.'

Jethro sat on the bed, gripped the whole of Ana Tai's sex, forced her back and kissed her mouth.

'Ana Tai!' exclaimed Auralie. 'He's a man!'

'Yes,' answered Ana Tai sweetly, raising her hips.

'Don't you want Sapphire?' asked Auralie jealously.

Jethro looked at the almost comatose figure on the bed. 'Yes,' he said, and reached out a hand and began fondling Sapphire's breasts.

Scarcely knowing what she was doing, Sapphire responded in a lazy, hazy way, her nipples stiffening under his caresses. She half closed her eyes and decided to enjoy Jethro. She would be abandoned, take risks, have fun. Sexual fun. And later, if she regretted it, she would tell herself she was drunk, so it didn't matter.

Sapphire watched Auralie slip off her skirt and jacket but keep on her high-heeled shoes and her hold-up stockings. She admired her friend's neat body, her small pert breasts and neat rounded bottom. Auralie climbed on to the bed and fastened her mouth over Ana Tai's; she snaked her hands up under the white shift and began caressing Ana Tai's nipples.

Sapphire gasped audibly with a sudden rush of pleasure as Jethro played with her breasts, raised her skirt and let his fingers trail up over her long white legs, until he reached the outer fleshy moist lips of her sex. She was not just feeling sexual; Sapphire needed to be ravished. She sighed and squirmed with excitement as his finger moved backwards and forwards over her silky blonde down. She opened her legs and spread her arms, enjoying the excitement of something forbidden and dangerous.

Sapphire turned her head to see what Auralie was doing. She was kneeling over Ana Tai's mouth and, putting her hands between her own legs, she displayed herself and moved her hips from side to side. Ana Tai rubbed a finger along Auralie's swollen labia, gently touching her stiffening bud.

Auralie tensed her muscles and jerked her hips forward as if asking for more; more pressure on her clitoris. Ana Tai obeyed; Auralie gave a tiny gasp of delight and began kneading her own breasts. Sapphire watched Ana Tai as she began to ease her fingers inwards, feeling the delight of the soft ridges and the tender juiciness of Auralie's vagina.

Ana Tai reached down her chained hands and grabbed at one of Sapphire's hard nipples. Sapphire raised herself slightly and put her head level with Ana Tai's moist opening. Auralie jutted her hips closer to Ana Tai's mouth, offering herself to the exotic girl, who buried her tongue in Auralie's sweet perfumed rosy flesh and licked her. Ana Tai moved her tongue along Auralie's swollen edges, teasing her, her nose devouring her special erotic smell; then she bit gently on Auralie's engorged clitoris. Auralie moaned with abandonment.

Jethro took hold of Sapphire's fingers and placed them on Ana Tai's belly.

'Stroke her,' he ordered as his fingers slowly, gently, tenderly, opened Sapphire's wet and hungry sex.

Sapphire quickened with anticipation. Then, when he placed his fingers at her sex opening, she trembled and he lunged. He plunged in, taking his fingers to the apex of her love channel. Sapphire squirmed and sighed, letting her fingers roam over Ana Tai's body and the young Asian woman's shaven and beringed sex lips.

Hesitating and unsure of herself, Sapphire allowed her fingers to proceed tenderly.

She savoured each second of pleasure; the pleasure of touching another woman's sex. Not used to the touch of herself, Sapphire became very excited by the softness and the yielding furls and ridges; she was fascinated and surprised by the strength of Ana Tai's inner muscles. They contracted around her fingers, clasping them, holding them, exciting her further and drawing her into hidden depths. Only very gradually did Sapphire completely penetrate Ana Tai's vulva, wallowing in her soft, creamy, sensitive wet sex.

She watched, fascinated, as Auralie bent over and kissed Ana Tai passionately. Then her attention went back to Jethro as he undid the fastening on her skirt and pulled it off, leaving her sex exposed. He removed her shoes and stockings. He bent down and licked her between her legs. She raised her hips.

'Turn over,' he ordered. 'Turn over and kneel.'

Sapphire obeyed him and her face was now at Ana Tai's sex, her rounded bare bottom high in the air.

Auralie knelt with her back to Sapphire and shoved her hips forward so that Ana Tai's tongue could lick and suck at her wanton pussy.

With speed Jethro removed his own clothing, put on a condom and came up behind Sapphire.

'Suck her,' Jethro commanded, pushing Sapphire forward. He stuck his stiff prick between her legs. He rubbed on the outside of her sex but didn't enter. He played and teased her, exciting Sapphire beyond endurance. He stroked Sapphire's round bottom, his hand climbing up her spine under her suit jacket. He was enjoying the sight of her semi-clothed, her long legs and her sex on show giving him immediate access and yet her breasts remaining tantalisingly half-hidden.

'Sapphire, I want to see you put out your tongue and lick Ana Tai; lick her between her legs. Lick her sex lips,' he commanded.

Jethro let his finger rub again and again on Sapphire's wetness but she didn't lick the other woman.

'Suck, I said,' he ordered, dipping his fingers into a saucer of oils. Then he began circling her tight puckered forbidden hole. Slowly he let his fingers ease their way into Sapphire's anus. As he suddenly thrust into her, she jerked forward and her head was forced between Ana Tai's legs. Excited and willingly impaled by Jethro's fingers, Sapphire squirmed and licked.

With every orifice plundered, Ana Tai was emitting squeals of bliss. Ana Tai pushed her shoulders back, making sure Jethro could see her erect nipples straining through the fabric of her shift.

'He's got a great cock and now he's learnt how to use it,' said Ana Tai proudly.

'And you can watch me screw Sapphire,' said Jethro, standing behind her, his fingers playing with her arse.

With his prick hovering, he let Sapphire feel the merest whisper of his stiffness against the moist wetness of her swollen sex. Then his cock began making small forays into her engorged and welcoming vulva. She gasped with excitement and lust. Jethro's prick instantly gained length. He jerked forward as if to enter her, but Sapphire, drunk on alcohol and desire, had other ideas and pulled back from him.

'I want them both to watch me being screwed,' said Sapphire brazenly. She took a short sharp breath of pleasure and anticipation then, swallowing a lump in her throat, she wiggled her hips and smiled. Capriciously she turned her head towards Ana Tai's sex and put her hands on the Asian girl's brown thighs.

'Now watch,' she whispered.

Sapphire wanted his cock sliding into her; that hard knob pushing her open, its long shaft inching its way upwards into her squashy pink swollen and lustful flesh. She wanted to feel the full impact of Jethro's pleasure, stretching her, taking her, fucking her, fucking her fast and furiously – his anticipation finally realised.

Auralie eased her body to one side so that Ana Tai could witness Jethro's entry. Sapphire rocked backwards and forwards and, little by little, Jethro's cock felt its way into her lascivious sex and was enveloped by her wanton willingness.

As he bent over Sapphire, he brought his hands round, kneaded her breasts and licked her neck. Then, when she had got used to his soft luscious gliding rhythm, suddenly, and with one quick movement, he thrust, pushing his thick engorged penis in up to the hilt. She devoured him, taking every inch of him. He rode her like a horse but she wouldn't let him come. She put her hands down between his legs; she felt his balls, squeezed them, and pressed on the base of his shaft.

'Oh yes,' said Ana Tai, sexily. 'Fuck her, fuck her.'

Sapphire saw the flash of jealousy cross Auralie's face, and wasn't as surprised as she would have been a few hours earlier when Auralie picked up a crop that was lying near, and slowly – but with great assuredness – trailed it along Ana Tai's sex lips, pressing on but never entering the Asian girl's soft juicy beringed wetness.

'No, madam, no,' moaned Ana Tai, enjoying Auralie's touch and moving her hips, trying to make the crop glide into her silken warm opening.

'Yes, I will – and don't argue with me,' said Auralie, standing up.

Sapphire, rocking on Jethro's cock, saw Auralie turn Ana Tai over on to her belly so that her sweet luscious soft brown buttocks were displayed ready for the crop.

'Sorry, madam,' cried Ana Tai.

Auralie poked her fingers into Ana Tai's vulva. Ana Tai let out little sighs of pleasure.

'You are very wet, very wet indeed,' Auralie said seductively, shoving her fingers up and down inside Ana Tai's sex, making her dance and squirm.

Ana Tai relaxed her bare buttocks. Auralie trailed the crop up between Ana Tai's legs, then, with tiny circular movements, poked first at her bottom hole and then at her soft open sex. The girl trembled with excitement as the thin hardness of the crop touched her rosy creamy-wet flesh.

In a flash Auralie brought the crop down on Ana Tai's thighs.

'Thank you, madam,' gasped Ana Tai.

'One is not enough,' said Auralie, sternly. 'Six stripes. And Jethro will administer your punishment.' She handed the crop to Jethro.

Jethro licked his lips in anticipation.

Sapphire realised that even though he was screwing her, there was a bond between him and Ana Tai. And that he desperately wanted to touch the young Asian woman but refrained. Every minute that went by, every minute that Auralie touched and felt and played with Ana Tai's private places, made Jethro randier and randier. Sapphire knew instinctively that he wanted to feel her lusciousness quivering beneath his touch. He wanted to touch the open wet juiciness at the top of Ana Tai's thighs, even though he was taking and pleasuring her. Jethro was yearning for Ana Tai's body – and Sapphire could understand why. She thought her big blonde heavy-breasted body compared badly with the Asian girl's sleek, slim figure.

Ana Tai caught and held her breath. Sapphire stuck her hips out, keeping Jethro's cock hard up inside her. Jethro brought the crop swishing down hard over Ana Tai's round buttocks. Between each stripe, Auralie rammed her fingers into Ana Tai's wet and wanton sex, and Jethro, suffering pangs of acute envy, thrust harder into Sapphire.

Sapphire could see that the exquisite mixture of pain and pleasure almost brought Ana Tai to the point of orgasm. Each time the crop came down, Ana Tai cried out, begging it to stop, but to no avail.

When her punishment was over, Auralie inspected the red weals on Ana Tai's bottom, then gently kissed and caressed the marks.

'What do you say?' asked Auralie.

'Thank you, madam, thank you,' she said.

'And how are you going to show your thanks, your true thanks?' said Auralie lecherously.

'Your pleasure is my pleasure,' said Ana Tai submissively.

Auralie, who now had her own legs wide apart, her thumb on her clitoris and two fingers inside herself, lay in front of Ana Tai's mouth.

Sapphire once again stroked the soft erogenous zone of Ana Tai's inner thighs. Facing Jethro, Auralie positioned her sex over Ana Tai's mouth and the girl sunk her tongue into Auralie's wetness.

'Thank you, madam,' said Ana Tai.

Auralie, sitting astride Ana Tai, gazed lasciviously at Jethro's prick charging in and out of Sapphire's sex. She slithered off Ana Tai's hot sweat-soaked body, leant forward and took Jethro's cock in her hands. Sensual and very erotic thoughts flooded through Sapphire as she felt Auralie's fingers tightening around Jethro's stiff cock and fingers straying on to her wet sex and swollen sexlips. Jethro began to shake and pant. The tantalising sensation of Auralie's hands on his prick was almost too much for him to bear. He was close to coming, but Auralie gripped his penis at the base and held his orgasm back.

'Feel her,' Jethro ordered Sapphire.

Auralie took Sapphire's forefinger, hooked it around her own, then trailed it along the top of Ana Tai's legs. 'She's very wet. Sapphire, put your tongue just where I've got my finger.'

Sapphire moved her head and did as she was told. Sapphire licked at the outer rim of Ana Tai's vulva. Auralie splayed Ana Tai's sex lips so that Sapphire's tongue could lick easily at her soft juiciness.

'She wants to be fucked,' said Auralie, stroking Jethro's phallus. 'Take her. Take her fast.'

Jethro moved back from the kneeling Sapphire and

positioned himself against the chained woman. Ana Tai remained utterly motionless. Auralie aimed his prick at the entrance to Ana Tai's sex. Jethro placed his hands on the girl's breasts and thrust his cock into her willing and wanting sex. With the force of his enthusiasm, she arched. He lifted her up against him and started to pound. Auralie began to feel herself with soft tantalising strokes. Ana Tai rolled and heaved, and rocked and swayed, taking every last inch of him. Their bodies were totally together, blended.

Sapphire moved to one side, lay on her back and watched. Auralie found a whip with a thick handle and rubbed it between Sapphire's thighs; Sapphire swayed her hips licentiously.

'Jethro, what are you doing?' roared his business partner, Petrov, charging into the room and grabbing hold of Jethro, forcing him to withdraw from Ana Tai.

Sapphire looked up with blurry vision to see who it was who had so noisily invaded the lazy sexy heat of their room. She recognised Petrov and was quite surprised. He did not seem to recognise her. She turned her face away but raised up her hips, giving him full sight of her beautiful, soft, white and rounded bottom.

'You should have been with me, not here, screwing,' said Petrov angrily; but he was instantly captivated by the sight of Sapphire's buttocks.

'Got well-laid,' replied Jethro flippantly. 'Anyhow how did it go? Did my new partner turn up?'

'No, he did not,' said Petrov.

'He didn't?' cried Jethro. It was Jethro's turn to be both surprised and angry. 'He didn't turn up? He didn't arrive?'

'That's what I said,' said Petrov.

'Then something's gone wrong,' said Jethro, jumping off the bed and hurriedly putting on his clothes.

'Where are you going?' asked Petrov.

'The Exchange.'

'Oh, you think it's that important?'

'Oh, yes,' said Jethro. 'Something real bad.'

'Aw, come on,' said Petrov.

'No. Come on, nothing,' replied Jethro. 'If my new partner hasn't kept his appointment ... Hell, Petrov, that's real bad news. He was bringing thirty million sterling in cash.'

'Then ...' Petrov looked wistfully at Auralie and Sapphire lying on the bed. 'Then I'd better go with you.'

'No, you stay here,' said Jethro.

'Are you sure?' asked Petrov, feeling relieved. Money was nice but sex was better.

'Quite sure. I'll sort it. Come along, Ana Tai,' said Jethro, unpadlocking Ana Tai's chains and lifting her off the bed.

'Hey!' said Auralie. 'Jethro, that's my woman.'

'We'll talk about that,' said Jethro.

'No, we won't. You're a man, a married man, and she's mine,' shouted Auralie.

'Now's not the time to discuss it, Auralie,' said Jethro. 'I think it is.'

'I know it's not,' said Jethro.

'Hey, hey, I'm not a piece of merchandise,' said Ana Tai. 'I'm not going anywhere – except to take a bath and then go to sleep. So you can put me down, Jethro Clarke.'

'Yes, ma'am,' he said.

Ana Tai marched out of the room, quickly followed by Jethro.

'Auralie,' said Petrov, seeing the crestfallen look on Auralie's face, and revealing his huge stiff prick throbbing and erect. 'Stay with me and play. You've got another lovely little friend here.'

Petrov was admiring Sapphire's long legs. He bent over her, put his hands out and rubbed her buttocks suggestively.

Auralie dipped her fingers in the oil and rubbed some over Petrov's cock, then on Sapphire's body.

Petrov began rubbing his cock. 'You, you're the one I want,' he said.

Petrov's cock twitched and stirred, betraying his intense sexuality. Auralie stroked Sapphire's breasts and rolled her over so that her rump was available for Petrov's whip. Sapphire didn't realise what Auralie was intending and stared into the other woman's eyes with growing lust. Sapphire wriggled her bottom, raising it slightly and enticing Petrov.

'Auralie, I wouldn't want to stop your pleasure,' said Petrov, 'but who is she? What's her name?'

'Sapphy,' said Auralie. 'I thought she should have some fun. She got a little drunk but I think she's had the fun.'

'I'll give her some more,' said Petrov. 'She's gorgeous. I want to fuck her.'

'Don't know if I want to let you,' said Auralie, nibbling on Sapphire's earlobes while stroking her breasts.

'Auralie, obey me,' commanded Petrov.

Auralie ignored him.

'Then this is for insolence,' said Petrov. He lashed at her. He struck Auralie again and again, catching her soft belly and the precious sweet soft flesh at the top of her thighs, giving her the feeling of exquisite pain curdled with pleasure. Auralie bit her lips and tried to lie still, accepting her chastisement.

Petrov smiled lecherously. He eased his hands down between Auralie's legs and found the fleshy pad between her vulva and the puckered orifice of her anus. Lightly he fingered that patch, exciting her; her excitement thrilled him, making his cock stiffen further. It made him roll his hips, and made his mouth salivate with unharnessed desire.

He'd punished Auralie; now he'd screw Sapphire. Petrov dipped his hands into the bowl of oil. With care and very slowly, he massaged every inch of Sapphire's body while she was stretching languidly and kissing Auralie full on the mouth. Petrov's fingers went round and round, down Sapphire's spine, across her buttocks and then up along and down through her crease.

'Hold my cock,' commanded Petrov, keeping his own hands busy and moving his body slightly so that his long stiff penis was pointing at Sapphire's stomach.

Sapphire's long delicate hands gripped Petrov's large erect prick. She held him at the base and cupped his balls. She gave tiny slippery caresses to the collar ringing its head, moving her finger over its neat cap, and watched droplets of liquid appear in its slit. Then, in one firm movement, she pulled the skin hard back down; she pressed, holding momentarily at the bottom of Petrov's quivering shaft before starting up again.

Sapphire could see that her actions pleased Petrov. He obviously liked a woman who knew how to handle a cock. Especially his cock. Petrov began to pant.

'Oil my prick,' Petrov ordered. He leant over the bed and picked up the whip. He stroked it lovingly and flicked the strands apart. Then he held the ends of the long thin leather strips so that she was able to see its cruel bulbous-ended phallus-shaped leather handle.

'You're too tight,' he whispered, bringing some rope from under the bed and quickly tying Sapphire's hands. 'Bend over, keeping your hands out above your head, your bottom raised and your feet slightly apart.'

Sapphire had no alternative but to obey. Petrov wasn't satisfied. He took a couple of pillows and placed them under Sapphire's belly. He fondled Sapphire's wanton moist sex, making sure she stayed wet and wanting, then tapped her legs apart with the whip.

As he struck Sapphire across her neat bare buttocks with the long-tailed whip, she jumped with the sudden flash of pain. Tears sprang into her eyes. Auralie quickly embraced her.

'No, no; go with it, Sapphy,' she said. 'It's wonderful; it can be marvellous. Let him do it.'

With precision, Petrov began to skim the whip across Sapphire's bare buttocks. Then he brought it down hard, marking her with a deep dark welt. With each stripe she experienced a curt pain, coupled with a refined sense of pleasure as the tail of the whip seared her soft inner skin.

'Raise your buttocks higher,' Petrov ordered.

Sapphire obeyed. Then she felt her flanks parting and slowly Petrov inserted the well-oiled head of the whip into Sapphire's tight back passage. Flushed with shame, she let her head droop. She knew it was senseless to struggle. She must go loose and accept the invasion.

Slowly Sapphire's well-lubricated channel began to take the invasive instrument and embrace its pleasure. Her muscles clutched at it as it passed upwards and let it go easily on the downward stroke. Sapphire opened and ripened. She wanted more. Deeper. Faster.

Aware of Sapphire's mute acceptance of his cruel thrusting leather phallus, Petrov pushed the bulbous head up harder. Then, languorously, he slid a hand round her belly and gripped her sex.

Sapphire was panting. The pain and pleasure was exquisite. She was rolling backwards on to the dildo. The leather whip strips were dangling enticingly between her legs. Petrov caressed her swollen red and wanton flower, up and down, up and down. Her entire body was quivering. Give me more, give me more, she was secretly yelling.

'Play with me, Auralie,' Petrov ordered, letting his hands ripple down over Sapphire's belly and thrusting the leather whip-end backwards and forwards into her newly-stretched anus.

From her bent-over position, Sapphire glanced at Auralie rubbing Petrov's cock, seeing the way she took his hard erect and throbbing phallus, stroking his glans, playing with his balls. Sapphire flashed back to her night with Everett. Instantly her emotions towards him were of anger and longing, though neither had the chance to be uppermost. Her thoughts were dramatically cut short by the sight of a large burly Asian servant walking into the room.

'Master Petrov,' said Kim Long, watching his master lying on the bed, his cock being played with by the redhead and the whip handle lewdly hanging from the blonde. 'Do you need any assistance?'

Kim Long was trussed into a black leather body harness which encircled his massive, erect cock, and his balls were thrust through a silver ring in the leather. He held a long whip.

'Can I suck your cock, master?'

'No, but you can fuck me,' said Petrov licentiously. He squirmed and wriggled his buttocks to the edge of the bed.

Kim Long's huge brown hands came down on his master's flanks. He spread Petrov's cheeks, displaying his crease. He put his huge prick to the opening, pressing slightly.

'Hard,' cried Petrov. And Kim Long plunged into his depths. 'And you – suck me.' Petrov yanked Sapphire close to his cock head as he squirmed with every thrust of Kim's prick. He loved the twin feelings of Kim Long's large sac banging against the padded flesh between his buttocks and his balls and his cock rammed up hard inside. Sapphire took his phallus slowly into her mouth.

Petrov turned his head towards Kim, who picked up the crop which lay on the bed. Petrov nodded, then withdrew his prick from Sapphire's mouth. Kim Long brought the lash down hard on Sapphire's rump. The pain scorched her. She jumped. The leather whip handle in her bottom began to ease out.

'Don't you dare let go of that,' said Petrov, pushing the handle back again. 'And keep your hands above your head.'

Kim held the short crop at Sapphire's mouth. 'Kiss it,' he said.

Sapphire bent her head and kissed the lash.

Kim scourged her again across her buttocks. Again

and again. Harder, more cruel. And Sapphire jumped, and screamed.

Sapphire turned her head to look at the big brown man. She found something deeply erotic in the sight of him, a leather collar round his neck, chains connecting the collar to a leather apron over his navel, with his cock hard and stiff sticking through the cock ring. She wondered what his cock would feel like inside her. Almost as if the servant read her thought, she received another stripe across her flanks, stinging and bringing tears to her eyes. She felt humiliated and angry, yet wet. Very wet. And Petrov kept touching, feeling and caressing her body, invading her sex.

Sapphire trembled; her knees shook and her womb tightened. There was an unreal quality to the state she was in. In her wildest dreams she'd never thought that she would have been ordered by a man, almost enslaved by him and obeying his commands – obeying and enjoying. Enjoying the freedom of total eroticism, the sensuality. She should have found it deeply humiliating. Instead, it was deeply thrilling. Sapphire was loving her role of slave, a pleasure-slave being pleasured.

Sapphire watched again as Kim, with his stomach muscles tight and his balls like two stones, thrust harder and harder into Petrov's anus. Kim dropped the whip. He snaked his hands round Petrov's waist, took hold of his long full phallus and rubbed it with the same rhythm with which he was ploughing him. He knew exactly what his master wanted: perfection. Kim Long lay over Petrov, kissing his shoulders; he sucked, leaving red-ring marks, and came. They came in unison. And Sapphire was left depleted, unwanted, not given release. And Kim Long smiled with pleasure that she had been denied his master's satisfaction.

The two men relaxed and fell asleep.

The two women lay looking at one another, watching the men deep in slumber. Auralie drew Sapphire to her and stroked her breasts and her belly.

'You want to come, eh, *chérie*?' she asked.

'Yes,' said Sapphire.

Auralie played softly and gently with her body, bringing Sapphire to her climax. Then, leaving the two men where they were, they gathered up their belongings and tiptoed out of the room. Sapphire wasn't tired. She was invigorated by her extraordinary experiences – and hungry.

The Hand of Amun

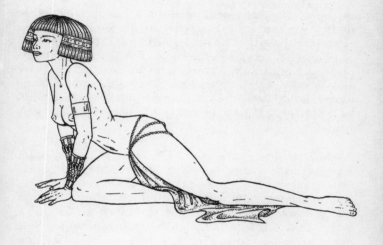

Juliet Hastings

In the mysterious world of Ancient Egypt, Naunakhte finds herself a willing servant to the god Amun, by whom she has been marked since birth. Yet, before she can begin her service as the Hand of Amun, she must be purified from mortal carnality. In this extract the slow and heavily scripted religious rite begins, while Naunakhte is transported to the utmost peaks of sensuality, towards the ultimate ecstasy of union with the god Amun.

Aside from the recent novel *The Hand of Amun*, Juliet Hastings has written four other Black Lace books: *Crash Course*, in which a female management consultant runs an unorthodox training course for three young men; *Aria Appassionata*, where life begins to imitate art as opera singer Tess Challoner falls for the male lead; *White Rose Ensnared*, where sensual affairs take place during the War of the Roses; and *Forbidden Crusade*, set in the Holy Land in the year 1186, against a backdrop of lust, religion and the Crusades. In addition, she has written short stories for Black Lace, including the lyrical *The Gilded Cage* for the first *Pandora's Box* anthology.

The Hand of Amun

All day she waited alone, watching the brilliant sun pass across the sky. She was dressed in the crumpled dirty gown in which she had fled from Khonsu's house, and she felt ashamed of its ragged state. She found herself hoping that she would be given clean raiment before the rite, as if she was more afraid of looking dishevelled than of what they might do to her, and she could not restrain a laugh at her own foolishness.

Every time she heard a footstep in the corridor outside her bolted door she tensed, wondering if they came for her. All day the footsteps passed her door, but as the shadows lengthened and the light became bloody with sunset she heard the tread of heavy feet approaching. She got up from her stool and looked towards the door, and despite all her attempts to calm herself she began to tremble.

The bolt was flung back with a crash and the door opened. A priest stood in the doorway, robed in white and flanked by medjay carrying spears. Naunakhte wrapped her arms across her breast and breathed fast. Then she saw the priest's face and realised that it was the same young man who had read out the choices of the oracle – the scribe whose dark eyes had wished her victory.

It was an untold relief to see a face that she associated with kindness. She stepped forward eagerly, ready to ask him about the rite. But he held up his hand in the gesture that enjoined her to silence. 'Say nothing,' he commanded her. His voice was firm, but she thought she detected a little quiver beneath its surface. 'You may not speak until you are purified.'

'But – ' Naunakhte began.

'Silence! Or must I order the medjay to gag you?'

At his words the medjay on either side of him stepped forward. They were tall men, dark-skinned, glistening and muscular, with broad wristguards of bright copper glittering on their strong arms. One of them wound a broad strip of linen to and fro between his big hands and watched Naunakhte with piercing eyes, as if he desired any opportunity to force the linen between her flinching lips, bind it across her gasping mouth and compel her to silence. Naunakhte stared at them in horror and disbelief.

The young priest's voice softened slightly. 'I am sorry,' he said, 'but the rite must be obeyed. You may not speak until your purification is complete.'

His face showed that he would have liked to be kind. Naunakhte lifted her hands towards him, palms uppermost, begging him in silence to help her. He turned his head away as if her beseeching eyes hurt him, and to the medjay he said, 'Bind her.'

Without a word the medjay moved towards her, their faces set and stern. Naunakhte retreated, step by step, until her back was against the wall and she could go no farther. They laid their hands upon her and for a moment she was ready to scream with terror and hopeless resistance.

Then she remembered the purpose of this unknown rite. She was to atone for her flight from the temple; to offer her body in submission as penance for the gift of herself that she had given to Khonsu. Whatever they did to her now was to restore the honour of the god. If she desired once again to be the handmaiden of Amun, she must let his priests do what they wished with her.

She lifted her head and stood quiet and proud as the medjay bound her. They tied strong soft ropes about her wrists, then lashed them securely to each end of a wooden rod as dark and polished as their skins. The wood was smooth with age and cunningly carved to allow a secure purchase for the ropes. It was grooved also in the centre and it was as long as one of her arms, so that her hands were held wide apart a little below the level of her waist, palms turned upward as if in supplication.

The young priest watched as the medjay secured her, his dark eyes darkening further. 'Good,' he said, and his voice was a little husky. 'Bring her.'

The medjay each put a hand on Naunakhte's shoulder and guided her through the labyrinth of the temple. She recognised her whereabouts quite quickly and realised with a chill of anticipation that she was being led towards the sanctuary of the god. Her heart leapt. Perhaps she would be required to submit to Amun himself. She looked down at her bound hands. The wooden pole pressed against her belly and the soft ropes chafed gently against her wrists, restraining her utterly. She shuddered with expectation and desire.

They were nearly at the gates of the sanctuary when suddenly the medjay turned aside. Naunakhte could not prevent herself from glancing over her shoulder in yearning. The young priest saw her look and lifted his shaven brows. 'You are not fit to enter the presence of the god,' he said, quite coldly. 'You may not come into his sanctuary until you have been purified.'

Naunakhte wanted to demand that they purify her at once. But she restrained herself, for she had no wish to be gagged.

Ahead of them a great door opened, revealing a high

room aglow with the light of the setting sun and glittering with torches. Naunakhte bit her lip against a cry of surprise and fear, for the room seemed to be full of men. Clad in the white robes of priests they clustered towards her, and their whispers sounded like the rustle of bees in a hive. Suddenly she was afraid, because her hands were bound and there was nothing that she could do to resist this encroaching horde. She tried to catch the young priest's eye, seeking reassurance in his face, but he would not look at her.

The crowd of priests got close to her; so close that she could see their mouths wet with lust for her, and smell their hot breath. Then they withdrew, folding back like the wings of a great bird, and formed into two ranks. A little way from her stood Merybast, the high priest, tall and stately in his long robes, wearing around his neck a great collar of gold and gems. Naunakhte's breasts lifted and fell with her quick breathing, and she knew that when her eyes met the high priest's he would see that she was afraid.

Merybast smiled a little as he looked upon her, but it was not a reassuring smile. He smiled as if he was well pleased to see her standing before him bound and helpless. His hands clenched into fists at his sides, and he said in his strong, clear voice, 'The victim is prepared. Let the rite commence.'

The high room filled with the heavy beat of a drum, sounding alone like a great heart. The medjay who had held Naunakhte's shoulders withdrew and she almost cried aloud to them to stay, not to leave her alone with this crowd of men with white robes and intent, hungry faces. She looked wildly from side to side and then her eyes fixed on the face of Merybast as he moved slowly towards her, step by step.

At last he stood before her. His deep eyes looked into hers and he licked his lower lip thoughtfully. Then he made a gesture with one hand, and the young priest darted forward clutching another rope and cast it quickly around the centre of the long pole to which Naunakhte's hands were bound. She gasped as the rope began to tauten, lifting her hands before her. Glancing up wildly she saw that it ran over one of the heavy beams of the ceiling and down again into a corner of the room. It was tightening inexorably. Her hands were level with her breasts, with her face, with the crown of her head. At last, when another inch would have caused her discomfort, the lifting stopped. She tugged helplessly at the wood, but could not shift it. Her hands were lifted high above her head, spread apart by the polished pole, and she could not free herself. The drumbeat suddenly ceased, and there was a breathing silence.

Merybast licked his lips again and nodded in slow satisfaction. He extended one hand and touched the crumpled linen of Naunakhte's gown, then frowned in disapproval. 'Strip her,' he commanded.

On either side the priests jumped to obey him. They tore and ripped at the linen and stripped the rags from Naunakhte's limbs. She moaned in protest, but could do nothing, and in moments she stood before Merybast stark naked.

Nudity had never seemed shameful to Naunakhte until this moment. But now, bound and powerless to protect herself, and surrounded by pair after pair of hungry eyes, she panted with shame and struggled vainly until she realised her ultimate impotence and closed her eyes and let her head hang back in despair. She was achingly conscious of the fact that the peaks of her breasts were tight and that the lifting and spreading of her arms tautened the tender swells of flesh, offering them to the watching eyes as if she were a wanton whore.

How could the Lord Amun want her to suffer this degradation, this exposure and humiliation? How had she deserved it? She moaned in hopeless protest and her long, dark hair swept against the lush curves of her naked flanks as her head rolled from side to side.

Then Merybast spoke again. 'Let her body be cleansed before she undergoes her penance.'

Naunakhte shut her eyes more tightly, trying to shut out what they might mean to do to her. Her body was rigid with resistance.

But then she felt sweetness and silken delight. Cool, delicious water was rubbed softly along her backflung throat. Trickles of water ran from the nape between her shoulder blades, coursed between her breasts, traced the lines of her ribs. She shuddered with the pleasure of the water's caress.

And, after the water, hands. Strong hands, gentle hands, hard hands, soft hands, smoothing that cool water along each limb, moulding the shallow orbs of her breasts, teasing out the dark puckered flesh of her nipples. Naunakhte drew in long, deep breaths and let them out in sighing gasps of astonishment. Every inch of her body was sensitised to the myriad different touches that were awakening her lust.

Strong, hard fingers coursed up the delicate flesh of her inner thighs, wakening goosepimples on her back and shoulders. Soft palms cupped the weight of her breasts, lifting them and squeezing them together. Her swollen nipples were trapped in the warm hollowness of a hand's centre. A delicate touch slid down the side of her taut neck and she shivered and moaned with startled joy.

The cool water and the exploring hands caressed every morsel of dust and sweat from her shining limbs. She stood helpless. Her eyes were closed and her head hung back as if she were in a dead faint, but the slow remorseless heave of her body revealed her arousal. She moved like the faint, oily swell on the surface of the sea which betrays the approach of a great storm, a storm that will tear the sky and the water with furious passion.

Her body was drowned by the approach of erotic bliss and her mind began to sink into the trance of the servants of Amun. Her moist lips gaped open, sucking in the warm, dark air. Behind her a slow voice chanted, 'You are being made clean for the god. As your body is cleansed, so will your spirit be cleansed. The penance of the temple shall erase the legacy of Seth.'

Naunakhte wondered dazedly how the priests of the temple could have known that Khonsu was Seth made flesh, with all that great and terrible god's fascination and danger. A faint image of him appeared to her; Khonsu lying naked beside her, his hand reaching out to caress her breast, his lips curled in his cool, mocking smile.

Then firm fingers traced spider's tracks down her throat and on to her breasts, found her nipples and pinched them so hard that she gasped. The voice behind her whispered, 'Open yourself to the god. Let his presence cleanse you.'

At once the god was there, summoned by his faithful acolytes. Naunakhte's body tightened as she sensed his presence. Now the hands that touched her were the hands of Amun, the hands of god laid upon his faithful handmaiden, and his divinity and power were such that the hands were many.

'Oh Lord Amun,' she whispered, 'come to me.' She drew deep breaths of bliss and smiled as every part of her body, every inch of her damp skin, was teased and caressed by the hands of the god she adored. Her breasts were swollen and tender with desire, and the peaks of her nipples rose to the touch of subtle fingers. Between her legs her sex was as heavy as a dew-soaked flower, parting its glistening petals to reveal its soft, moist secrets. On the shutter of her closed eyelids she saw the god, golden and shining, naked and beautiful, his magnificent phallus thrusting forward in full erection, ready to take her.

Her trance deepened. The approach of the god filled her ears with a rushing sound like a great wind, and her whole body shook. She arched her back, thrusting her breasts forward, and above her bound wrists her fists

103

clenched and then opened spasmodically. She thought that she cried the god's name aloud, but in fact her slack lips let out only a helpless moan.

Then a strong male voice commanded, 'Enough.'

At once the hands withdrew. Naunakhte's trance faded and broke. She gave a little groan of protest and clutched at the wooden pole to give her the strength to lift her heavy head.

Merybast stood before her, his dark eyes glowing beneath his greying brows. 'Good,' he said, 'good. Naunakhte, do you feel the presence of the god?'

How could he ask it? Naunakhte replied in a husky, tentative whisper. 'Yes. He is here.'

The high priest slowly nodded his head. 'You were indeed born the servant of Amun. Few women feel his presence when they undergo this rite.'

Naunakhte frowned in puzzlement. 'Is the rite over, then?'

At that Merybast smiled. 'Over? Oh no.' His smile widened slightly. 'It is barely begun. And, for the remainder of it, Naunakhte, I shall not permit the god to entrance you. You must experience everything in your own person. Do you understand me?'

'Yes,' said Naunakhte, swallowing hard. She understood what the high priest said and she wanted to be obedient, but how could she promise? The god came to her at his desire, not hers. 'But what – '

'Enough.' Merybast raised his voice to a snap of command. 'Take her to the altar!'

At once Naunakhte was surrounded. The priests reached up to release her bound hands from the restraining pole. She gasped as her arms fell to her sides, the loosened ropes still fastened firmly around her wrists. But before she could relish the sensation of freedom she was seized on every side, then lifted bodily and carried at shoulder height across the room.

Turning her head, she saw the altar. It was a massive piece of rose-pink granite, more than six feet square. Its sides were carved with the story of the god in hiero-glyphs and it was polished as smooth as glass. Let into its top, an arm's length apart, were two loops of gleaming bronze.

Between the bronze loops was a carved indentation. Naunakhte twisted her head and began to struggle with sudden terror, because the altar looked like one of the great rock tables on which a beast might be sacrificed, carved with grooves to carry away the dying animal's blood. She heaved and writhed between the restraining hands, imagining that the moment they bound her between those fierce loops they would set the sharp bronze to her offered throat.

Then Merybast was standing beside her. 'Be still,' he commanded her sharply. 'What do you fear? The god does not demand your life. This is a rite of penance, not of sacrifice.'

Naunakhte stopped struggling and lay still. She was afraid, but she trusted Merybast. He would not lie to her. The priests carried her over to the altar and laid her down. Her body fitted comfortably into the shallow carved depression in its surface and her thick hair cushioned her head. They tied her hands to the bronze loops, offering her naked breasts to the torchlight and the coffered ceiling.

For a moment Naunakhte closed her eyes and prayed to Amun to protect her from whatever was about to happen. But then Merybast's voice spoke again, sharp and commanding. 'Naunakhte. Speak now of what took place between you and your lover Khonsu.'

Shocked, Naunakhte opened her eyes. Merybast was standing beside her, looking down into her face. His eyes were hot. Naunakhte turned her head aside in shame and whispered, 'I don't understand.'

'You are to be cleansed,' said Merybast coldly. 'We must cleanse all those parts of you which he polluted. Speak, Naunakhte. What did he do to you?'

Slowly Naunakhte realised what it was that Merybast

meant her to do. He meant her to speak aloud the secrets of Khonsu's bed, to recite everything that they had shared in lust and passion. A scalding blush burned her cheeks. She glanced up into Merybast's face and tugged helplessly against the ropes which secured her wrists. Aloud she whispered, 'I can't.'

'You must,' insisted Merybast. 'But I shall help you. Where did he pollute you, Naunakhte? Here?'

And without warning he thrust his strong fingers between her thighs and slid them up into her, deep into her wet, open sex. She cried out and tried to pull away, but it was too late. Two fingers were buried deep inside her, moving in and out very slightly, so that she moaned.

'Here?' insisted Merybast, sliding his fingers in and out once more.

Naunakhte's sex clenched helplessly around his invading hand. Merybast's palm brushed against the taut bud of her clitoris and she sighed in pleasure. When she gasped, 'Yes,' she did not know whether she answered him, or begged him to continue.

'Very well,' said Merybast sternly. His fingers withdrew and Naunakhte whimpered with loss. 'And here?' He reached for her mouth and touched her parted lips, then stroked the tip of her tongue. She tasted her own arousal on his hand.

'Yes,' she whispered. She could not prevent herself from licking lasciviously at his finger, relishing the faint salty sweetness of her juices.

'Even so.' Merybast took his hand away and Naunakhte tensed, knowing at once what he would do next. She was not disappointed. The high priest pushed his hand between her closed thighs, forcing her legs apart. She moaned as he stroked his finger along the dewy lips of her sex, drawing slick moisture from her. Then his hand moved further back and his fingers probed and stroked at the delicate entrance of her anus.

'Here?' His voice was hoarse. His finger probed steadily until it opened the little satiny flower and gently, determinedly, penetrated her.

'Yes,' Naunakhte groaned helplessly, squirming as Merybast's finger slid deep into her tight anus. 'Yes, oh yes.'

Merybast thrust his finger into her again. He seemed to relish her faint cries of pleasure and the sinuous writhing of her golden limbs. He smiled a little and at last withdrew his finger, drawing it beneath his flaring nostrils and smelling it voluptuously.

'Good,' he said softly. 'Now I know the extent to which you must be purified.' He stepped back and lifted his hands. 'Let the rite begin.'

For a moment there was silence; the silence of expectation. Then once again the drum began its steady, remorseless double beat. Its vibrations struck Naunakhte's ear through the very granite of the altar, so that she felt she lay like a child upon the muscular chest of a great cold giant, listening to its thumping heart.

The priests of Amun stood around the altar. They pressed as close as a flock of white birds. As the drum beat, they began to chant, a low murmurous sound like the rumble of thunder. They invoked the god, calling to him to come in his power and strengthen the sinews of Merybast as he carried out the rite.

A movement beside Naunakhte caught her eye and she turned her head. She saw the young dark-eyed priest removing Merybast's long linen robe. Beneath it the high priest was naked. His smooth oiled body was thick and solid, impressively taut for his advancing years. He looked heavy. Between his legs his penis stood up, swollen and erect, and Naunakhte swallowed as she looked at it. It was much larger than Khonsu's: massive, huge and hard, almost as large as the phallus of the statue of the god.

The priests began to clap their hands in time to their chanting and the beating of the drum. Slowly Merybast advanced up the steps at the side of the altar. He was holding the base of his penis in the ritual posture of the god. He stood upon the altar with one foot on either side of Naunakhte's neck, looking down into her wide-open eyes.

'Great Amun, father of all things,' he intoned above the chant, 'give power to my penis. Make my phallus strong to purify this sacrifice.'

Slowly he sank to his knees. Naunakhte shivered as the high priest's rampant phallus came closer and closer to her face. She tried to remain still and calm, but despite her intentions she tugged helplessly at the bindings that secured her wrists, trying to free herself.

Now Merybast was kneeling over her, astride her face. He grasped firmly at his penis and began to stroke it, sliding the velvet-soft skin up and down over the engorged rigid core. Her eyes gazed up at the swollen scarlet head, so smooth and shining that it seemed about to burst like an overripe fruit.

'Naunakhte,' said Merybast, 'open your mouth.'

Fear and lust fought within her. She writhed on the cold stone as terror chilled her spine and desire softened her limbs and melted warmly in her liquid sex. She was afraid of Merybast, and she was afraid of her own helplessness. But at the same time she longed to taste his phallus, and her soft thighs parted and shook as she yearned to feel a hot penis entering her.

'Open,' repeated Merybast. Naunakhte let out a little helpless moan and licked her lips, smoothing them with her saliva to allow Merybast to penetrate her mouth more easily. She saw him point his penis downward and closed her eyes just before she felt it nudging against her lips and parting them, driving its way deep into her throat.

He thrust himself so far into her mouth that for a moment she was afraid she would choke. He tasted of salt and costly perfume, sandalwood and attar of roses. She opened her jaw and relaxed, and Merybast's massive phallus slid further into her; in and in until his dangling testicles brushed against her lower lip. She tried to moan, but she was smothered by his presence.

Her hands pressed flat to the cold stone and her body arched unconsciously upward, offering the soft mound between her legs for the possession of a man. The feel of Merybast's penis within her mouth made her long to be taken. The glistening folds of her sex quivered as she clenched her inner muscles, impotently clutching at emptiness.

After only a few thrusts Merybast withdrew. His phallus gleamed with her saliva. He knelt over her for a moment, breathing hard. Then he stood up and commanded, 'Offer her to me.'

The priests around the tomb leant forward and caught hold of Naunakhte's legs. They held her by the ankle, the knee, the thigh. All along her limbs she felt the tightness of their clasping hands. They pulled her legs wide apart and held her very still. Lascivious fingers squeezed at her flesh and she moaned with ecstatic expectation.

Merybast stood between her spread thighs, masturbating. His hand slid smooth and fast up and down the length of his cock. She stared up at him, her mouth slack with desire, and Merybast smiled grimly and lowered his body on to hers.

He was heavy, so heavy, and through his perfume she smelt the odour of his body, rank and intense like a rutting beast. He put his hands on her bound wrists and snarled with pleasure as if it aroused him to feel her beneath him, restrained and powerless. He pushed his face towards her and his hot breath brushed her cheek. Naunakhte moaned in protest and turned her head aside. She tried to struggle, but his weight pinned her down and her legs were held completely still by dozens of male hands. She twisted her head from side to side and Merybast chuckled and leant towards her and licked her throat.

The touch of his hot, wet tongue shot through her like

a dart of fire. Naunakhte cried out and ceased to resist. Merybast dragged his tongue again up the length of her golden throat, then set his teeth to her neck as if he would worry her like a dog. She moaned with pleasure to feel him biting her. Her own immobility and helplessness filled her with the joy of utter submission.

Merybast's huge penis throbbed between her open legs, twitching as it brushed against the wet lips of her aching sex. His teeth dug again into her throat and he shifted his weight, bringing the broad, hot head of his phallus closely against her body. His heavy buttocks were taut with readiness and she knew that soon he would move. How that giant member would fill her! She longed for it almost as she had longed for the penis of the god Amun. But this longing was not divine, it was mortal. She was fully conscious, far from the golden glow of divine trance, and her body was warm and tingling with lust. She wanted the high priest as a woman wants a man. She wanted him to possess her.

Merybast lifted his lips from her bruised neck and shut his eyes tightly. His hands gripped hard at Naunakhte's wrists and his body tensed as he thrust. The head of his penis nudged its way between the lips of her sex and began to penetrate her. She moaned with joy and Merybast gasped as his thick, erect phallus slid slowly into Naunakhte's moist vagina; deeper and deeper until it was entirely sheathed in her warm, trembling flesh.

For a moment he was still. Naunakhte whimpered with delight at the sensation of that massive penis wholly imbedded within her. She moved against him and tried to lift her hips towards him so that he would take her, but still the priests held her completely motionless. She could only wait, shuddering with expectant bliss, until Merybast was ready.

At last he bared his teeth, drew in a long hissing breath and pulled his penis almost free of her clinging sheath. Naunakhte moaned with loss, and then her moan turned to a gasp of pleasure as he slid himself into her once again. She began to pant in rhythm with his thrusts, glorying in the steady pounding of his body against hers. Her spine tensed as the sensations grew. Merybast lay heavily upon her and the skin of his broad chest dragged against her flushed, straining breasts and her taut, puckered nipples. The lips of her sex were swollen and tender, her clitoris was engorged and protruding, and the friction of Merybast's loins rubbing against her began to drive her towards orgasm.

Again she cried out, and, as if this was a signal, Merybast withdrew from her entirely. Naunakhte let out a little whimper of disappointment and opened her languid eyes.

Merybast stood up, shaking his head in disapproval. 'Your pleasure is irrelevant to the rite,' he said sternly. 'Contain yourself. You are not yet purified.'

Naunakhte's lips parted in a soundless gasp of realisation. Every part of her body which Khonsu had entered was to be purified by the penetration of Merybast's huge cock. That meant – she swallowed hard – that meant that he was going to insert his member into her anus, that narrow orifice which had made Khonsu gasp at its tightness. Surely it was not possible! And yet she desired greatly that he should try.

Her face must have shown that she had realised what was in store for her, because Merybast smiled coldly. 'Yes,' he said, 'you have guessed, Naunakhte. And you shall watch.'

Watch? How? Naunakhte frowned and wriggled protestingly against the priests' restraining hands. Merybast stepped back a little from her and issued another abrupt command. 'Prepare her. Let her be oiled and made ready. And then place her so that she may see what I do.'

At once the priests caught hold of Naunakhte's legs even more firmly. They held her by her ankles and calves and lifted her buttocks bodily from the cold stone.

Naunakhte gasped in surprise, then gasped again as the priests pushed her legs forward, further and further, until she was standing on her shoulders and her thighs were spread and parted directly above her face. She could see right up into her open sex. It was moist and pink and quivering with need, and behind it was the tight brown flower of her anus.

'Oh gods,' Naunakhte whispered, astonished and aroused.

The dark-eyed priest lifted a little flask above her parted buttocks. He tilted it and a thin stream of aromatic oil poured downward. The oil fell on to Naunakhte's crease and she heaved in reaction. Slowly the priest massaged the oil into her tender skin, anointing the delicate, satiny membrane that surrounded her puckered rear hole. Naunakhte trembled and moaned. After a few moments he began to slide his fingers very gently into the hole itself, opening her softly and delicately. The pleasure was intense. Naunakhte let out little shuddering cries and her eyes opened wide as she watched the priest's long, dark finger gently pushing in and out of her flinching anus.

'She is ready,' the dark-eyed priest said after a moment.

'Good.' Merybast came and stood over her, his huge erection aimed directly at her offered crack. 'Hold her buttocks apart,' he ordered. 'Spread her open.'

Naunakhte whimpered and tensed, clenching her cheeks together in instinctive denial. But the priests caught hold of the tender skin of her flanks and tugged at the firm orbs of her opulent backside, spreading the cheeks apart so that her oiled bottom hole was presented lewdly for Merybast's attention.

He stood over her and directed his penis downward. It was wet and shining with the juices of her vagina. He guided the smooth head to the spot, and Naunakhte watched in disbelief and fear as the scarlet glans rested against her anus and prodded, first gently, then harder.

He was too big, too big. It was impossible. Naunakhte moaned and closed her eyes, resisting desperately.

For a moment Merybast thrust vainly, butting the head of his cock against her like an angry ram. Then he said, 'She is afraid. One of you caress her, fondle her, give her pleasure. She will soon forget her fear.'

At once a gentle hand ran along the soft flesh of Naunakhte's inner thigh, sliding towards her wet, eager sex. She took a deep breath and opened her eyes and saw it was the young priest, smiling down at her as his hand reached her mound of love. He stroked the swollen lips, very gently, and parted them to reveal the dark entrance to Naunakhte's vagina and the tiny rose-pink bud of her clitoris. She stared in fascinated anticipation, then sighed with delight as his finger slipped into her. He penetrated her first with one finger, then with two, then withdrew both fingers, wet with her moisture. She moaned as he began to stroke her clitoris, very gently and dexterously, quivering the pad of one finger deliciously against the little throbbing bead while with the other, he rimmed the entrance to her vagina, entered her, withdrew, entered her again.

Pleasure flooded through her. She moaned again and arched her hips upward, welcoming his touch. But she was betrayed, for the pleasure relaxed the taut muscles of her sphincter, and even as she cried out with bliss Merybast lodged the head of his cock in her anus and thrust hard. The great shelving glans eased its way slowly inside her, fixing her as a peg fixes wood. Merybast nodded and the young priest withdrew his hand. Naunakhte looked up, gasping, and saw the swollen tip of Merybast's cock buried within her arse.

'The final road,' Merybast whispered. He put his hands on Naunakhte's thighs, pressing them even further apart, and leant his weight into her. Inch by inch his erect phallus disappeared into the little gaping mouth of her anus. Inch by inch he penetrated her, and she was utterly overwhelmed by the sensation. It was as if he would split her limb from limb, tear her as a lion tears its prey, and yet it was ecstasy too; a dark, forbidden ecstasy.

The impossible was achieved – the whole of Merybast's penis was buried in her. She stared up at their joined bodies, hardly able to whimper. Slowly Merybast moved his hands, shifting them up the soft skin until they brushed against the dark mass of her pubic hair. He teased her, fluttering his fingers against the flushed lips of her moist vulva, but avoiding her clitoris.

'Please,' Naunakhte moaned. 'Please.'

'As I said, your pleasure is irrelevant.' Merybast shifted his weight to allow himself to withdraw his gleaming penis from her anus, then drove into her again. His face was contorted with pleasure. For a few moments he fucked her arse with strong, steady thrusts, making her cry out with bliss and frustration and the shadow of pain. Then his rhythm changed, becoming jerky and hurried. 'Lord Amun,' he whispered, 'it is too much, too much. I cannot – ' And with a gasp he withdrew from her. Naunakhte cried out with shock, because as his penis sprang free Merybast grabbed it and began to rub it furiously. He pointed his phallus at Naunakhte's face and masturbated violently. The thick rod of flesh leapt in his hand and jolted as he began to come. He shouted aloud as his orgasm possessed him, and his thick white semen pulsed from the tip of his penis and fell on to Naunakhte's gasping face. Hot liquid caught in her eyelashes and slithered lewdly down her cheeks, wetting her panting lips. She gave one desperate cry and then was silent.

For a few moments the only sound was of Merybast's heaving breath. Then he said, 'Release her.'

Naunakhte's hips were lowered to the cold stone and the priests busied themselves around her, freeing her hands from the ropes. When she was released she lifted herself on one elbow and rubbed her hand over her face. Merybast's seed was slick against her skin.

'Naunakhte,' said Merybast, 'your formal purification is complete. But now the priests of Amun must approve your service.'

With a thrill of excitement Naunakhte looked around her. The priests were watching her, their eyes bright and their penises erect beneath their robes. Merybast went on, 'If you are willing, you shall be free while they take their pleasure with your body. If you are not willing, you shall be tied on the altar while each of them possesses you, one by one. Which will you have, Naunakhte?'

Naunakhte's whole body was trembling with arousal. She had been on the brink of orgasm, and now all she desired was to reach her peak. She replied without thinking, 'I am willing.'

A susurration of excitement filled the high room. Merybast nodded slowly and then turned away. Naunakhte looked from side to side and saw the priests glancing at each other and then unknotting their kilts, letting the linen fall to the ground behind them. One after another they stripped. Naunakhte quivered with anticipation as she saw so many penises, all stiff and ready to pleasure her.

She knew which one she wanted to taste first. Glancing quickly around, she caught the dark eyes of the young priest who had officiated at the speaking of the oracle. She sat up a little more and held out her hand to him, and he smiled and moved towards her.

'Take me,' Naunakhte said. She leant back, meaning to stretch her body out for him upon the cold stone. But he caught her hand, holding her up.

'There are many of us,' he whispered, 'and all want to taste your beauty, Naunakhte. One at a time will never do. Come, trust me.'

He guided her down from the altar. She went willingly, shivering with anticipation. The young priest lay down upon the floor and opened his arms to her. 'Lie on me.'

His penis lay flat against his belly, stiff as a piece of wood. Naunakhte eagerly straddled him and took hold of his cock, lifting it until she could guide it into her. She sighed with bliss as he slid up inside her.

'Now,' whispered her friend, 'lean forward, Naunakhte, so that another may take his pleasure with you.'

For a moment Naunakhte did not understand. Then she felt the warmth of another man kneeling behind her, parting her buttocks and sliding his stiff prick along the crease of her arse. She was startled, but if a phallus in one orifice brought delight, then surely it would be even more wonderful to accept two at once? So she leant forward and groaned with pleasure as the unknown penis pressed against her anus and slowly, deliciously, eased its way within her.

'Good,' hissed the young man beneath her. He lifted his hips, thrusting himself deeply into her, and as he did so the man behind her also thrust. Naunakhte cried out, astonished by the power of the sensations that now seized her.

And then her cry turned to a gasp as hands caught her by the hair and pulled back her head. Another man stood before her, offering his erect penis to her open mouth. She whimpered with delighted submission and parted her lips, then moaned with pleasure as he pushed his phallus into her mouth.

All three men moved at once, sliding their pulsing erections at will into her sex and her mouth and her anus. Naunakhte closed her eyes and weltered in lubricious joy. Every part of her was filled, aching and scalding with bliss. Other penises pushed against her spasming hands, begging for her attention, and without even looking at them she grasped them and slid her fingers up and down, up and down. There were hands knotted in her hair, phalluses wrapped in the thick black locks, fingers brushing at her breasts and teasing her tight nipples. The man with his cock in her anus cried out and clutched at her buttocks as he ejaculated, then he withdrew and at once his place was taken by another man. Naunakhte writhed with delight and ground her turgid vulva down upon the body of the young priest whose dark eyes had looked at her with kindness. She arched her back and he lifted his hands and grasped her breasts and she knew that she was about to orgasm a fraction of a second before pleasure burst within her, radiating from her loins like the fiery streamers of the noon sun. Her belly jolted and shuddered, but she was fixed upon the three penises that penetrated her. They moved faster now, driving into her rigid body with deliberate force, raising her time after time to new plateaux of pleasure. She uttered a smothered, agonised cry, and for long moments her whole body was tense with the torment of orgasm. Then she relaxed, slumping forward in the fainting aftermath of ecstasy.

After that first, immensely powerful climax, Naunakhte did not fully recover her senses. Her body was soft and pliant in the hands of the priests. They turned her this way and that at their pleasure, placing her in one position after another, each one more lewd than the last, and one by one they took her, sliding their penises into her every orifice. Her skin, her sex, her mouth and her hair were wet and sticky with their congealing semen, and after a while they laid her on the altar and licked her clean. They lapped at her nipples and dragged their tongues lovingly over her breasts and belly. One of them glided his face between her legs and began to suck her sex, caressing her clitoris with his lips while his tongue burrowed deep into the moist well of her vagina. He seemed to relish the taste of her, and when they pulled her upright and parted her buttocks so that another of the priests could sodomise her he stayed where he was, his face pressed to her thighs, lapping steadily at her clitoris. Two more of the priests sucked at her swollen breasts while another of them kissed her, thrusting his tongue into her mouth and biting her lips. Naunakhte cried out in helpless delight, and, as the man behind her grunted and thrust his prick harder and harder into her bruised and tender anus, she convulsed again in the throes of an orgasm even more powerful than the last.

She hardly knew when they had eventually finished with her and laid her slumped and panting upon the granite altar. Every part of her ached dully, as if she had been beaten, and yet the pain was pleasure too. She moaned and stirred faintly for a moment, then lay still.

She must have fallen asleep, for when she woke with a start the high room was dark and quiet. One of the temple girls was standing beside her, wiping the sweat and semen from her body with a damp sponge, and the Lady Hunro was stroking her face.

'You have been purified, Naunakhte,' said Hunro softly. 'I am glad. Welcome back to the temple, little lotus flower.'

Naunakhte's whole body felt as soft and liquid as molten wax. Every pore of her skin was soaked in sensual satisfaction. She could not speak, but she smiled.

'The inundation is beginning,' said the Lady Hunro, returning Naunakhte's smile. 'Today the Nilometer showed that the waters rose by two cubits and a span. Soon it will be time for the festival of Opet, when the god travels to Luxor.'

She did not seem to require an answer, so Naunakhte stretched to allow the girl to sponge her breasts, and raised her brows curiously.

'Naunakhte,' Hunro went on, 'I have a part in the Opet festival. I expect that this will be my last year as high priestess, that next year there will be a new god's wife of Amun. I would like you to sit beside my throne on the god's barge, Naunakhte, and watch what I do.'

Naunakhte's eyes widened. The Lady Hunro implied that she, Naunakhte, would be the next Hand of Amun. She was amazed and delighted, for if she became the Hand of God she would legitimately be able to enjoy the body of the god himself. But her joy was marred by an undercurrent of fear. She wanted to ask how the Lady Tiy would take this news, but she did not dare.

'Yes, lady,' was all she said. Then she remembered Tiy's cold green eyes and her threat of poison, and she shivered.

Fresh Meat

Miranda Stephens

Fresh Meat and *Flight of Fantasy* are two stories by Miranda Stephens. Her style is raw, fresh and honest. These stories make no pretence to romance; they're down and dirty and all the more wonderful for it.

Fresh Meat

She had seen him in the transfer bus to the hotel and whispered to her friend, 'Fresh meat.' A seventeen-year-old boy, unaccountably alone; strong-shouldered, slim, curly-haired, shy, alone and all alone. At a beach disco she said, 'Dance with me,' and he had agreed reluctantly because, as fresh meat, he had not seen her as a sexual creature with a need to be filled. She was with her girlfriend on the same package holiday as him; she was a proper grown-up, then, and not the page-three girl for whom he had ground his cock into the mattress and come gasping so many times. He did not suspect her kind of body because he was fresh meat.

So his six foot of unknowing new strength and her five foot three of experienced lusts stood on the little disco floor and moved to their own rhythms. It was not the aunty dance he had expected from a proper grown-up. She reached up under his arms to his shoulders and slid her hands down the long beautiful muscles of his body to his hips, manipulating him to the edge where the dance floor met the sand and the straightness of his back met the roundness of his newly formed man's arse. She held him too close and forced his body against hers so he would become unbalanced and have to use his strength against her. She could feel his muscles working under the taut skin and thrill to it because if he did not brace himself against her they would fall, and falling with him hard and her ready and wet in the sand was what she had come on holiday for. This was a special treat: fresh meat; no more than seventeen; a sauce made just of dew.

Now in the dark on the sand she tasted him. He was confused: shirt wide open, this proper grown-up woman licking him, her tongue curling over his nipples – worse, her tongue in his armpit where the delicious dirty sweat was gathering. Her hands roamed across his chest. It was covered with just enough light-auburn hair to mat the liquids of that hot holiday night. Under his jeans, she explored him. He tensed, which made her even more determined to open him up so she could take his cock in her mouth, and put a licked finger into his anus and feel the weight of his balls.

She lay on him, her body light to his new strength. His hands developed a sex of their own without his meaning it, and they moved under her silk blouse and across her woman's body – which was different from stroking the printed page-three girls. He found the line of her neck which became her slim strong shoulders sliding into the line of her spine which melted into the thrill of her arse – which he did not yet dare to plumb with his fingers – and he felt down around the globes to her thighs. Under her white skirt she was naked and messages came back through him while his hands explored her. The messages went straight to his balls and drove his cock up hard and she felt his hardness and knew the play was hers. This boy was ready to become a man and she would take and shape him and make him hers and use him for her experiments. She would ask him questions: what his fantasies were; who he had wanted; what he wanted to do to her; whether he had done it with a girl or another boy. She hoped he had so she could thrill to that as well. She would ask him what he felt and would seem to be concerned by his feelings, but what she actually had was breathless lust for his fresh meat – hung to fuck her brains out.

She sat up and, taking his ankles, opened his legs. Seeing his cock hard under the fabric of his jeans, she put one hand there and said, 'Look at me.' She was wise and, putting the moon behind her, she showed him her breasts, silhouetted through her blouse.

'Now I'm going to show you how to enjoy me,' she said. 'Lick my breasts, suck my breasts, hold and squeeze my breasts.'

She liked saying it and she felt his cock – already iron hard – react as she did. 'You can look at me and touch me whenever you want to feel the weight.'

She took his hands and placed them over her breasts, through her blouse. She asked him if he liked it but he could not speak. He felt the weight of her and, wanting more, he moved to the buttons of her blouse.

With a killing stroke she slapped his face so hard his world spun. In shock, the pain mixed with his new experiences to drive him to the edge of orgasm.

'Do what I tell you,' she whispered. 'There are rewards I can give and I will show you pleasures but you must learn to know what your woman wants, same as she knows what you want.' She slowly rubbed the bulge made by his hard cock and his balls. He thrust up against her hand and she smiled. 'Lie back and relax,' she said.

He lay back, the pain of the slap mixing with the pain of his full cock. She crouched over him.

'You are going to have me,' she breathed. 'You are going to have all of me, but take your time and learn to enjoy me.' She sat up and very slowly unbuttoned her blouse, letting her tits spill out, the shimmering skin catching the light of the moon. She bent forward and brushed his chest with her hard nipples. Almost involuntarily his hands moved to her and she caught them, pinioning his wrists to the sand. Moving up, her nipples brushed his mouth. 'Now suck my tits,' she ordered, as her own breath became more ragged. He did so, while she pulled up her long skirt and rubbed her wet cunt against his hard, softly hairy, new man's thigh.

Fresh meat learns fast, she thought, as his mouth on her nipples, together with the hard thigh between her legs, started that slow explosion in her centre which would soon take her over if she let it.

She released his arms and slowly pulled down the zip on his jeans, dragging them off, releasing his rock-hard cock. The hair around it, and on his legs, was gold and beautiful in the moonlight. He lay naked and spread-eagled on the sand while she stood up and, in the light of the moon, slowly stripped for him, leaving only her gold sandals.

Placing one beautiful sandled foot on his cock, pushing it down on to his belly, she gently let the heel brush his balls. His face contorted in ecstasy and fear. She said, 'Now take your time or I will make you come with my foot and never let you touch me again, and you will never know how it feels to fuck me. That is what you want, isn't it? You want to feel me draw you in, surround you, suck the come out of you. So suck and kiss every inch of me. Do to me what you dreamt of doing while you masturbated when you were a kid. Now it's real, so enjoy it all with every part of you. You have to fuck me with your eyes and your mouth and your beautiful skin but most of all fuck me with your brain. Watch how you make me come so I can't help it.'

She lay on the sand stark naked. He did as she asked and kissed her sandled toes; he could see the beautiful female strength and slenderness of her feet and ankles. His gaze moved up her smooth legs, glorying in the view of her hips and flat stomach and wonderful tits, so full they spilled down her like cloudbursts. Her body was not muscled like his; it was soft and yielding but still strong. Burying his tongue in her cunt, drinking her, he found her clitoris, although he did not know that's where he was. He tongued her urgently.

In her mind she begged him to lose control, to take her as he chose, violently or sweetly, but for God's sake fuck her before she exploded. She, knowing the trigger, slowly drew her fingernails across his balls; it worked like an electric shock. His cock rammed her desperate sex, plunging and sawing at her. She turned him on his back; now there was his heaving chest and tight-muscled stomach, his cock and the bush of hair around it and his balls lit by the moon. They were hard and filled with come and yet the skin so smooth she wanted to eat him; that would be for later, because she knew he was ready. Sitting astride him, she guided his cock into her, feeling his balls against her arse. She heard him gasp as he filled every inch of her, and she moved to pull the action of his cock across her clitoris. As he drove into her and opened his eyes, which had been shut against disappointment, he saw her there naked, astride him in all her beauty with the moon behind her. He lifted her whole body up by his thighs and back so she was flying on him, pinioned on his driving cock. They came and flooded each other. New meat sauced with dew.

He was young and lusty for her, and hard again in minutes. She laughed, not at but with him – at the strength of his sex and the effect she could have on him.

'I want you to watch me come,' she said. 'You'll enjoy it. Kneel at my feet, where I can see the effect on you and watch.'

She lay full-length in the sand, the fingers of one hand stroking with the lightest rhythm, just inside her labia. Her touch was so light that he could not believe she would enjoy it. Her other hand, caressing her breasts, squeezed her nipples with a more urgent tempo. She gazed at her beautiful, naked young man in the moonlight and dreamt of educating him to please her. The thought filled her with a delicious sense of wickedness.

'Hold your balls with one hand while you stroke your cock with the other. Make it huge for me; make me mad for it,' she breathed.

He did as he was bid, enjoying the experience of being fucked by her eyes. The rhythm of her own frigging became faster, her fingers penetrated deeper, the wetness soaking her hand, while the other still could not get enough of her own breasts. The sight of her held him spellbound; his cock became so full he thought he would explode with the pressure of needing to come.

She panted, 'Form a ring with your fingers. Apply pressure under your cock, just above your balls.' He pumped himself achingly slowly, under her breathless instruction, opening his fingers at the key moment, putting off when he must come and jet his hot sperm over her.

She put an ankle on each of his strong, young shoulders and curved her back to form an arch that gave him a perfect view of her hand, now furiously frigging her clit while her other hand, exhausting the pleasure of her breasts, sought her own anus and lightly penetrated it while she looked deep into his eyes.

'Yes, yes now,' she cried, her body vibrating with the pleasure of it while he contracted the ring of his own fingers on his cock, dragging the come from his balls in a long stream of spunk while he arched forward to drench her tits with it.

On the sand that night she taught him how a woman is and what a man can be. There was no part of her he did not kiss and lick. He savoured the flavours of her mouth and tongue, and the taste of his own come on her breasts and in her soaking cunt.

He tasted the sweetness of her buttocks and the adventure of parting them to discover how she worked. He begged her to pee on him and she crouched over him and drenched his chest. There was the button of her anus which he discovered would, when lubricated with his tongue and her juices, dilate and open to his cock so he could fuck her that way too, the curves of her arse deliciously caressing his balls.

By dawn they had exhausted every plane and curve, orifice and muscle of both their bodies. Sated, watching the sun rise, they lightly caressed each other and talked.

'You know this isn't love,' she said. He laughed; he knew love was another book. 'This is just sex, but it's beautiful in its own right. I wanted you when I saw you on the transfer bus from the airport.'

This was a game he was starting to understand. 'What did you want me for,' he said with a serious voice and a smiling face.

'I thought you were a virgin,' she said. 'I wanted to be the first to have your big cock inside me; I wanted to see your tight, strong arse pumping in to me. I wanted to feel the strength in your arms gripping me. I wanted to be fucked by you and filled up by you till I was so full I spilled your come out of my cunt on to the sand. All of which you duly did. So, are you satisfied?' she asked with a grin.

'Not any more,' he said. Her lust-filled words had pumped his penis up hard again.

'Jesus! Kids nowadays. What do you want now?'

'You came here with a friend,' he said. 'I saw you both looking at me on the bus. I want you both together.'

'You learn fast, fresh meat and well hung,' she said, as a private joke. 'She'll be in bed at our hotel; we'll give her a nice surprise.'

Flight of Fantasy

Miranda Stephens

Flight of Fantasy

She sat in the window seat, he by the aisle, a spare seat between them, on the flight to New York. Seven hours chasing the low afternoon sun west across the Atlantic, illuminating and silhouetting her, a show that only he was in a position to enjoy. He could not believe his luck. Under cover of his newspaper he studied her minutely; she was not so much pretty as extraordinarily beautiful. Tiny gold hairs on her neck and a sleek sheen to her skin caught the light of the dying sun through the aircraft window. Large rounded breasts filled out the silk of her dress. Three inches of deep cleavage invited his gaze.

She was ripe and full of womanhood; her cream silk dress showed off her bare, brown shoulders, their smoothness accentuated by the crossed supporting straps and the wisps of hair at the nape of her neck. Her legs were crossed, revealing five inches of slim calf tapering to a slender, strong ankle sloping towards him. Absorbed in her book, she had shed one shoe, revealing a delicious, shapely foot. She dangled her other shoe as many women do so maddeningly, just obscuring her gorgeous, suckable toes.

Her strong, sexy face seemed to have laughed a lot,

and he thought she had probably flirted with most of the interesting things life had to offer. He could see she was intelligent and warm. A curvy woman; he thought she was exciting. Speculating that she had a really dirty laugh, he saw that her blue eyes were shot with a glint of gold, and her hair was short, accentuating her femininity still more.

Against the sunset, he saw she neither wore nor needed a bra. Her breasts so close and so full combined with her perfume to stimulate his imagination and his fantasies.

He closed his eyes, irresistibly picturing her stripping slowly for him, her brown, strong hands pushing first one then the other strap from her shoulders, the silk slipping down, tumbling from her breasts like a slow waterfall to rest around her waist. She would know the effect this glorious spectacle would have on him and delight in her power to create a hard, potent bulge in his trousers. She would kneel and brush her nipples against his crotch, the scent of perfume rising from her unfettered breasts weakening his legs. Gently folding her arms around his waist she would press her breasts against the outline of his rampant cock, sending him rolling back on to the bed in the New York hotel suite they would share.

She would undress him, her fingers seeking out every erogenous zone on his body, caressing him as though his pleasure was precious and necessary to her survival.

Then he would lie naked on the bed, his cock magnificently huge against his belly, and watch as she positioned herself in front of the window, the dress falling from her in silky slow motion, leaving only the sheerest panties. She would place the sole of her foot against his penis, fondling him gently with it while demanding that he drag the wispy silk knickers off her. He would reach up and slowly rub his fingers against the thin silk stretched over her mound, feeling the damp, softly coiled hair beneath them. Then, insinuating his fingers beneath the fabric, he would explore the lips of her hot, wet hole. Her breath coming in gasps, she would whisper for him to fuck her, her beautiful voice enlarging and exploring the word 'fuck' as though it was itself rich and precious. He would tease her with his fingers so she could barely stand, undulating against him to increase the blessed pressure. He would finger-fuck her with fast, light strokes, brushing her clit until she nearly came, before stopping a moment too early and ripping the soaking panties off her.

With a gasped scream of frustration and pleasure, but mercifully naked at last, she would straddle him, lowering herself on to his erection until his cock filled her. Deep inside he would seek her core. She would lean forward, her nipples close to his mouth begging for succour. His hard shaft would move against her clit while the ridge around the full head pulled at the sensitised spaces inside her. She would move him against her clitoris very, very slowly, exciting that wonderful, deep liquid of a woman's eyes when she is being fucked.

Disengaging herself from his rock-hard penis, she would lick the smooth, swollen head of it, mixing her own juices with his on her tongue and then, with two fingers, take the liquid from her mouth and rub it into her large, soft nipples, squeezing them to hardness, pointed, deep red.

She would crawl over him and rub her sex against his face, drenching him in her scented juices, her hands behind his head pulling him in to the soft, hot, wet hair around her mound. She would use his nose and chin to open up her beautiful quim. She would taste of pure sex, fresh and delicious; she would make his tongue serve her clitoris while her own hands rubbed her nipples and squeezed her breasts. His hands would explore the perfect globes of her arse. She would gyrate her hips on him, faster and faster, her head back, her back arched, breasts thrown out. She would come, his face drowning in her heat and wet as she slowly collapsed over him.

With his cock still hard and ready he would turn her gently on her front, marvelling at the combined strength and softness of a woman's back.

Languid from her adventures on his face, she would be hot. Beautiful sweat pouring from her, combining with the juices of her coming to slick her body, she would be supple and pliant. He could take her as he wanted and she would want him to be as demanding as she had been. Now she would want to be had any way he liked. The thought excited him still more. She wants me to fuck her; she's dripping for me; she wants to be filled; to be had slowly. I'm going to have her all.

He would straddle her bare arse, his rigid cock lubricated by her juices lying between her buttocks; his balls caressing her soft skin sending a current of electricity through his brain telling him to explore and enjoy her as she deserved.

Taking a bottle of warm oil, he would pour it slowly between her shoulder-blades, rubbing it in and spreading it till she glowed like a soft, warm golden animal, the oil adding a fourth dimension to the thrill in the curves of her body. He would oil the beautiful domes of her arse and, parting them, would lubricate her anus, his fingers tantalising her by circling it before pressing gently in, forcing her to raise herself up to meet him and increase the beautiful force. His hands would enjoy the wet heat between her buttocks. Finally, he would drive himself into the depths of her cunt.

He would stop masturbating her and she would groan in frustration. Still on her front as he had commanded, she would replace his hands with her own, fingers feverishly stroking her clitoris, desperate to come again yet not wanting to, waiting to see what more he would do to her.

With the warm oil, he would run his hands down her ribs to where her breasts swelled, crushed out by her own weight. He would lift her just a little to fill his hands with her gorgeous tits, nipples still diamond hard in lust for him.

Turning her over and pulling her arms up to lie above her head, he would work the oil thoroughly into her breasts before moving his hands down over the swell of her perfect woman's stomach to her wet mound. He would work her cunt again, finding her clitoris with a single finger while three more fingers imitated a cock – sliding in and out till she would scream in desperation for him to fuck her with his big, hard penis. Removing his hand, he would deny her for just a little longer, holding her wrists so she could not masturbate.

Completely slick from the oil and their joined sweat, he would amuse himself, sliding his cock in the cleavage between her breasts while on his upward thrusts she would use her ravenous tongue to lick the moisture from his cock end.

At last he would be ready; he would give her what she was gagging for; he would fuck her brains out. He would tease her at first with his cock end just inside her while his hands played with her full breasts. Then, without warning, he would ram deep into her, extracting an involuntary scream as she was filled. He would be suffused by the heat and wet inside her that demanded all his sweet, hard fucking.

He would turn over, holding himself hard inside her, and she would ride him, gyrating her hips, her cunt muscles rippling and sucking him up into her, desperate to pull the come from him, his balls in delicious lubricated friction against her oiled arse, her breasts shiny and heavy with his massaging. That fallen-angel look on her face as she leant forward to drown his face in her scented hair would almost bring him off. One of her hands would slowly find its way down behind her to his balls. Sitting upright on him, full of his cock and laughing her dirty laugh, she would say, 'Now I'll have you, you bastard.' She would drag her fingernails gently, slowly, across his balls, and he would come, exploding up into her with hot foaming come, and she would scream as she matched him with her own orgasm, her body falling limp on his as the last thrusts spent into her.

'Ladies and gentlemen, the captain has switched on the seatbelt sign, and we will be landing in ten minutes.' Jerked out of his fantasy, he glanced nervously at the woman next to him. Her eyes were fixed between his legs on his very real erection. She allowed her gaze to follow the line of his lean body till she looked him squarely in the eye. Holding his gaze steadily, she smiled and, bringing her seat back into the upright position for landing, she arched her back, framing the silhouette of her breasts for his benefit in the aircraft window. 'Why not?' she breathed.

The Name of an Angel

Laura Thornton

Clarissa is a well-respected university lecturer. Her life is one of academia and cultured conversation until the insolently sexy Nicholas St Clair enters her world. While she is delivering a class on erotic literature, she realises that the gorgeous seventeen-year-old is playing with himself. Clarissa is far from offended, however, and looks forward to seeing him in every English class. Suddenly her position, and the age gap between them, no longer seems to matter as she finds herself becoming obsessed with this mysterious young man. In the following extract, Clarissa invites Nick to her house. Unprofessional, maybe, but she finds him irresistible.

Laura Thornton is an American author who lives in the UK. She is an academic and has written extensively about the Gothic tradition of romantic and erotic fiction.

The Name of an Angel

*A*nd so it began. When Clarissa had to face Nick in class after they had first made love, she was terribly nervous. She wasn't sure how she could possibly act the disinterested lecturer when she had passed two sleepless nights mentally reliving the thrill of his body as it so expertly handled hers. Nearly crazed with the anticipation of seeing him again, she was also concerned about the signal she wanted to send. She certainly didn't want the rest of the class to guess at her obsession, nor did she want Nick to see clearly how much she wanted him now that she had had the chance to taste him. So Clarissa dressed extra carefully for class that day, not wanting to appear either too distant or too familiar; her tightest clothes seemed to her to be too much of an invitation, but she didn't want to appear dowdy. Therefore, she chose a lightweight wool apron-front dress that skimmed her curves rather than clung to them, a blouse that buttoned demurely at the throat, and a single choker of pearls. Hoping to strike the right note of attractive but professional university instructor, she held her head high and walked assuredly into the classroom.

She needn't have worried, however; all her care and concern were for naught. Nick wasn't in class. Frustrated

141

and disappointed, Clarissa struggled to concentrate on the day's lesson while straining to keep an ear out for the tread of Nick's boots in the hall, her eyes continually darting to the door, hoping to see his tall, rangy frame. He failed to materialise for the entire 60 minutes, however, and when Clarissa finally dismissed her class she tasted the bitterness of thwarted expectations and silently cursed herself for her impatient desperation to see him. Now that she had experienced Nick's body for herself, she felt bound and tied to him in a way she'd never felt to another lover, and she fought to maintain her equilibrium and to distance herself from the memory of what had happened. As she abandoned the empty room and turned towards the stairs leading to her office, she forced herself to view what had happened as a mistake, promising herself she'd forget about it and somehow try to treat him as just another student.

Later that day, though, when heading towards yet another departmental meeting, she saw him; he was leaning casually against the stairs surrounded by laughing classmates, among them, Clarissa noted unhappily, the blonde-haired girl she'd seen him with a few days ago.

Damn him! she ground out to herself silently. How dare he! It occurred to her that, sensing how desperately keen she'd be to see him, no matter how nervously, he had purposely stayed away as though to torment her further, prolonging her desire to lay eyes on him again. Thorns of angry humiliation invaded her body as she considered the possibility that the sex they'd shared had been no more than an amusing challenge to him, a dare he'd set himself. Horrified by the possibility that he had entertained his friends – perhaps even some of her own students – with the tale of how he'd fucked his English teacher, Clarissa prepared to accost him where he stood, using the power of her position as lecturer, and demand to see him in her office. However, she immediately thought better of it. Her horror deepened as she imagined him defying her authority in front of his friends and refusing to meet with her, and so instead she turned on her heel and strode off in the opposite direction.

He was waiting for her by her car as she approached it after the meeting, his back leaning against the window, his hands shoved deep in his pockets. He smiled full in her face as she neared the driver's side, and he appeared annoyingly arrogant, as though she had arrived at that place solely to see him rather than to drive herself home. Again it occurred to her that he knew exactly how much he'd angered and hurt her today by staying away from class, as though he were trying to avoid her.

'Hey, Clarissa,' he called out affably, towering over her with his tall, lean body. 'On your way home?'

'Why the hell weren't you in class today?' she nearly shouted at him, unable to appear as cool as he.

He grinned at her, and shrugged offhandedly. 'Oh, that,' he said dismissively, as though it were no matter. 'Sorry I had to skip the lecture today.'

Stung by the brevity of his reply, Clarissa merely unlocked the door to her car, then paused to look at him. Damn, but he's sexy, she thought to herself, unwilling to admit the force of her desire that was already propelling her round to his side of the car to unlock the passenger's door. 'You missed an important class today,' she said crossly, hating to hear herself sounding like a primary-school teacher. 'Get in.'

Hardly able to believe herself, Clarissa roughly shoved him inside, slammed his door, then jammed herself into the driver's seat – and immediately stalled the car in her agitation at being so close to him.

'Damn!' she cried, and he laughed aloud and reached over to caress the thin circle of her gloved wrist with his beautifully long fingers.

'Hey,' he said soothingly, 'it's OK.'

She looked at him and, unable to stop herself, reached over to kiss him, her lips briefly enclosing his before her tongue slipped in between them and swept across the inside of his mouth. His unshaven cheek rasped against hers as he drew her towards him and began to reach between her legs when, abruptly mindful that they were still in the faculty car park, she pushed him away and started up the car – successfully this time.

'Are we going to your house?' he asked offhandedly, still keeping his hand up her dress and between her thighs.

'Where else?' she gasped as his fingers inched up the lace banding of her French knickers and began to stroke aside the auburn clutch of curls that covered the lips of her sex. 'Are you offering to take me to yours?'

He merely laughed and continued to stroke, and Clarissa tried to concentrate on her steering as Nick's fingers slyly parted the rapidly unfurling leaves of her blossoming vagina and slipped inside, two of them, to slide in and out of her while his thumb covered her clitoris. Clarissa nearly lost sight of the road as Nick's hand lifted her slightly upwards then down again so she was sitting fully on his palm, two fingers pushing against her plush inner walls while his thumb continued to agitate the ripening bud of her eagerly emerging clitoris. He smiled a little when Clarissa glanced at him, as though merely amused by the quickening pulse of her vagina which was widening and moistening around his fingers, but one quick grope on her part assured Clarissa that he was finding his manipulation of her every bit as exciting as she. He had a taut, promising bulge in the front of his trousers, and she thought she could feel it leap a little under her fingers before she withdrew her hand to resume steering. Clarissa felt a sharp pang of loss when her difficulty in manoeuvring the car around a particularly tight corner caused Nick's fingers to slip momentarily out of her heaving vagina. But he rapidly resumed his position, his increasingly powerful finger-thrusts making her cry out, partly in pleasure and partly in panic, as the car skidded briefly out of her palpitating control. His eyes fixed on her face, Nick reached over to slip his other hand down the front of Clarissa's blouse, clasping her breast and passing his palm around her stiffening nipple while his lips sought her throat. His warm tongue moved tantalisingly around the milky softness of her flesh, and he shifted position slightly in his seat so that he could bury his mouth at the base of her neck.

Such an intensifying of pleasure proved to be too much for Clarissa, who forcefully shoved Nick away from her while lifting herself off his hand and replacing it firmly in his lap.

'That's enough!' she said primly, trying to conceal the near-climactic ripplings of sensation which continued to reverberate along her now achingly empty sex. 'Do you want me to have an accident?'

'Safety first,' he admonished her seriously, then tipped back his head and laughed – not at her expense, she hoped anxiously. Again it struck her that Nick found a certain degree of amusement in her panting response to his touch, as though he savoured the power her desire for him had over her, while he remained curiously detached.

As Clarissa pulled into her driveway, Nick let out a low whistle of appreciation. 'Nice house,' he commented, admiring the neat bed of marigolds and azaleas which bordered her front garden.

Clarissa said nothing, but led the way into her cluttered but tidy front sitting room, now thankfully free of boxes, where she deposited her load of books and gestured towards the aubergine-coloured sofa. 'Drink?' she offered.

He nodded. 'Please,' he said, studying the crammed wooden bookshelves, Tiffany lampshade, framed black-and-white modernist prints and, incongruously, a set of cosy family photos skewered lovingly to a ribbon attached to the cheery yellow wall above the menacing hulk of her computer. She watched him examine the intricate ivory curves of her chess set, picking up the pieces and fingering them curiously, as though he'd never seen one before. As Clarissa handed him his foaming glass of beer, she watched him puzzling over a replica of an Oxford gargoyle, then moving on to consider a porcelain Chinese vase, causing Clarissa's stomach to tighten in fear that he might drop it. He turned towards her with an inquisitive lift to his eyebrow.

'All yours?' he asked, indicating her curios with a tilt of his head. 'You bought all these yourself?'

'Inheritance,' she said shortly and, she hoped, with finality. Clarissa absolutely did not want to go into the details of her family history with Nick; although not by nature an excessively private person, she felt that she had already shared enough of herself with him, and she wanted to keep as much of her personal life apart from him as possible. She had a deep irrational fear of opening up her life to him as though it were something constructed merely for his amusement. She expected nothing more out of this affair than a mutual giving and taking of pleasure, and she was determined to keep as much of herself as possible separate and inviolable, revealing as little of her life to Nick as the fates allowed.

As if on cue, however, the phone rang sharply, jarring both Clarissa and Nick, and she froze, her gaze locked with his, as the shrill, insistent ringing continued.

'Aren't you going to answer it?' Nick asked, watching Clarissa closely.

'The answering machine will take it,' Clarissa nervously replied, desperately hoping that the caller wouldn't turn out to be someone from work.

As the answerphone clicked on, however, Clarissa realised with deep dismay that it was ex-boyfriend Graham's voice that came loudly into the room, sounding a bit strained, his accent a little too affected.

'Ah yes, Graham here,' he was saying, his stilted formality grating on Clarissa's ears, as well as his exaggerated pronunciation of the Queen's English. She couldn't help but contrast it unfavourably with Nick's warm, rich Midlands lilt.

'I'm ringing to remind you of our plans for tomorrow night,' Graham continued. Damn! She had forgotten that she'd agreed to meet him. He went on with his message to add conversationally, as though she could answer, 'Please don't arrange anything else, as these bookings are rather hard to come by, and it has been so long since we've been out together, you know.'

He sounds as though he's expecting a reply straight away! Clarissa thought angrily to herself. As though he knows I'm standing here listening to him, but can't be bothered to pick up the phone – which, of course, was precisely the case.

Nick's eyes met Clarissa's in amusement, and it was with great relief that Clarissa heard Graham finally ring off, vowing to herself to ring him back tomorrow morning and cancel their damned date.

'Husband? Boyfriend?' Nick casually inquired, regarding her over the rim of his glass.

'Neither,' she answered abruptly, then moved away from Nick, nearly backing herself into a corner as though his very presence in her house was making her uncomfortable.

Apparently sensing her discomfort, Nick replaced the mask he was holding on to the carved occasional table and stepped backwards a bit. 'Is my being here making you nervous?' he asked gently. 'Am I invading too much of – ' he laughed ' – your personal space?'

She stared at him, aghast. Really, it was maddening the way he already seemed to know so much about her! Hoping to catch him off-guard, Clarissa deliberately set down her beer and pressed her body firmly against his. 'Invade away,' she invited, her arms reaching up to him.

As he brought his mouth down over hers, Nick lifted Clarissa up easily in his arms and inquired around her probing tongue, 'Where's the bedroom?'

'Through there,' came her muffled reply as she

pointed with her arm towards the doorway leading to the stairs. Despite her rising excitement, she maintained enough detachment to be impressed by Nick's ability to co-ordinate kissing her with watching where he was going as he carried her up the narrow, winding staircase and into her surprisingly spacious bedroom. He laid her down on her large, Egyptian-cotton quilt and then stepped back a bit to survey the contents of her room. Clarissa congratulated herself on having finally shed the last of those prissy Laura Ashley patterns that had disfigured her house as Nick's eyes travelled round her room, taking in the muted mauve, teal and strawberry tones of the walls and the intricate scrollwork of her big brass bed. Framed prints of vaginal-looking flowers and erotically contorted dancers covered her walls; there was a beautiful antique oak armoire in the corner, and arched brass lamps were placed strategically about the room. Clarissa sat on the bed removing her pearl choker and watched as Nick wandered over to her low mirrored dressing table and ran his fingers over the cut-glass bottles of perfumes, lotions and oils. He held up a particularly ornate atomiser with an old-fashioned black bulb and pressed it slightly, releasing a spray of spicy floral scent.

Clarissa was intrigued, and a little bemused, by Nick's apparent fascination with the way she lived her life. She wouldn't have thought that he'd be interested in how she'd personalised her intimate living-space, and it occurred to her that he was trying to lay claim to her by exploring the margins and details of her house the way he'd explored the folds and crevices of her body. If knowledge was power, then it certainly seemed as though Nick was trying to learn enough about Clarissa to extend the control his body already had over her.

When at last he turned to her on the bed and came to lie beside her, running his hands over her body as he'd run them over her bottles and jars, Clarissa was keen to do something to redress the imbalance of power. She rolled on top of him and began to move her mouth slowly over him, starting with his lips and moving across to thrust her tongue in his ear, and then below to kiss the place where his head joined his neck, turning his jaw away to allow herself greater access. As she moved lower to trail her tongue along the contoured ridges of his pectorals, unbuttoning his shirt along the way, Nick's hands slid down the arch of her spine to cup and squeeze the muscled curves of her rotating buttocks as she undulated her hips against him – but she stopped him.

'Uh-uh,' she said warningly, her mouth against his nipple. 'Don't touch me now.'

He said nothing but merely clasped his hands behind his head while Clarissa's tongue sought out his stiff brown nipple and her hand moved downwards to rub against the protruding bulge in his jeans. She enveloped the organ, rolling her hand around it and moving steadily upwards and downwards in a smooth, slow rhythm. As she did so, her left hand finished unbuttoning his shirt, and then she pulled away and commanded, 'Take it off.'

Nick looked at her and grinned, still saying nothing, then neatly stripped off his shirt and dropped it on the floor. 'Now yours,' he said, reaching for the straps of her dress, but she slapped his hands away and said, 'Uh-uh – I told you, no touching.' She considered him thoughtfully a moment, then, lifting up her dress so she could comfortably straddle his hips, she deftly unbuckled his belt and drew the leather length rapidly out of the loops of his jeans, saying, 'I see we'll have to do something to prevent your hands from getting in the way.' He glanced at her questioningly and she ordered, 'Roll on to your side,' pushing at his hip and lifting it up to help him oblige. 'Hands behind your back now,' she told him, and then pressed his wrists together and threaded the belt through and around them, securing it by fastening the buckle and then testing its tightness.

'Too tight?' she asked a little anxiously, then fought to regain her control. She had, after all, done this before, but never had it afforded her the thrill it did now, feeling herself exert a form of dominance over this incredible young man who held her in such thrall.

Nick shrugged, clearly struggling to contain his excitement, as though to show it would be giving something away, and said, 'It's OK.'

Clarissa regarded him a moment, silently admiring the way his muscles bulged underneath the smooth skin of his arms, now tautened and strained by the confining belt. She ran first her fingers, then her mouth along the lines of the arm closest to her, and tongued the sensitive crease inside his elbow. She then drew her mouth down to his wrist and kissed the sensitive flesh before nudging him again on to his back and locating the deep indentation of his navel with her tongue. Clarissa licked up and down the sides of it, savouring the rough, male taste of him and smiling to herself when she heard a low murmured moan of approval. She briefly pressed her cheek against the hollow formed by his stomach beneath his ribcage, then sucked one last time at his salty, textured navel.

Rearing back on to her heels, Clarissa then tugged at Nick's boots and, with some effort, finally pulled them off, careful not to muddy her blouse with the soles. She then eased off his socks and hesitated at his toes, thinking about sucking them, then decided she'd wait until after he'd had a bath – hopefully with her. Instead she bent over the fly of his jeans, briefly bared her teeth at him with a low growl, and then nipped at the fly, gripping the fabric around the top button with her teeth. It had taken her years of practice, but Clarissa was now justly proud of herself for perfecting the art of unbuttoning a man's fly in this manner. Denim was a tough business, but Nick's trousers were well worn and it took but a few firm jerks of her head – like a dog with a particularly juicy bone, she always thought – to release the set of five buttons from their tight little enclosures. Noting that again Nick wore no underwear, Clarissa wondered to herself whether he'd planned on seducing – or being seduced by – her today, or whether it was his usual practice to allow his cock to abrade freely against the front closure of his trousers. She considered asking him, but the shut-eyed look of tremulous anticipation on his face as she slipped off his jeans convinced her such a trivial issue could wait to be resolved.

At last Nick lay naked on the bed, Clarissa sitting beside him fully dressed, and she paused to admire the length of him, his hands tied helplessly behind his back, the skin of his chest and arms pulled tightly enough to display his flexed muscles and his cock dancing a little in expectation, as though trying to attract her attention. Clarissa's eyes absorbed the sight of that long, thick shaft, noting its swelling plum-like tip and already imagining the taste of it on her tongue. She took a firm grip on his penis, feeling it pulse and quicken beneath her fingers, and she smiled down at him, her own body tensing with erotic arousal.

'Comfortable?' She smiled, and was enormously gratified to see him wince a little at her deferral of his pleasure, the tip of his cock already beginning to emit a thick drop of lush, pearlised liquid. Eager to send this boy out of his mind with delight, Clarissa bent over and caught the silken drop on her tongue, swallowing it down and positioning herself between his slim, muscular thighs. 'Mmm,' she purred, looking up at him and nearly mewling with satisfaction, 'let's see if there's more where that came from.'

And then she began in earnest, gripping his cock with her lips and drawing him deeply into her mouth, her tongue slipping under the foreskin and circling round the steely hardness of his shaft. She worked her way around the circumference of his cock, concentrating on keeping her tongue soft and wet, taking in as much of the violet-and-rose-coloured length of it as she could.

She tried to position it so that the head was enclosed in the tender patch of her mouth where her molars ended and her cheek met her gum, and then she shifted so it was pointing down her throat. She sucked up and down the jutting rod, covering up her teeth with her lips, and she could feel her jaw muscles bulging as Nick's hips jerked in rhythm with her mouth. Clarissa slowly slid his cock out of her mouth and glanced up at Nick, whose face was contorted with pleasure, and she whispered, 'Lie still. Open your legs.'

Obediently his legs spread for her and she took his balls in her mouth, the soft sac reminding her of the texture of moleskin, so sensual and delicate was its feel. Clarissa sucked gently at his testicles, her fingers circling the cushiony pad behind the scrotum, feeling the pulse tick and beat with her movements. Releasing Nick's balls, Clarissa ducked her head lower and stroked that sensitive spot with her tongue, then, grasping Nick's thighs and pushing them further apart, she sucked at the core of his body where his legs joined his pelvis. Feeling Nick struggling against the belt that bound his wrists, Clarissa sensed his time was near, so she tugged at his hip, causing him to roll back on to his side. Sliding her fingers down the sweat-moistened cleft between his buttocks, Clarissa found the tiny, tight opening, and, parting the tightly muscled globes of his backside, she inserted her tongue, slowly licking at the pink-and-beige lining of the crease that divided his buttocks. Using the moisture from her mouth as a lubricant, she worked her finger inside, feeling the rectal walls unfolding around it while she continued to suck gently at his anal entrance. Nick gasped aloud in delight – or was it shock? – and Clarissa wondered if he'd ever been penetrated in this way before. She twisted her finger in further, then firmly pushed it in and out while she pressed her mouth against his backside one last time. Finally she rolled him on to his back again and moved upward to claim his cock with her mouth. She drew the length of it deeply into her mouth, then slid it back out so that only the head remained between her lips. She withdrew her finger so that she could concentrate on relaxing her jaw as she felt the blood start to pound in the jerking, throbbing shaft, and she knew Nick's climactic moment had come. There was that momentary pause in Nick's movements before his sperm jetted forth into her mouth, and he arched his back and tensed, muttering a single, nearly silent 'ah' of ecstasy. Clarissa stayed absolutely still, simply gathering the fluid in her mouth before withdrawing slowly to swallow it down, wiping off the salty, slightly bitter drops that fell from her chin as she moved away from Nick and bent over to unfasten his belt.

'Wow,' Nick exhaled as he sat up and flexed his aching wrists, grimacing as the blood began to resume its circulation. '*Where* did you learn *that*?'

Clarissa smiled and straightened her clothes, then reached forward to brush Nick's hair back from his eyes. 'Years of practice,' she answered throatily as she leant forward to kiss him, testing to see whether he'd pull away. Not many men could stand to have the taste of themselves revisited on their tongue, but Nick kissed her with force, working his tongue around hers as though extracting every drop of himself from the interior of her mouth. Clarissa was pleased with herself for pleasing him so well, as though this were a competition of sorts to see who could retain erotic dominance over the other.

As if guessing her thoughts – damn, he's good at that, Clarissa thought to herself in annoyance – Nick pushed her back down on the bed and said, 'And now, my dear, it's your turn.'

Unwilling to succumb so easily, despite the vibrant excitement which was rampaging through her body, Clarissa resisted Nick's gentle push, sat back up and lightly jumped off the bed.

'Let's have some supper first,' she suggested cheerily,

then absorbed his blank-faced expression. 'Or ... perhaps you'd rather not.' Even though Clarissa was reluctant to share too much of her private life with Nick, that didn't include dinner – or perhaps, she thought, eating together was just too chummy, too much of a boyfriend-girlfriend thing that Nick might not want. I guess it's pretty obvious, thought Clarissa to herself, that he only wants me for sex; perhaps that's the only activity he's willing to share.

His shuttered look rapidly dissolved, however, and was replaced instead by a sly, almost cunning expression. 'Of course, Clarissa,' he said. 'I'll eat with you. What are we having?'

Relieved to recall that she had done a week's worth of shopping the night before, Clarissa waited until Nick was dressed then led the way to the kitchen and directed him to chop up vegetables, blend a salad dressing and peel fruit while she threw together a chicken stir-fry, saffron rice and poured a significant amount of brandy into the fruit salad. Clarissa was a little startled to discover that cooking together was an easy, comfortable affair, cosy even, and she felt that she and Nick worked naturally together in such a domestic environment. She started to instruct him on how to lay the table when, with a wicked glance, he stopped her. 'Let's eat in your bedroom,' he grinned, and searched about for a tray. Clarissa followed him up the stairs with a bottle of champagne, and they set up a little picnic on her bed, feeding each other with chopsticks.

'This is fun,' Clarissa chirped happily, dabbing her napkin gaily at Nick's chin to catch a dribble of soy sauce. She then stopped guiltily and clapped a hand to her mouth. 'I guess I'm not acting very much like a lecturer,' she said, half to herself and half to Nick. 'And don't think I'm looking for anything more involved than this!' she snapped defensively.

Nick laughed and settled back against the pillows. 'Tell me about yourself, Clarissa,' he said, ignoring her previous remark and pouring them more champagne. 'How did you get into teaching?'

Clarissa stared at him for a moment, surprised he was even interested, then decided his question was somehow intended to trap her into revealing enough of herself for him to maintain some sort of hold over her. She was still unable to satisfactorily analyse why it was she wanted him so badly, and she was determined to maintain as much of an emotional distance between them as possible. Clarissa doubted she was more to Nick than just a momentary fling, an amusing sexual diversion heightened by the illicit thrill of her age and position. She suspected that her passion for him ran deeper than his did for her, and so she was anxious not to appear too eager to share confidences or to imply that this was in any way anything other than a casual affair for her either.

So, instead of answering his question, Clarissa put the tray on the floor, drew a deep draught of champagne into her mouth and placed her lips on Nick's, letting the liquid flow into his mouth from hers. She kissed his neck while he swallowed, and then his hands were everywhere on her body, under her dress, over her breasts, circling her waist and inching between her thighs. She gave herself up to the indescribable waves of blissful sensation that were flooding her nerve endings, suddenly inflamed with the need to feel his flesh upon hers. She lunged at the buttons on his shirt, nearly ripping the garment from his body, when his hands caught at her wrists and held them away from him, needing only a fraction of his strength to imprison her.

'Uh-uh,' he said, mimicking her earlier admonition. 'No touching, remember?'

Clarissa lay back and closed her eyes while Nick unbuttoned the straps of her dress with one easy flick of his long fingers, then pulled it over her head, undoing the buttons at her waist so that the whole thing came off. He then nipped at the buttons of her blouse as she had done at his jeans, but her buttons were tiny and tightly fastened, so with an impatient grunt he undid as many as were necessary to simply lift that over her head as well. Clarissa wanted to tell him to be careful, that it was expensive Italian silk, but she was so mesmerised by the feel of his fingers on her body she could hardly breathe, let alone speak. She now lay before him, clad only in her bra, panties, stockings and suspender belt, and she felt herself tremble as she awaited his touch, for he had withdrawn his hands and now simply sat looking at her. She experienced the way his gaze passed over her body as though it were a tangible, tactile thing; she felt his eyes caress the heaving swell of her bosom, the striated planes of her stomach, the fullness of her rounded thighs. She held her breath in anticipation of the feel of his mouth, fingers, body, but he merely held himself back, smiling a little as though he sensed her mounting frustration while he considered what to do with her.

Feeling a little silly, finally, Clarissa started to sit up in protest when she saw him sip at his glass of champagne as though he were going to ignore her, but with one easy sweep of his arm he gently pushed her back down and then spilled some champagne on to her breasts, causing her to gasp in surprise and discomfort at the icy-cold liquid. The chill was quickly replaced by his heat, however, as Nick's tongue plunged into the pool on her chest and lapped at it slowly, trailing over the cleft of her cleavage and licking away the last sparkling drops. He grinned at her again, then expertly unclasped the front closure of her cream-coloured bra as though he'd received personal instruction in the ladies' undergarment department. Clarissa helped herself out of the underwired entrapment, tangling up the straps in her haste, and then felt her breasts quiver a little as Nick dipped his finger in his glass and drew intricate patterns on her stiff pink nipples with the champagne. The delicate alcoholic drops tickled her breasts, heightening their sensitivity as Nick bent his head and licked at her nipples, drinking in the fizzing wine. He lingered at her breasts for a while, alternating the warm softness of his tongue with the now only slightly cool drops of champagne, and then trickled a path to her navel which he sucked up with his mouth. There was no sound in the room other than the splash of the wine and the swishing sound of Nick's lips; Clarissa was afraid to sigh or pant too loudly lest she break the tingling spell of their passion. Desperate for Nick to do more, yet unwilling to relinquish the feel of his tongue in the well in her stomach, Clarissa was both relieved and disappointed when he finally reached behind her to unhook the itching lace of her frothy red suspender belt. He then unrolled one dusky-blue stocking down her right leg, did the same with the left, then dangled them teasingly in front of her, close enough for her to smell the lingering scent of her perfume on the silky fabric.

'Let's see,' he drawled, trailing the edge of one stocking down the length of her stomach. 'Should we use these to tie you up, like you used my belt?' Playfully he grabbed at her wrists, wrapping the nylon tightly around them, then pulled it slowly away, like a conjurer unfolding a magical scarf. 'Or perhaps we should tie up your ankles?' He indicated the scrollwork at the foot of the bed as though he would anchor her feet to that, and then chuckled a little at her reaction as he let the stockings float down to the floor. 'No?' he queried, examining her face. 'Maybe we should leave that for another time?'

Although Clarissa generally enjoyed being tied up, and yes, more than one lover had used her own stockings for that purpose, the idea of lying helpless before Nick, passively awaiting his moves, wasn't something that appealed to her; indeed, the prospect of adding to her vulnerability was much too disconcerting. So it was with great relief and a rush of internal moisture that Clarissa lifted her hips to allow Nick to ease off her panties, obviously deciding against tying her down that day. Once he'd discarded them, consigning them to the heap that was the rest of her clothes, he settled himself on the floor by the side of the bed and grasped her shapely calves, dragging her to him so that her sex was poised on the edge of the bed directly in front of his mouth.

'Close your eyes,' he commanded against the softness of her inner thigh, kissing the curve where her leg met her body. 'Let this be a surprise.' He then gently pushed her legs apart, placing one foot on the floor and setting the other one next to her pillows so she was spread wide apart. Closing her eyes, Clarissa waited with a beating heart to see what he'd do next; expecting the heat and strength of his tongue, she cried out in shock when she felt something cold, wet and slightly squishy being quietly inserted into her.

'What the hell is that?' she demanded, sitting up and nearly kicking Nick in the head, but he quickly rose to his feet and nudged her back down.

'Patience,' he whispered. 'Just wait.' Arranging her back into position, he gently prodded another cold, wet object inside her and then, putting his mouth squarely at the entrance to her vagina, he sucked out whatever he'd put in and then rose above her so she could see his face. He held a slice of melon from the fruit salad between his teeth and Clarissa felt a sudden thrilling jolt as he bent over, slipping the fruit between her lips and watching while she swallowed it, tasting her own sweet-as-honey juices on the piece of honeydew as it went down.

'So that's what that was!' she hooted, and then, wildly aroused by such a novel use for fruit, she breathlessly awaited the feel of Nick's warm, wet mouth which contrasted so favourably with the icy chill of the fruit and the sharp, acidic sting of the brandy. Clarissa shivered in exquisite pleasure every time Nick slid in another plump slice or segment of grapefruit, pineapple, melon or strawberry, and she clenched her interior muscles around each piece, coating it with the flavour of her own inner juices. She couldn't tell if the moisture running down her now-luscious crevice and in the cleft between her buttocks was from Nick's mouth, the juice of the fruit, or her own vaginal creaminess. She felt as though the heat of her musky dampness might soften and melt the fruit, so aroused was she, and she thrilled to Nick's obvious enjoyment as he simultaneously devoured her and the dessert she so temptingly offered him from between her thighs. Eventually, the pressure of Nick's mouth against her syrupy vagina was driving her close to the brink of orgasm so she waited until he'd swallowed the last succulent sliver of strawberry and then, turning back the folds of her labia so the shining pearl of her clitoris was clearly visible, she murmured huskily, 'Kiss me here. I want you right here.'

Nick surged forward and laid his tongue against the dewy sweetness of the nub of Clarissa's pleasure, which had also been bathed in the fruity juices which flavoured the rest of her. He licked and sucked at the peaking bud, his long soft tongue sweeping over and around it until Clarissa came in convulsions, her whole body shaking with the force of her climax. The waves of shrieking rapture had barely subsided when Clarissa, desperately craving penetration, lunged at Nick's jeans, tearing at his fly in her frenzy to get at his cock. Laughing, Nick held her off a little with one hand while he reached in his back pocket with the other.

'Whoa,' he said, trying to restrain her. 'Calm down. All in good time. Look what I brought with me.'

Clarissa stared in amazement at the shiny red condom packet he held triumphantly above her, and a heady smile of delight curved her lips.

'Go on,' she said, nodding at the sheath. 'Let me watch you put it on.'

Nick's fingers fumbled with the buttons of his shirt, which he finally drew off, and then he hastily removed his jeans, his cock springing proudly forward as though reaching out towards her body. Clarissa watched while he grasped it in his hand with obvious familiarity and jiggled it a little so that the head fitted securely into the ringed opening of the condom. He pinched the tip of the sheath, expelling the air, then rapidly rolled the condom down until his blushing, swelling penis was entirely enclosed. Clarissa found the sight of him handling his shaft deeply erotic, and, as soon as he was safely wrapped up, she reached up to him and pulled him down on the bed so they were body to body, skin to skin, flesh to flesh.

'The first time we've held each other while both completely naked,' Nick mused aloud, and then pressed his body even closer to Clarissa's, saying, 'Let me just experience the feel of you.'

Overwhelmed by his unexpected tenderness – like the time he'd first kissed her in her office – Clarissa felt tears start to well up in her eyes at the same time as she savoured the feeling of Nick's naked body against hers. She kissed his mouth, tasting her fruited flavour which still clung to his tongue, and rubbed against him, trying to tell where her skin left off and his began. When Nick ran his hands along the sides of her body, she could feel the softness of her own skin as though his hands had become hers, and the velvety texture of his chest against her own seemed to mirror the silken softness of her breasts.

Unnerved by this intimate, unlooked-for closeness, she deliberately pushed him off her and rolled him on to his back, throwing her leg across his hips so that she was centred across his cock, kneeling fully astride him; then she leant a little forward, guiding his pulsating staff into the secret depths of her slightly sticky vagina. Once he was fully inside her, she paused for a moment and he held still within her, their eyes meeting, each gauging the other's reaction. Slowly she began to move, sliding up a little and moving back down while he rocked his hips and answered her motions with strong, probing thrusts. Clarissa moved now up and down, now forward and back, rubbing her clitoris against the bone of his pelvis and the base of his cock. She rode him long and slow, her buttocks clutched in his hands, her breasts braced against his chest as she leant forward to kiss him. They moved together in silence, looking into each other's face and listening to each other's breathy, hushed sighs. The bed creaked softly under them as their tempo began gradually to increase, their accelerated rhythm heightening and intensifying their pleasure until Nick was pounding away inside her while Clarissa arched her back and shut her eyes, her knees abraded by the heavy cotton of the quilt, her hands tucked up high beneath Nick's shoulders. As Clarissa's orgasm began to rip through her, she heard Nick's voice through the pounding of the blood in her veins saying, 'Open your eyes, Clarissa. I want you to look at me.'

She looked at him then, a faint flush on his cheeks and his sensual lips slightly apart, and she wanted to hide from the intensity of emotion that swept through her. As Clarissa screamed her pleasure aloud, she felt Nick's own ecstatic spasm, and his body rocked hers as he gave one final thrust, shuddered and lay still.

He lay quietly within her for a moment, then, turning away his head, he withdrew completely, gently nudged her off him and disappeared into the bathroom, taking his discarded clothes with him. While he was gone, Clarissa quickly dressed in a pair of leggings and a jumper, then dawdled nervously about, unsure of how to act once he re-emerged. She felt naked and exposed, not because of the sex they'd shared, but because she felt that some indefinable emotion had surged forth from within her and was clearly visible on her face. She didn't want Nick to think that this had been anything more than an extraordinarily pleasant evening; after all, she still had to grade his essays and assign his homework.

Thus she struggled to maintain somehow a coolly professional demeanour.

When Nick emerged from the bathroom, dressed and obviously ready to go, she hesitated shyly, then forced herself to say lightly, 'Well, I guess I'll see you in class.'

He smiled a little at the absurdity of the situation – at least, she hoped that was the source of the smile – and said, 'I suppose so.'

She followed him down the stairs and then paused at the door as he opened it.

'Well,' she said again, feeling awkward and uneasy – something she never usually felt with a lover. 'See you in class.'

He nodded, smiled and left, shutting the door firmly behind him.

The Stranger

Portia Da Costa

It's not every day a handsome young man dressed as a Victorian poet throws himself into your arms. This is what happens one night, during a storm, to the widowed Claudia in her country cottage. A stranger to her and to himself – he has lost his memory – it's not easy to tell whether he is an accomplished trickster with a hidden agenda or just a beautiful young man with a bad case of amnesia. Whatever he is, he manages to reignite Claudia's sleeping sexuality. This extract is taken from the beginning of the story, when the stranger has found shelter in Claudia's house.

Portia Da Costa's name will be familiar to those of you who have been reading Black Lace books from the early days. She is a prolific and talented author of erotic novels and *The Stranger* is her sixth book for us. Her other titles are *Gemini Heat*, which features identical twin sisters who compete with each other for the attentions of an enigmatic art dealer; *The Tutor*, which is about a librarian employed to educate a young man who has led a sheltered life; *The Devil Inside*, a story of extra-sensual perception; *Gothic Blue*, a haunting tale of erotic love across the centuries; and *Continuum*, about a clandestine society devoted to erotic punishment. *Shadowplay*, her forthcoming novel, will revolve around a louche young man who believes he is the reincarnation of an artist.

The Stranger

*H*e was awake, and sitting up in bed, actually watching the storm. He no longer seemed quite so afraid of it.

'Hello. Is everything all right?' Claudia asked him, peering cautiously around the door when he had answered her knock. She gestured towards the sky, which obligingly lit up with a distant bolt of lightning. 'Is the storm still bothering you?'

'Not so much any more, thank you.' He gave her a small shy version of his smile, which made her quiver. 'I think both it and I have calmed down a bit now.'

Knowing exactly how foolish she was being, because in his new, more rational state he could well find her attentions embarrassing, Claudia closed the door and walked across to the bed. The stranger gave her an unfathomable look as she approached, which almost made her turn and run, but when she reached him he smoothed his hand across the coverlet at his side. Claudia took this as an invitation, and settled down facing him with her kimono arranged carefully over her thighs. Too great a display of flesh might alarm him.

You stupid bitch! she told herself, as the stranger

165

regarded her levelly, and she felt her loins melt like honey on a stove. *He's young and he's beautiful. Even if he is some kind of runaway, or mentally disturbed, why the hell would he want you?* And yet something in her heart told her she was doing herself an injustice, and a gross one. Her nascent self-confidence reminded her of her powers.

'You must be wondering what the hell is the matter with me,' said her companion softly. 'Beating your door down in the middle of the night ... Screaming and fainting and cringing ... I hope I didn't frighten you too much?'

'No, not too much,' answered Claudia, her pulse and hormones in turmoil. Gerald's pyjamas seemed to fit the young man perfectly, and their rich blue was undoubtedly his colour. It made his smooth, milky skin almost luminescent in the lamplight, and turned his eyes into twin chips of aquamarine. Against the white pillows, his damp hair appeared black.

'You're certainly a bit of a "happening" though,' she said, clenching every muscle in her body to control herself. She wanted to lunge at him; to kiss him and caress him. 'It's not every night that a handsome young man dressed as an Edwardian poet throws himself into my arms.'

The stranger laughed; a simple act that affected Claudia profoundly. She knew that at any second she was going to do something unthinkable, like tearing off her kimono and throwing herself into his arms. *If he would have her.*

'I wish I could explain everything,' he said, shrugging. 'The clothes, the screaming, everything – but I can't.' He looked at her seriously, his face a complicated montage of emotions. She sensed that he had been genuinely flattered by her reference to him as 'handsome', but that he was also still a little desperate and confused.

'The thunder was just the last straw.' He sat up straight, then reached out and grabbed her hand. 'I don't know what's happened to me ... It's ... It's all a huge blank ... A blur.' His fingers were like steel around Claudia's, but even the pain of his grip was exciting. 'I remember bits of yesterday, and today. All mixed up ... But I can't remember anything else! Not a thing.' His eyes were shining now, and his mouth working with the effort of holding back his distress. 'This must sound so stupid! You won't believe me ... I don't even remember my own name!'

'But I *do* believe you,' said Claudia, twisting her hand out of his grip, then reversing the process to take his hand in hers. 'The same thing once happened to me. I fell off a horse, banged my head, and I didn't know who I was for two weeks.' She paused, felt her own body shaking, then looked down and realised that she was caressing his hand with her thumb. 'But it all came back to me ... And I'm sure the same thing will happen for you.'

'I hope so,' he said, suddenly sounding a little better. He looked down at her thumb, still moving against his skin. 'I would have liked to at least have been able to introduce myself.'

Ah, the social niceties. Her mind was red with lust, and she had almost forgotten them.

'My name is Claudia Marwood.' She twisted their fingers into the conventional grip of greeting, and her companion did the honours, shaking her hand.

'And I'm – ' He grinned and shrugged.

'The man with no name?'

He smiled again, then scrunched up his face, as if a physical effort might prise free elusive knowledge. 'Is that from a film?' Claudia nodded. 'Well, I've just remembered my first fact. Thank you!' Leaning forward, he suddenly touched his lips to hers.

It was like being hit by the lightning outside. The fleeting contact of his mouth was electric, and filled Claudia with such a wave of passion that she couldn't breathe for a moment.

This is insane! she thought. She was making a complete idiot of herself. 'I'd better go now and let you get some rest,' she said, and made as if to get up from the bed and run for it.

The hold on her hand turned to steel again. A carefully gauged, velvet-covered steel, but steel nevertheless.

'Stay.' His voice was husky, already changing. 'Please!'

She should have asked why, but she knew why. In the dim light, his blue eyes were steely too, and alive with a message that was unmistakable.

'Are you sure?' she asked, then had to smile, knowing that under any other circumstances this was a question the man would ask.

The stranger nodded, answering her smile with a beautiful and very masculine one of his own. 'At the moment it's the one single thing in the whole world I *am* sure of.'

Claudia was imprisoned by him. At the centre of their stillness, she felt the balance of power tilting on its fulcrum; her lost boy had found his way and taken command.

'Let me turn the light out,' she said faintly.

'Must you?' His voice was teasing now: deep and intense, but flirtatious.

'Yes, I think I must,' insisted Claudia, fighting not to go under entirely. She drew a deep breath when he released her, then she reached out and flipped off the lamp.

'I can imagine you,' he said, as she slipped off her robe, feeling glad of the darkness to hide her confusion. It was a long time since she had bared her body for a man, and even longer since she had been naked before a new lover rather than her husband.

The stranger lifted the covers and, shaking with nervousness and longing in equal parts, Claudia slid into bed beside him.

'Don't be afraid,' he said, and then she was in his

arms, her bare skin against the cotton of his pyjamas, her mouth sought by his for their first true kiss.

Expecting boyish haste, she was astonished when he began to kiss her quite slowly. His lips were gentle and mobile against hers, and the pressure they exerted complex. Without thinking, she opened her mouth and his tongue darted forward, accepting her gift, searching and finding her own tongue with its tip. He tasted strongly of spearmint, the toothpaste she had left for him, and she wondered why she had never realised how such a common flavour could seem so exotic.

His hold on her was measured too, hands flexing just enough to keep her against him; no grabbing, no groping, no force. His body was warm and firm through the cotton that covered it, his erection a hot brand against her thigh.

Suddenly, his self-control seemed to rip away the years from her. She became the impatient adolescent, surging against him, anxious to explore his body and touch and caress it. She scrabbled at the buttons of his pyjama jacket, trying to bare him. She wanted to taste and devour him.

'Hush!' he whispered, reaching between them and taking both her hands in his. 'There's no hurry ... I'm not going anywhere.' He gave her fingers a little squeeze, then eased her on to her back and made her lie still, her arms at her sides.

'You're very lovely, Claudia,' he said, letting his long hand settle at last on her breast. 'So soft and warm. You make me feel so safe here.'

His fingers cupped her curves, first one, then the other, as if he were weighing and assessing her, the touch light and infuriatingly playful. Claudia longed for him to squeeze her; to be rough and forceful, to take her breath away, to ravish her. She shifted her thighs, trying to rub herself against him.

The stranger laughed softly. 'I never realised I was so

desirable. Did you want me this much when you were watching me by the river?'

Shocked to her marrow, Claudia began to struggle, but the stranger was too quick for her, stopping her mouth with his lips and stilling her body by the simple expedient of pressing his own down potently upon it. Somewhere miles away, the thunder rolled again.

He knows I watched him! How could he know that? Who is he? thought Claudia frantically. She felt fear, and yet the fear excited her even more. Her body seemed to be burning underneath him and her nipples were so engorged that they were hurting, chafed by his weight yet sending sublime bolts of feeling to her groin.

The stranger could be a consummate trickster, she realised, the confusion and amnesia just a smooth and very clever act. And yet she didn't care. His thigh was between hers now, and his pyjama leg was wet where it pressed against her crotch. It was obvious that she was so aroused she couldn't think straight. He laughed again, the sound vibrating in her mouth.

Claudia broke away. 'How did you know it was me? Why didn't you call out? Say something?'

'I wasn't sure I was right,' he said more quietly, almost penitently. 'It was just a feeling . . . I didn't *know* there was anyone there.' He sighed and grew still. 'Everything was so weird . . . I could have been hallucinating . . . Imagining things.'

The lost boy was back again, although, against her leg, his penis was still a man of iron's.

'I shouldn't have been spying on you,' murmured Claudia, putting her arms around him and feeling him shiver in response and move against her. 'I should have made some noise or something . . . Given you a chance to cover yourself.'

'I would probably have run a mile,' he answered, his equilibrium, momentarily lost, now returned. He rocked slightly, caressing her with his erection and sliding it closer to her sex. 'But I feel much better now. More together. More used to you.'

It was Claudia's turn to chuckle. 'Yes, I think you can be of some use to me.' She reached down and clasped him through the cotton pyjamas, feeling a rush of lust, and of confidence, when he gasped.

The young man was bigger and harder than Gerald had ever been, although her late husband had possessed a penis to be proud of. Claudia quivered inside. Her vagina fluttered as if to express its hunger, demanding she get on with the entertainment she had promised it.

How good could he be, this man who had stumbled into her life out of the storm? It was readily apparent to her that between the sheets, at least, he was surprisingly sure of himself, and he had the natural grace and the body of a good lover. And he wasn't a callow boy, despite his spaced-out behaviour when he had fallen into her arms. She sensed again that he could well be older than he looked, and excitingly experienced in the ways of physical love.

Time to find out.

Releasing his cock, she took his hand and drew it down between her legs. His face was against her neck now, and she felt him smile, slow and knowingly, against her skin. At her crotch, his long, rather tapered fingers began delicately combing the soft hair over her pudenda, parting it neatly, then pressing inward between the tender lips it covered.

He touched her very lightly, hardly more than a brushstroke, on her clitoris – and Claudia cried out, the tiny organ was so sensitised. She had known she wanted him, but she hadn't known how much. The almost ethereal contact had brought her heart-stoppingly close to orgasm, and she lay there panting, astonished by her own reaction.

'More?' enquired the stranger, against her throat. Claudia heard the familiar note of masculine arrogance in his voice, and she wanted to laugh with delight at how complete and diverse his approach was. He seemed to move from foundling to superlover in almost an instant.

'Yes! Much more!' she said fiercely, then grabbed his head, digging her fingers into his soft, tousled curls, and pulled his face down to hers so he could kiss her while he fondled her sex.

Again, the delicate, drifting touch; again the response out of all proportion. His fingertip lingered longer this time; too long for Claudia to be able to contain herself, if she had ever wanted to.

Climaxing, she cried out with joy against his gentle kissing lips and felt her vagina beat and pulse like a racing heart. He circled his finger, making her orgasm extend like a long, exquisite note, or a cadenza. She cried out again, her body jerking as she clapped her hand over his, and felt the minute flexing of his tendons as he cleverly caressed her.

'You ... You –' she gasped, arching upward, riding the fabulous wave. 'Goddamn you! Who the hell are you?'

'I don't know! I really don't!' The stranger laughed, looking down into her face from just inches above it, his eyes like pale fire in the darkness. 'And right this minute, I can't say I care!'

And as she climaxed once more, and even harder, he kissed her again.

Moments – or what could have been hours – later, Claudia moaned, 'Enough! I need a minute or I'll have a heart attack!'

Obligingly, the stranger withdrew his hand and let it rest upon the sweat-sheened curve of her belly. The touch seemed compassionate, almost protective, the pads of his fingers resting on the operation scar that was masked by her pubic hair. In some other situation, Claudia might have been anxious when he traced its lightly puckered length, but she was still floating too

172

much to care about anything. Lifting her weighted eyelids, she looked up.

The stranger had flung back the covers and was lying
on his side, half propped up on one elbow, studying the
movement of his hand upon her flesh. Her dark-adjusted
eyes saw his serious expression, and the long, gleaming
line of his torso where he had unbuttoned the jacket of
his pyjamas.

'This must have hurt,' he said, nodding to the little
cicatrix.

'Yes it did, but not for a long time ... And I hardly
think of it now.'

'I'm glad,' he said, regarding her steadily again, his
light-blue eyes so vivid they almost frightened her. Then,
leaning down, he kissed the little scar and the soft hair
that tangled across it like a veil.

Claudia shuddered and he immediately straightened
up again. 'Do you want me to ...?' He left the question
hanging, but she knew his meaning.

She did want him to, but she could also see the
aroused state of his body; his erection pressing hard
against the blue cotton of his pyjama bottoms. It was his
turn, she decided, reaching out to touch him.

'Let's save that and concentrate on *this*,' she said,
running her finger over the hard length of his flesh
beneath its thin, cotton covering.

'I'd be delighted to,' he said impishly, unfastening the
button and letting his stiff cock spring free. 'Is it as
impressive close up as it was from a distance?' He hefted
himself playfully, as if offering his manhood to her as a
choice *objet d'art* for her approval.

'Of course it is, you vain creature!' she said, laughing
and reaching for him, using his penis to tug him – very
gently – towards her. He gave her the marvellous smile,
then squeezed his eyes shut, sighing. 'But do you know
what to do with it?'

'That's one thing I *can* remember,' he replied, deftly
extricating himself from her grip, then sliding over her

again. 'It's coming back to me very clearly now.' He poised himself, hovering, the glans of his cock just touching the entrance of her vagina. 'Is this right?' he enquired, pushing a little, the very tip of him finding its niche with perfect ease. He rocked his hips and a little more of him slid inside her. As he held himself above her, his face was like a pale, beautiful mask in the darkness: his eyes unblinking, his lips parted, his expression half fierce, half loving. He looked like a god; a demon lover; transcendental.

Frozen in the act of being possessed, Claudia felt a dizzying unreality overtake her.

What if her adorable stranger were even more of a happening than she realised? An angel, an alien, a supernatural being sent to pleasure and enchant her? He had the looks for the part, and the mystique. Even his weird clothes were romantic and other-worldly.

'Oh, please,' she murmured half to herself, thrusting upward, grabbing at him, wanting him even more for his strangeness. He slipped in a little further, his presence commanding and his girth a challenge to the moist tightness of her channel. His eyes were still wide open, observing her face and reading the lineaments of her soul as he took her.

'For God's sake, fuck me, whoever you are!' she cried out, dying for him to invade her.

'Gladly,' he growled, as he completed his incursion.

There was no unreality about the stranger's penis inside her. He was all too real. Claudia felt a sudden urge to cry again, as she had by the river. At last! She had a man inside her. Living, breathing, hot and hard. She didn't know his name, but her body seemed to have known his for ever. He fit into her so accurately he might have been made for her; he felt more right for her than Gerald had ever done, although her husband had never disappointed.

Deliciously impaled, she tried to move beneath her nameless lover, but he held her still and tamed. She scrabbled at him, wanting to hug him tighter and explore him, but by some sleight of hand and body, some physical trick she could not unravel, he quelled her struggles. He pinned both her hands above her head with only one of his, and used his other hand, at the small of her back, to clasp her close to him.

'Hush,' he murmured again, kissing her throat and then her shoulder. 'Be still. Let our bodies get to know each other.'

'But mine does know you!' she wanted to shout, but somehow all she could do was pant and gasp. He was subduing her by just holding her and being inside her. His inaction was somehow vigorous and all-enveloping. He just had to be there; he didn't seem to need to move.

'You're wonderful. You're wonderful,' he chanted softly, his voice catching as if he too was feeling the happy urge to weep. Claudia felt his long eyelashes brush her cheek as he kissed her jawline, then her ear.

And then he did begin to move, so slowly, so very slowly, allowing her to feel the whole length of him sliding smoothly in and out of her. She savoured the strange blend of friction and slickness that was his very essence in motion against hers.

How could a young man exert such control over his own so obvious desire? She had expected haste, clumsiness, frantic thrusts and fumbling; yet he was so deliberate, so in charge of both himself and of her. She realised she was starting to come again, her loins melting in the age-old, unmistakable implosion. Losing mastery of herself, she thrashed in his hold, her body filled with a gorgeous, blinding violence; yet he gentled her, stopping her shouts with his mouth and bottling the fire inside her to increase and enrich it.

But when she had reached a plateau, relaxing into a long, dreamy orgasm that seemed warped and extended into a condition rather than an event, the stranger seemed to step up another gear. Flexing his supple body, he began to thrust more authoritatively, pounding her with a delicious force and fury. His kisses became powerful and devouring.

'Oh God!' he shouted, releasing her hands so he could slide both of his beneath her to grab her buttocks. He plunged into her as if he were trying to become her.

Engulfed in passion, Claudia felt consciousness slide sideways and fragment. She was a swirling feather being carried on a torrent, a dancer spinning down into infinity. But just as velvet darkness claimed her she felt the sensation of moisture on her face. Tears. Not hers, but the stranger's; warm and salty; the happy weeping of a sweet soul in release.

'Oh Claudia!' he cried, and came inside her.

It had taken Claudia all her willpower not to wake him as soon as she woke.

When a shaft of morning sun falling across her face had roused her, she had lain still for a few seconds, wondering if her senses were playing tricks on her. Then she pinched her own thigh, instead of that of the angel who lay in bed beside her.

Her handsome young stranger – her lover, she thought, rolling the innocuous little word across her tongue – had been sprawled across his side of the bed, his hair all tousled, and his smooth, pale face gently smiling. He had been fast asleep – as he still was now, a little while later – but a perfect icon of innocent temptation. Claudia had pinched herself again, to make sure that he was real, and she still bore the dark bruise upon her thigh.

You were inside me last night, she said to him silently. You touched me. You made love to me. I adore you.

Oh dear, this is far too drastic and far too soon, she thought, as she placed some clean clothing over the end of the bed for him. Luckily, the newcomer was of a very similar build to her Gerald, and, though her late husband had been well into his fifties, he had possessed the taste – in casual clothes – of a much younger man; not to mention the good looks to carry them off. As Claudia had not yet had the heart to send anything of his to a charity shop, there was plenty to choose from for the stranger. She had picked out denims and a soft white shirt for him, along with boxer shorts, clean socks and a pair of deck shoes.

Steepling her fingers to stop herself reaching out and caressing him, Claudia took another yearning, lingering look at her sleeping beauty. His long, rather elegant face; his soft, crazy hair; his sculpted lips. Those lips had kissed her with complete assurance last night, despite the fact that only a short while earlier those same lips had framed a cry of fear.

And she could still hear his heartfelt groan as he had climaxed.

Come away, you old lech, she told herself, gathering up the clothes the stranger had arrived in, for laundering, then turning her back on the very image of temptation.

Claudia made coffee then sat down at the kitchen table to enjoy it. In a little while, she decided, she would take him some of the tea he seemed to like so much – and serve herself to accompany it, hopefully – but for now she would allow the man his sleep.

Her coffee finished, she examined the velvet frock coat he had arrived in.

The coat was beautifully made, and bore the hand-stitched label 'Hawkes of Savile Row', which suggested it could be a genuinely well-kept antique garment rather than an item of fancy dress. It was rather dusty, and looked at the moment as if it had been slept in for several nights – which it probably had been – but with expert cleaning it could be made as good as new.

As she smoothed her fingers over the lush nap of the velvet, she felt something hard beneath the surface, near the hem. Turning the coat over, she discovered a small tear in the lining of its inner pocket, and, when she managed to work the hard object out through the hole, it proved to be a watch. A period fob watch to be precise; a very choice one that appeared to be made of gold. There was nothing to identify the stranger in any of the other pockets, either of the coat, the trousers or the waistcoat, which suggested he might well have been robbed or mugged or something, but the hypothetical thieves had clearly missed this hidden treasure. It had become caught somehow, and thus detached from its fob and chain.

Curiosity made Claudia flick it open, and she smiled when it proceeded to play a tinkly but melodious 'Blue Danube'. Twisting it around, she suddenly discovered that it was also engraved:

To my dear son Paul, on the occasion of his twenty-first birthday. Love, Dad.

Paul! Her lover's name was Paul.

'Paul. Oh, Paul,' she whispered, wishing the timepiece was magic and could whisk her back the requisite number of hours so she could sigh 'Paul . . .' as her mysterious lover entered her. So she could groan 'Paul' as he fondled her so beautifully that she climaxed repeatedly. So she could cry 'Paul!' in exultation, when they came together.

'Good morning,' said Paul shyly from the kitchen doorway. He was immediately the focus of Claudia's attention.

Seeing him again, her exquisite stranger-lover, she felt light-headed. Even in a pair of perfectly ordinary jeans and a plain white shirt, he looked as exotic and as 'different' as he had in his Edwardian finery.

'Paul,' said Claudia softly, rising from her seat and moving towards him, fishing the watch from her pocket as she did so. 'I think your name is Paul. I found this caught inside the lining of your coat.' When she reached him, she flipped open the case and put the timepiece into his hand. He smiled at the pretty little waltz it played, then looked closer to read the inscription.

'Does it ring any bells?' she asked, when he said nothing but just stared at the words etched into the gold.

'I'm not sure,' he said eventually, flicking the watch shut, then open again, then shut, as if the action itself might trigger a memory. 'Paul ... Paul ...' he intoned slowly and thoughtfully. 'It doesn't feel *wrong*,' he continued after a moment, 'but I couldn't honestly say for certain that it's my name.'

'I like it,' said Claudia, realising she did, very much. 'It suits you.'

'Me too,' said Paul softly.

She began to fill the kettle for his tea but did not manage it very well. As it clattered against the tap, he took it from her, placed it on the draining board, then slid his hands around her waist and hugged her to him.

Claudia felt as if her knees had turned to jelly. She drooped back into his hold, her breath suddenly coming in harsh, deep gasps. All he had to do was be close and touch her in the most innocent way and she was as mad for him as a panting bitch on heat.

Not that his touch *was* entirely innocent. Between her buttocks, she could feel the knot of his genitals pressing against her through several layers of fabric. He was erect again, as hard and as fabulous as he had been last night. Unable to help herself, she pushed backwards against him.

Feeling a little dazed, she looked up and saw their ghostly reflections in the window over the sink. Her own image was glassy-eyed and sluttish; her lips were parted and her nipples were two clear, telling smudges beneath her light T-shirt and her thin cotton bra. She couldn't see Paul quite as distinctly. His face was just a pale impression, where it was inclined over her shoulder as he pressed his lips to her throat, and his hair appeared as a wild, darker mass, a tangle of serpents against the sleek blondness of her crop. His long eyelashes were two crescents, a pair of silky, black fans; his mouth a flexing line as he kissed her.

'You give me this!' he said, his teeth grazing her skin as he rubbed his hard body against the cleft of her bottom. 'And I feel whole again. I don't need to know my name when I'm with you.'

Claudia leapt in his arms when he slid his hand down and cupped her crotch through her jeans. It was like being wrapped around by an electric fence; wherever he touched her, her body sizzled with energy. He laughed aloud as she shimmied against him, his chuckle intense and wicked as he kneaded her mercilessly between her legs.

'You make everything so simple for me,' he murmured, almost devouring her neck as he rubbed and rubbed her. The seam of her jeans was pressed tight against her clitoris, and she knew that her demon lover was aware of it.

'Oh Paul. Oh Paul,' she gasped, savouring his name as the lovely tension grew between her legs. He was stimulating her with his fingers and massaging her bottom with his cock. How close are you to orgasm? she wondered dreamily, as her climactic spasms began to ripple; then she cried out as their full force took her over. Her vulva was jumping and pulsing in his grip, and she knew he must be able to feel her reaction through the denim. He laughed again, as if confirming her supposition.

'Paul! Oh God, Paul, you're a bastard, you're adorable!' she yelled. She seemed to come and come and come for several minutes.

As her eyes fluttered open and she regained the ability to support herself, the first thing she saw was the kettle.

'What about your tea?' she said faintly, trying to straighten up.

'In a little while,' he said huskily, his voice sounding more domineering and older than it had done at any time so far. With a little bump of his pelvis, he reminded Claudia of his erection, then, sliding his hands down to her hip bones, he held her still while he ground his cock against her bottom.

'There's something I need right now far more than tea,' he said, then had the grace to laugh at his own statement of the extremely obvious. Releasing her, his hands went to the button and the zip of Claudia's jeans.

A whole slew of inconsequential thoughts whizzed through her mind as Paul went to work on her denims.

He was going to have her jammed up against the sink. What a cliché – but how exciting!

And what time was it? Eight? Nine? Ten? If it was the latter, she should have had her breakfast by now and be doing the dishes before her cleaning lady arrived. Oh God, what if Mrs Tisdale walked straight in, as she always did, and found her employer being shafted against the sink by a total stranger? Mrs Tisdale was a dear old soul and was always saying how worried she was for Claudia, being on her own. She would probably have rung the local police by the time Paul was finished!

And neither one of them had had any breakfast!

Such mundane considerations were blown away by the impact of Paul's fingers on her bare bottom. Within seconds, he had loosened her jeans, and now had both of his long, slender hands down inside them, and inside her knickers too. For a few moments, he just held her buttocks, a hand gripping each cheek, then he began to knead them and move them very slowly.

Claudia sighed, gripping the edge of the sink and bracing herself against it. She was aroused all over again by Paul's caress. He had gripped her bottom last night, while he was making love to her, but somehow now, in the presence of clothes and sinks and kettles, the intimate fondling seemed far more lewd and daring. She felt him circling the twin mounds of her flesh, stretching the tender groove between them, his little fingers rudely rubbing against her anus.

'You're so lovely, Claudia,' he murmured in her ear, at the same time gripping harder down below.

Claudia became too excited to keep still. She twitched her thighs, churned her hips, pushed against the hands that contained her, hoping to edge one of them down to stroke her quim. What would really be the nicest thing, she thought, would be for him to slide one hand down the front of her jeans, while still stroking her from the back with the other. She wanted to ask him to do that, but their relationship was too unusual, too tenuous. If she broke the spell, he might vanish like a dream.

But a dream with special powers, it seemed. Perhaps, she thought, as his right hand deftly relocated to exactly the part of her body she had wished it towards, the loss of his memory had created mind space for other abilities? He was either telepathic or just very, very clever. She shifted her thighs faster as, within her panties, he touched her clitoris.

'Again?' he queried, then, without waiting for an answer, he pressed down gently on the swollen bud of flesh.

Claudia let out a high, yipping cry and climaxed with a force that was just as piercing. Throbbing with pleasure, she retained just enough sensibility to keep her arms braced and prevent herself pitching forward into the sink with its soapy water. Otherwise, she was helpless; her lover's puppet.

While she was still pulsating, still panting, still coming, she felt him swiftly peel down her pants and jeans as far as her knees, then with equal dexterity release his penis from his clothing. She was still in orgasm as he neatly slid inside her.

He wasn't gentle this time, and he wasn't slow. As if fired by the novelty and danger of their situation, he fucked her quickly and powerfully. You've read my mind again, thought Claudia, her vulva beating.

Her mad, scary orgasm continued, soared anew, and her arms ached with the effort of keeping upright. She was bearing the weight and momentum of both of them, because Paul was busy with her breasts and her clitoris. After a few minutes of commotion, he shouted incoherently, his hands convulsing on her body while his penis leapt within it. Claudia bit her lip as her own sensations doubled.

They should have ended up on the floor, but somehow a miracle recovery prevailed. They found themselves laughing like teenagers as they scrabbled to right their clothing.

'I shall never be able to look at washing up in the same light again!' said Claudia, eyeing the soapsuds, whose silent deliquescence had accompanied their congress. The kettle stood abandoned on the draining board, but, as she reached for it, remembering the tea she had offered an aeon ago, Paul took her hand and led her back to the kitchen table. Pulling out a seat for her, he made her sit down.

'Allow me,' he said, returning to the sink and the kettle, and flashing her his sweet, sunny smile over his shoulder. 'It's the least I can do under the circumstances.'

Claudia watched him move around her kitchen as if he owned the place. Pretty sure of yourself now, aren't you, young man? she thought, observing his neat, economical movements as he assembled the crockery and made the tea with the assurance of one who prepared it every day of his life. The correct disposal and timing of leaves and boiling water seemed to be something that had remained in his memory when both name and identity had apparently gone AWOL. Could his little-boy-lost act be just a clever, almost award-winning performance?

She waited until he had poured them both some tea, and she had tasted hers – which was even better than the tea she made herself! – before she tackled him.

'So, Paul, what are we going to do with you?'

The Meeting

Alice Rowan

The Meeting, by Alice Rowan, explores what happens when a woman bravely arranges to meet the man she's been having phone sex with. According to our readers, this is a very popular female fantasy.

The Meeting

First time we spoke was by chance. He rang the owner of the farmhouse where I was staying for a holiday with my friend, Venice. She's not really called Venice, but she always goes on about the exotic places she'd like to visit, so somehow the name fits. Her real name is Ruth, but more often than not she's known as Ven.

Anyway, Ven had gone out with her brother – the owner of the place – to stock up on enormous amounts of food from some little supermarket on the edge of the nearest village. Ven's brother was a big fish in a small pond and the setting was perfect for him to parade himself in all his vulgar flamboyance. This part of rural France didn't know what to make of him – all fast cars and mobile phones and, of course, the regular grand parties.

This time it was to mark the end of our holiday and send us off in style. While they were out frantically filling trolleys with expensive party food, I sat planning ways to avoid the whole event. Difficult this, as the entire house was to be filled with people intent on having a good time. Most of them would be British, young and drunk by ten that evening. A few locals would be in attendance just to show how popular the brother was, and how he'd been accepted into the small community. That was what he liked to believe anyway. They knew a free evening out when they saw one.

I was pondering the idea of falling suddenly and violently ill, or going out and returning only when everyone had ceased to notice who was or wasn't present, and similar methods of escape, when the phone rang. Relief to hear a British voice – a Welsh one in fact. We carried out the brief exchange with no idea at all that we would one day spend an afternoon locked in pornographic poses.

The next time we spoke was also unexpected. I was beginning to return to my normal shade of bluish-white, and preparing for the great Surrey winter wrap-up. I was at a low ebb, with all memories of France fading into myths. The phone rang. It was him. Had got my number from Ven, and her number from the brother.

We talked easily, still not aware of what lay ahead. Friendly, polite conversation about our impressions of Ven's brother's place. We had some common ground – both found the brother thoroughly unpleasant and more than a little amusing. At least I had no further need for contact, but he worked with Ven's baby brother, so had a continuing struggle to do business with what he termed 'a wealthy young gorilla'.

Nothing more for weeks. Had forgotten about him. Then another phone call, and this time we talked for ages – much questioning and wanting to know about me on a more personal level, like who was my last boyfriend, and when. This was touching a nerve; I was in the middle of deep grief and inconsolable loss after the end of a wonderful affair with a man I was sure could never be replaced, and who I wanted more than anyone I'd known before. He had felt the same but managed to distribute this powerful devotion to most of the female population of the county. The constant strain of meeting women at work or in shops with whom I may be sharing this amazing man was too great and I gave him an ultimatum. He barely noticed and was off to the next in the queue before my tears had made puddles on my shoes.

I told my story, in modified form. He was a good listener and I liked talking to him. Still knew nothing of the day in York on that four-poster bed. You need to meet someone else – that was his advice. He felt that all losses could be cured by an instant replacement: on to the next thing and leave the last one behind was his theory. I made coy noises about not being ready, and not knowing how to go about it. The conversation went on and somehow we moved to the subject of sex. Very liberating and grown up.

Here I was, having a conversation about very intimate things with a man I had never even met. Both of us acted as if this was normal behaviour. I had never done it before and didn't know if I wanted to boast to my friends or keep it a shameful secret. Decided on the latter. But found myself hoping that it would happen again.

It did. The following morning. I was asleep and thought the ringing phone was my alarm clock. Kept pushing the off button to make the noise stop. When I finally picked up the phone, he was already in a state of considerable arousal. Had an erection like a pickaxe handle, he informed me. If it hadn't been for the Welsh accent, I wouldn't have known who was giving me this information so early in the morning. Have to admit though, I did notice one or two rather enjoyable reactions taking place in my half-asleep body. He told me morning was his best time and that after our long talk the previous evening he'd woken up with a huge appetite for sex.

Details then, in that exchange – the first of our long-distance telephone sex sessions. Sometimes we were gentle and built up slowly, throwing in the odd comment about work or Ven's brother. Other times, we would get straight to the point. 'Take your clothes off' was a good indication that we were in for a hot discussion. He liked me to give a commentary on this activity as I undressed. He would tell me what he was doing while he listened. I once got the receiver stuck in the neck of my jumper as I tried to take it off, and this provided some surprising excitement for him – the extra fumbling and sound effects heightening his passion. I think I knew what was happening even without his voice-over. The groans were unmistakable. Still nothing about the bodily contact that was to come, so to speak.

Met Ven for an evening of rude chatter and chocolate. Told me about her latest offer in the male companion department – her current lover's best friend. Had asked her if she'd ever had sex with a hoover, and followed it up by enquiring if she would be frightened by a large penis. 'In what way?' was all Ven could think of to say at the time, not wishing to appear too interested, or be misunderstood by saying something witty like: 'Why, do you know someone who's got one?'

We were both intrigued by the hoover question and spent hours giggling over the possibilities. Never be the same getting dust from under the bed from now on. Didn't tell Ven about my sex calls with the Welsh pickaxe. I thought she'd never believe me and would think I was trying to compete with her hoover man.

That night I called him. I'd felt agitated and unable to sleep. 'Hold on,' he said, 'I'll have to get back to you.' Had his mother there. They were in the middle of cocoa and interrogations about his hygiene habits. But he rang me back at two thirty in the morning. The whispered descriptions of his fist moving up and down his axe handle were the sexiest so far. My turn to make the groaning noises. Not announcing my orgasm in the same way he had, he found it necessary to ask, 'Did you come?' Confirming this, I noticed that he did too.

The pattern was set. Phone bills were doubling. This wasn't a one-off casual arrangement; this was the real thing. Regular intimate interaction between two people who had never seen each other. Never even described each other. This seemed unnecessary. We had all we wanted with voices, hands and imaginations.

One afternoon, after a short, intense call taken in my bath, water splashed everywhere, he said we should meet. We must; we owed it to ourselves. If it was this good on the phone, why miss out on the real thing? I was thrown into doubt, and feared the loss of yet another relationship. Stopped myself in my tracks to check that word relationship. Could hardly apply it here, could I? I would walk past this man and not know him, yet he'd witnessed me at my most abandoned. What if he took one look at me and lost the ability to ever have an erection again? If the sight of my naked body was less appealing than the image he had in his head? Or if he thought I was too fat, too pale, too undesirable? Seriously worried about shattering our illusions, I thought we should leave things as they were.

Several calls followed when the sex was rather dutiful – the telephone equivalent of a sulking match. Undercurrents were evident. Our relationship was suffering. That word again. Had to question myself. Maybe it would be an appropriate word if we met and if things took off from there. I'd been feeling better about the loss of the serial lover since I'd had the Welsh handle at the end of my phone. Perhaps meeting would put everything on a more involving, complete level.

I agreed. His terms. No seeing how we got on, or opt-out clauses – we had to agree we were meeting for sex, and would go through with it. It was too far to travel for pizza and polite conversation. And that was how we arranged it. No backing out. No second thoughts. Just drive two hundred miles, meet a stranger recognisable only by the way he sounds when he comes, and get in bed with him for the afternoon.

Felt nothing at all on the day. Got up at dawn and set off early for York to miss the traffic. Thought about anything but what I was about to do and arrived in a state of businesslike calm. He was late. This wasn't helpful. I looked far too closely at every man passing my bench and had some unwelcome smiles in return. Each time a man appeared in the vicinity, I would either hope it was my Welsh pixie, or pray hysterically that it wasn't, and that he'd keep walking. Finally, I rang his mobile phone. He was on his way. That evaporated my aura of calm. The whole thing suddenly seemed like a dangerous and foolish game. He could be a murderer. Or a mugger. Or a transvestite who would steal my clothes and leave me naked in some seedy hotel room with the local press taking notes for their gossip column as I was escorted out by the police . . .

And then, there he was. Shorter than I had imagined. Very well-dressed in a casual, expensive way – not my taste at all. All designer labels and aftershave. A diamond ring on his little finger. Immediate realisation that much of what we find attractive is visual. This, rapidly followed by realisation that the visual element somewhat lacking on telephone.

We were both pretending not to be nervous. Went to have lunch, which was a good idea – plenty of wine helped to blur the edges of what this meeting was really about. I could have taken the opportunity to run. I could have gone to the toilet and never come back. Something had hooked me, though, and I found myself wanting to go through with this experience – almost for its own sake. Something bizarre to look back on. Something daring and exciting. Or perhaps it was just the temptation of that pickaxe handle.

Lunch was lovely – a spa hotel. Very civilised, and increasingly sexy. Nothing obvious or inappropriate for such a public place – rather, the presence of a subtle tension between us. We played little word games, referred to various phone calls: our own private code. This was bloody exciting. A big turn-on. Time for the meeting.

Found a hotel. It was decent-looking, tasteful and

quiet. We held hands as we went upstairs to our room. The first physical contact we'd had. About to be followed by quite a lot more. He opened the door and let out a humourless laugh of disgust.

'There's a fucking four-poster bed in here,' he exclaimed.

I quite liked the idea. Until I saw it. It wasn't grand or romantic. It was cheap, tacky and embarrassing. But it broke the ice even more and we had a good laugh at the whole situation. We used the bed as our reason to get very giggly.

Suddenly he was gone. Just got up and left the room. I thought he'd changed his mind and decided to get out before anything happened that he might regret. But running water made me realise that he was in the shower. I sat on the edge of the bed then draped myself across it. Then I leant against one of the posts, reading a hotel brochure. They had a chain of establishments across the country, it said, catering for every need. That was all right then. Telephone sex partners meeting for the first time a speciality, maybe?

The gap under the en-suite door was allowing a constant stream of male perfume to enter the bedroom. I wanted to open the window but thought it unwise, given the groaning we were about to make and our proximity to other rooms. So, hot – and with the beginning of a headache – I stood looking out of the window, leaning forward to see the view beyond the city.

That was how I remained during my first test ride of the pickaxe handle. He was still damp from his shower, and had crept up behind me with the same enthusiasm for sex that he'd had that first morning on the telephone. Didn't seem to matter that it was early afternoon – the quality of hardness was very much as described. But this man had not told the whole truth; he had been far too modest. We were, I felt, in the realm of much heftier tools. Big sledgehammer handles. Road drills which make the workman vibrate as he tries to guide his equipment through the surface.

Our phone calls had been the longest foreplay either of us had known – the urgency and intensity of this first time was inevitable. There had been no kiss or caress, no words or preparation. This warm, scented stranger had simply approached my black-skirted bottom, placed his hands on my hips, and eased up the close-fitting fabric to expose the very last remains of my summer tan – now emphasised against the contrast of black stockings. Pleased now that I'd worn my favourite type of underwear, after earlier indecision about being sensibly clad in cotton, or going with my usual indulgence: having delicious reminders through the day of naughtiness beneath a surface of respectability. Always enjoyed attending important meetings at work in smart suits while being aware of the pressure of little suspender buttons on my thighs as I sat facing serious professionals. Knowing, while they didn't, that cream-coloured silk was sliding against my skin as I moved. And, on this occasion, the secret was shared as the sledgehammer slowly rucked up my skirt and pushed his hammer head into me, and found his way easily into the floaty looseness of my French knickers. My private pleasure in sensual undergarments is increased when a man appreciates it too – the Welsh pixie was certainly doing that. His appreciation was thick and hard, and radiated heat inside me which spread from my slippery anticipating vagina to my stomach. He pushed the full length as far as he could, each time pulling my hips on to his groin to make deeper contact. I locked my arms into supports and let my bottom stick out rudely while I stared with unseeing eyes at the view from our rapidly misting window.

As had become customary in our phone calls, he gave prior notice of his orgasm – entirely unnecessary but very exciting because he only got halfway through the announcement before the event took place. His ultimate spasm made him ram into me with such force that I banged my head against the window pane and left little spidery marks on the steamed glass where my hair pressed in this shared shuddering moment, so long-awaited at the ends of our separate telephones. He had been right – this was too good to miss. The meeting had got off to a very promising start; now it was time to discuss the remaining agenda.

While I rearranged my clothes, he pulled on a soft towelling robe and then we kissed tenderly in the middle of the room. Both finely tuned to each other, we recognised that our fantasies were being brought to life with no boundaries other than our own – and these were likely to be few given the electric current we created between us. The kiss was acknowledgement of mutual passion, sexual appetite and greedy expectation. Warmth and wildness were equally mixed in the moist atmosphere of his shower and our mingled intimate aromas.

Never thought I'd hear him say, 'Keep your clothes on,' but he told me to do just that as he gestured for me to sit on the floor, with my back against the wall. I took the chance to gather physical details about my voice-over man while he stood in front of me. Very hairy legs, hard calf muscles, and a glimpse of tight thigh where the robe fell open. So hungry for physical contact, I wanted to push my face into the fluffy robe and breath in newly washed skin, nibble inside his thighs, reach up to stroke his stomach, his bottom. Hard to control myself as this masculine presence dominated my senses. He knew what was happening and smiled a wicked little smile as he bent to kiss me deeply but briefly. Stopped abruptly and walked away. He sat opposite me, his back against the other wall. There we faced each other, at the foot of the as yet unused four-poster bed. Having dealt with the first item on the agenda without discussion, we were now ready to focus on other pressing business.

My turn first. Told him I wanted to see what I'd heard

so many times. 'Show me how you make yourself come. Do it as if I wasn't here, unselfconscious and wild. But don't actually come. Not yet. Just get very, very close to the edge,' I heard myself say. He agreed, then made his own request for the same. 'Don't hold back, don't put on a performance – let go, lose yourself, do it like you do on the phone, and talk me through it.' Then he added that I was allowed to come. He would stop himself while he watched what he had listened to so many times – this time not having to wedge the handpiece in the crook of his shoulder as he used both hands to speed up the friction. We agreed a few other needs and desires and left the rest to see where our once-in-a-lifetime mystery sex meeting would take us.

He wanted my clothes to stay on, so I found the pulsing place calling for pressure inside the privacy of my black satin knickers. This helped to hide my shyness, but the need for touch helped me forget coyness, and my middle finger found such sliding sensitivity and heat that I felt the first stages of arousal had already been achieved. Though it could never match the pickaxe, the hard little knot of nerves in my clitoris were attempting to compete in a display of excitation. No need for the transfer of saliva, or gentle stroking to encourage lubrication; today I was starting halfway through, as if my rude thoughts had manifested themselves into physical entities and been present since the meeting commenced, slowly rubbing and nudging, probing and circling. And then – such a treat – I'd had the test ride. The sort of powerful coupling usually followed by limpness, disinterest and sleep. How lucky to find a man who would begin in such a way. Little wonder really that my finger now found such swollen readiness. I had been doubtful that he would be able to resist orgasm as he showed me all the stages of his personal method of masturbation, from light finger movements at the top, through to the blur of a fast-moving, tight-squeezing fist. But it was me who was in danger of rapid climax now. I felt a direct line of sensation from my clitoris to my vagina, both areas aching for movement and pressure. It didn't help to slow things down when I looked across the room to see his parted knees pulled close to his chest, and the stiff, red sledgehammer being gently rubbed between his palm and his thumb. Obviously, he was using only light pressure, but the sight made my stomach churn and tighten, and I asked if I could take off my clothes to give more freedom of movement. He gripped the handle more firmly and gave it a few very long strokes, right down to the roots. As he did so, my hips pushed forward, trying to close the space between us, and my finger pressed harder under my French knickers. I repeated my request. 'Just your knickers,' he said, as he slowed down again and used fingertips on the shiny, hard head of his axe handle. I slid them off and opened my legs fully, with my feet touching sole to sole. All traces of shyness totally gone, I was shamelessly sharing with my Welsh stranger the most intimate parts of me. Not only that, I was allowing him to see what I had only ever carried out in the privacy of bedroom or bathroom. It felt incredibly naughty, and a hundred times more exciting than solitary sex.

Remembering the instruction to let go, I felt I had permission to be really free, so I used the fingers of my left hand to push at the entrance of my vagina, and my two middle fingers to apply hard pressure now on my ultrasensitive little knot. Looking down at myself, I realised that my skirt was now up around my waist, revealing pale thighs and black suspenders to frame the hot place between my legs. Letting my gaze travel to the opposite wall, I took in the view of the whole man – back pressed against floral wallpaper, eyes narrowed in rude, sexy expression, legs now spread out straight and parted – and then I focused on the only area of movement. His hands on that pickaxe. He bit his bottom lip now as he got closer to coming. Two fists, one above the other, held the pickaxe away from his stomach, out into the room, and made determined rhythmic glides up and all the way back down again. 'Tell me,' he said. 'Talk me through.'

Told him I was way past the point of no return, that I needed to make firm circling movements with my fingers and, as I did, so the need to be entered increased. Told him my hips were moving of their own accord, and that all my feelings were starting to distil down to one place – and that watching him lose control was intensifying the whole experience. Felt myself go to another level and knew I had to have that fullness inside me as I came. To have that thick hardness to contract on to as the ripples of my orgasm quaked through me. Couldn't stop myself saying please. 'Please enter me just as I come, please, please just let me have it inside me. But don't stop what you're doing until then.' Once again, my Welsh pixie performed beyond expectation, and was suddenly in front of me, masturbating furiously, with the taut end of his penis almost touching my hot vagina. We had close-up views of what we were doing to ourselves and neither of us seemed shy about watching intently. He was moving his fist very fast, and that image was my step to the next level. 'Please – now,' I said in an amazingly calm voice. And he did – he pushed in just enough to tip me over the edge, making me force my hips towards him and take the full length of him into me. He pulled me on to his kneeling lap and let me slide and grind on the pickaxe as I juddered through several false endings of the most exquisite orgasm. For once, he had no need to ask if I'd come. However, I was stunned that he hadn't. He still had the same quality of erection from the beginning of the meeting.

Not wishing to waste such a wonderful opportunity, I led him to the small armchair in the corner. My idea was to explore the smoothness of that tight, pink skin with the inside of my lips, but he pulled me on to his lap and kissed me passionately before turning me over and surprising me by biting my bottom. He spanked me, too, and I began to feel a tingling glow on my buttocks as his stiffness dug into my tummy. He stood me before him and undressed me, then let me suck and circle him with my mouth. It was like pushing my lips over the ripe skin of a nectarine. I then moved my mouth along his length as far as I could. He seemed to like this because he had to ask me to stop through gritted teeth.

We transferred our meeting to the four-poster bed and he smiled as I picked up my silk scarf. He allowed me to pull off his robe and bind his wrists to one of the posts. I left him there and took my turn to disappear to the bathroom, carrying my heap of tangled clothes. I gave him a running commentary as I smoothed stockings up my legs, slipped the silky chemise on over my head, then fastened hooks and eyes on my suspender belt. But I couldn't find my satin knickers, and told him I was unable to return in such a state of undress. His turn to say please. Said his cock was throbbing with the need for stimulation and he was helpless to relieve the sensation bordering on pain. After one more plea I returned to the bedroom, stood at the side of the bed and asked my lovely Welshman what he wanted. He wanted to come. He wanted me to assist him with this. I was willing, but first a delay while I slowly undressed. He tried to roll over and find something to push against but it didn't work, and the pickaxe made little jerking movements as he lifted his hips off the bed and said please again.

My slow-motion striptease was accompanied by his groans and deep breathing. I didn't untie his wrists. I mounted him and took my turn at controlling the pace. Kept it light and took in only half his length. Then we both needed more, both needed deeper thrusts, and I set him free of his handcuffs, let him show me again what enthusiasm he had for our joint interest in these basic pleasures. True to form, he told me when he was about to come, and I'm sure he told people in the neighbouring rooms too, but we were beyond caring about the sensibilities of others, and at that moment could only let the fierce responses of our finally connected bodies overwhelm us.

Having made good use of the four-poster, the armchair and the carpet, we made our way to the shower, deciding we were not clean enough to do such dirty things to each other. It was one of the wettest afternoons of my life. We seemed to communicate via secretions rather than words. Sweat made us shine. Saliva made us slippery. And other juices flowed freely between us. The shower seemed like our natural element and, as hot water made little dents in my flesh, I pushed his head down between my breasts and over my glistening abdomen to the hidden heat so he would need no further instructions on where I wanted his mouth to be.

Stopped for tea at about four, and there seemed little to say. Most communication had been physical. We were exhausted, but still engaged in further non-verbal interaction. That last time was particularly powerful. Perhaps there had been something in the tea. His erection was magnificent – almost too good to place out of sight. Almost. When it did disappear from view, I couldn't utter a sound. Just as well we were not on the telephone now. I was in paradise on that four-poster bed, with my telephone, and my road-drilling Welshman, who smelled like the cosmetics department at Boots but knew how to make the most fundamental connection and remove all sense of loss. Couldn't stop smiling on my journey home. Wasn't sure if it had actually happened until I stopped for petrol and could hardly walk. A delicious disability. Couldn't make up my mind if I should tell Ven – she would either be shocked and never speak to me again, or she might feel obliged to explore the hoover question further. I don't know if I want to be responsible for the outcome of that.

The Succubus

Zoe le Verdier

Adele King is a talented ballet dancer but the company for which she performs is in danger of losing its funding. When wealthy patron of the arts Rafique wants a private performance at his luxury house in the English country-side, Adele is chosen to dance the role of the Succubus – a mythical sex-crazed demon. However, this is against her nature. She isn't naturally inclined towards exhibitionism and is happy with her boyfriend, Jamie. But staying at Rafique's house has a strange effect on her and the other members of the company. In this extract, Adele begins to realise that Rafique can help her to lose her inhibitions.

Zoe herself is a trained ballet dancer who now works in television, making arts documentaries. Her other Black Lace titles are: *The Seven-Year List*, about a group of young people who meet up seven years after leaving school to see if they've realised their ambitions and desires; and the forthcoming *Mixed Doubles* about the kinky lives of the tennis-club set in Home Counties Britain. She has also written several erotic short stories, including *The Man Across the Street* – a tale of voyeurism – which was published in *Sugar and Spice*, the Black Lace anthology of original short stories.

The Succubus

There was a door opposite Adele's bedroom. Foster unlocked it and ushered her into the cold, dark corridor beyond. They walked for several silent minutes, descending into the belly of the house before windows announced their arrival at the back of the Manor. Going up a narrow, steep staircase lined with blazing torches, Foster knocked before opening the door and standing aside for Adele to enter.

'Enjoy your meal, Miss King.' He blinked, the first time she had seen him do so.

Her jeans were blasphemy in the splendour of the room. Even the ceiling was well-dressed. The surface was a carved honeycomb pattern of hexagons, and in every wooden frame the white rose of Yorkshire had been delicately painted. The high, oak-panelled walls also served as a picture gallery, each panel holding a portrait. There were long-haired men with pointed beards, wearing capes and slight smiles; women in beautiful, tight-bodiced gowns, their hair piled high in elaborate bouffants, eyes shining demurely; children sewing, riding, or sitting with their dogs. All stared down enviously at the table.

Stretching the length of the room from the door to the

red-velvet-curtained windows, the table was so laden with food that its highly polished surface was barely visible. Ornate, silver candelabras perched between the plates, their delicate lights flickering on the sumptuous feast. Hunger growled in Adele's stomach as her eyes greedily moved from one dish to the next, like a child in a sweetshop wanting everything. Slowly, she walked along the length of the table, passing ten chairs before she came to the end. There, sitting on a high-backed, ornately carved throne, was Rafique. The tastiest dish of all, she smiled to herself, thinking she had never seen a man so well-suited to a dinner jacket. The men she knew always seemed uncomfortably aware that they were dressing up; Rafique, with his luscious skin and the opulent wave in his glossy black hair, looked like he'd been born in a tuxedo.

He held out his hand as she approached, and smiled. 'How do you feel?'

She placed her fingers in his. Her eyes fell down his long legs to his black shoes, then across the wooden floor to her scuffed trainers. 'Distinctly underdressed.' She looked up. 'I wanted to change, but Foster wouldn't let me.'

He caressed the back of her hand with his thumb. 'You look lovely.' He pulled her closer. Hooking his arms around her waist and legs, he scooped her on to his lap and kissed her. Adele closed her eyes and rested her arms on his shoulders. The now familiar scent of his after-shave filtered through to her brain. The warmth of his tongue spread over hers and as his kiss reached deeper and deeper into her soul, she felt her innards turn to liquid and flow away. One of his hands was on her neck, beneath her hair, the other eased underneath her T-shirt and up on to the curve of her breast, fingers settling around her shape as if that was where they belonged.

His face pulled away. Sighing, he slowly opened his eyes. 'Are you hungry?'

'I'm always hungry.' For you, she added silently.

He nodded. 'You do have a good appetite.' His dark eyes glittered mischievously, and Adele suspected he had read her thoughts, as usual, and was sharing her innuendo.

'I just can't stop myself. I should diet, but I haven't the willpower.'

'And why on earth would you diet?'

'Dancers aren't supposed to have hips.'

'Who says? When I go to the ballet, I want to see women.' Rafique ran his hand down her back and on to her rump. 'Real women. With curves.'

Adele shrugged. 'It's all very well having curves, but pity Jamie and Alexei. They have to lift me.'

'Pity them? They have one of the best jobs in the world.' He stood, gently sliding Adele from his lap. 'Let's eat.'

Adele drifted towards the table. She gazed longingly at the nearest bowl, piled high with king prawns doused in an oily sauce. 'Is Foster bringing plates?' she asked, noticing that there weren't any empty ones. She looked around the room for a cabinet, but there was no other furniture. 'And cutlery?'

His body pressed against her back. Reaching around her, he tenderly squeezed her breasts. 'We don't need plates,' he breathed into her hair. 'Come on.' He grabbed her hand and led her purposefully away from the table.

He pushed at a panel holding a portrait of a fey young man in hunting dress, and a doorway opened up. Inside the adjoining room, a porcelain roll-top bath held centre stage beneath a cloud of steam. A pile of white towels waited on the red-tiled floor.

Slightly confused that the talk of food seemed to have been forgotten, Adele looked up at Rafique. 'I've just had a bath.'

He pulled her inside and closed the door. 'You're going to have another.'

'I'll look like a prune.'

'A peach.' Standing in front of her, he peeled her top over her head. 'You'll look like a peach; smooth and ripe.'

Moving behind her, he unhooked her bra and pushed it from her shoulders. Realising that it was pointless protesting, and that she didn't want to anyway, Adele kicked off her trainers, unbuttoned her jeans and discarded them on to the floor. Rafique took off her knickers, palms sliding over her buttocks on the way. Then he turned her by the hips to face him, and reverently kissed her soft mound of pubic hair. 'Goodbye,' he whispered.

'Pardon?'

He didn't answer but led Adele to the bath, holding her hand as she stepped over its high side. She sank into the heat, wallowing in the perfume as it enveloped her senses. Rafique took off his jacket and hung it on the back of the door. He unhooked his cufflinks and put them in his pocket, then rolled up his shirtsleeves. Picking up a small wooden stool, he brought it to the side of the bath and perched on its worn seat.

'Stand up.'

Steam rose from her skin as the soothing water trickled off her. Adele watched his dark hands dip into the water, wetting the soap he clasped. Moving between her legs, he rubbed the slippery bar all over her groin, spreading the lather over her strip of tight curls. Putting down the soap, he produced a razor, and looked up at Adele with a lustful, longing glint in his eye.

'What are you doing?' she gasped, her body tense as she already knew the answer.

'I want to see you naked.'

'I am –'

'I want to be as close as I can to the bare, naked you. I want to see *you*. All of you.'

Carefully, he raised the blade. Gently pulling her skin taut with one hand, he swept the cold metal over her pubis.

He worked with clean, swift movements, eyes glued

to his fingers, sweeping away the hairs with a man's well-practised skill. Adele felt his breath on her as his face leaned closer, totally absorbed in his task. She shifted her stance, lifting one foot on to the side of the bath, her hands steadying herself on his shoulders. He shaved the very tops of her silky inner thighs where they curved inwards, and the inner edges of the fleshy mounds covering her sex. His fingers were deft and businesslike, never still as they mauled her tender skin to enable him to reach every fold and crease. The feeling was incredible; his eyes so close to her, his soapy fingers brushing against her swelling clitoris, opening her silky labia, but never lingering. Watching his concentration made Adele's thighs quiver.

'You're done.' His face was full of fierce admiration.

Squatting to wash off the lather, Adele looked down at herself. Her fingers delightedly, inquisitively discovered her new nakedness, shocked at the pleasure it gave her to feel smooth skin where there had been thick curls.

'It looks beautiful.' Rafique's fingers twitched hesitantly over her bare mound as she stood again, like a sculptor afraid to spoil the perfection of his own work. 'So sexy.'

Head bowed, Adele's fingers brushed over his and pressed them on to her skin. It was sexy; incredibly so. The flesh which had been hidden since puberty was unbelievably soft and like a peach, its smoothness was pleasure to the fingertips. She felt as if the essence of her womanhood had been stripped and laid bare, ready for worship from eyes, lips and penis. A different dampness from that of the bath began to well up inside her.

Rafique unfolded a wide towel, motioning for Adele to step into it. He held her tight, drying her quickly with urgent strokes. When he had finished, he gently pulled at the band holding the weight of her hair up in a pony tail. Releasing the soft waves, he ran his fingers through them from her temples, combing her hair on to her shoulders. He paused for a moment, framing her face in his warm hands, his gaze very serious. Then, as if he had suddenly remembered something, he smiled. 'Come on,' he said, grabbing her wrist. 'I'm starving.'

Back in the dining room, they stood in front of his throne. 'On the table,' he motioned, the familar aggression burning in his features.

'Yes, Master.' Adele hitched herself up, shuffling backwards into the gap Rafique had cleared, until the backs of her knees fitted against the table's edge. Beneath her naked sex, the wooden surface was cool and hard, in contrast to her pussy which felt softer, warmer and damper than ever before.

Rafique dipped a finger into one of the silver goblets, and pushed the tip inside her mouth. The dark-red wine, smooth and rich, awoke her taste buds. 'I'm not your Master any longer, Adele. There's nothing more I can teach you.'

She suckled on his skin, drawing every trace of wine from his fingertip. Looking up at him, she noticed something different in his eyes tonight; lust was there, as fierce as ever, but there was a sorrow too, a ruefulness that she couldn't explain.

'Tonight, we're equals. If there is something you want me to do, you must tell me. Tell me what you want.'

Adele smiled wistfully. For a split second she wondered what the others in the company would think. Would they believe it if they saw her, naked on the table, her sex bare, and a beautiful man offering his services? Then she banished them from her mind, along with her old self. She mourned the passing of the old Adele, but only in the same way a greedy, money-grabbing relative might grieve. She had never liked her. Now that she was gone, the new Adele, the real Adele, could enjoy the spoils.

Taking a deep breath, she filled her lungs with air and her body with anticipation. Her eyes scanned the length of the table stretching out behind her. 'I want to try everything. I want to taste it all.'

He reached for the nearest plate. Holding it in the palm of one hand, he picked up a tip of asparagus and dangled it above her waiting lips. Adele stuck out her tongue, her eyes fluttering to his to watch his reaction, intensely aware of the barely hidden agenda in her suggestive movement. Tilting back her head, she sucked the firm, green tip between her lips, and chewed on its perfectly cooked texture. 'Mmmm. Another.' He lifted a second shoot. This one was dripping with butter, and a droplet of it dribbled off the asparagus and on to her lower lip. She wiped her mouth with the back of her hand.

'Let me do that.' Rafique bowed his head and sucked her lip into his mouth, gathering the butter from her skin. She wondered whether he could taste her arousal.

Having cleaned the spill, he put down the plate and reached for another. Salad this time; plump tomatoes, sliced and laced with olive oil, slivers of cucumber, red, green and yellow peppers, all laid intricately on crisp radicchio leaves the colour of the wine. Patiently he fed her, seeming to relish each fresh taste as much as she did. Vinaigrette smeared her mouth and chin, sharp and oily, and again he dipped his head, licking her fastidiously like a cat cleaning itself.

'Those,' she pointed, as he pulled away and waited for instructions.

He placed the dish on her lap, shocking her with its coldness. With a faint and satisfying crack, he broke the prawn's back and peeled off its shell. Waiting expectantly, he lifted the tasty morsel to Adele's open mouth.

'Oh God,' she murmured, overwhelmed by the flavours mingling on her tongue, challenging her to recognise them. There was an Eastern note to the flavour: ginger, lemongrass, peanuts. Beyond that, appearing like a wicked afterthought only when her teeth dug into the succulent flesh, there was a sudden hint of fire: chillies, their heat taking her breath away.

'A drink,' she begged, and he held the goblet up to her lips. The wine did nothing to quench her thirst. Longingly, she eyed his cool mouth. 'Kiss me.'

Putting her drink back down, he rested his hands either side of her hips and leant his body into hers. His kiss was slow, tentative, a contrast to his usual urgency, as if her mouth was a delicacy being savoured for the first time. Adele lifted her hands on to his back. Beneath his shirt, she could feel the sharp edges of his shoulder blades moving. She opened her eyes and was shocked to find his open, too. The intensity of his gaze warmed her inside more ferociously than the hottest, most potent chilli could have done.

She pushed him away. Skinning a prawn for him, she touched her greasy fingertips to his lips as he greedily ate. He took another from her, then another, sucking the juice from her fingers between mouthfuls. They took turns feeding each other until the dish was empty.

Without a word, Rafique picked the next plate; strips of smoked salmon, drizzled with zig-zags of dill-flecked mayonnaise. Chilled and sharpened with lemon juice, the rich, luxuriant taste quickly calmed the memory of the hot prawns. Gulping greedily, Adele and Rafique soon cleared that plate, too.

'Still hungry?'

'I'm just like you.' He took a gulp of wine. 'I'm always hungry.'

Adele brushed the plate out of her lap. Neither was watching and it fell to the floor, spinning loudly for a moment before it settled into silence. Spreading her legs, she pushed at Rafique's shoulders. 'Eat me, then.'

He slumped to his knees. Reverently, he rested his trembling fingers on her thighs. He gazed at the naked smoothness of her pussy, his head swaying slightly like a snake in a hypnotic trance; then he fell on to her.

He licked all over her soft mound, tasting her afresh

as he had done with her mouth. Moaning quietly with unrestrained pleasure, he kissed the gap where the widest part of her triangle of hair usually lay. Slowly, methodically, he moved downwards, covering every spot that had been hidden from him before, until he reached her pouting labia. Like the dishes they had devoured, her pussy lips were succulent and moist. He opened her with one lap of his tongue, and delved inside.

Adele gasped with delight, pushing food out of the way as she lowered her body on to the polished wood. Her hair spread out around her face and she lost her fingers in its softness as Rafique pushed deeper and deeper. Her hips twitched frustratedly, hunger eating her up.

'Come here,' she moaned. 'I want to taste you.'

He joined her on the table. Standing over her prone and quivering body, he unzipped his trousers. He was wearing nothing underneath, and Adele reached up like a drowning man, as his long, dark cock appeared.

Turning around, he splayed his legs in a wide kneel astride her hips. Like a slavering animal, Rafique's penis lowered inexorably towards her mouth. Then his taste filled her; musky, salty and warm. Adele strained her neck to pull his velvet-coated hardness further inside. As she began to suck and lick, his insistent lips pressed once again to the mouth of her sex, and wetness lapped at her like the tide slowly coming in over her body. They seemed to feed on each other for an eternity. Sometimes, Adele froze as Rafique sparked intolerable sensations deep within her, then gluttony would overcome her again and she would suck on his long prick with renewed gusto, and it would be his turn to momentarily lose his rhythm. Like wolves at a carcass they gulped ferociously, shuddering and writhing together and eagerly drinking the juices that overflowed from their ecstasy.

'More,' she pleaded as he stood, one hand clutching

his trousers, the other his forehead. She knew how he felt; she was dizzy too, insane with desire. 'I'm still hungry, Rafique.'

'What do you want?' he asked, breathlessly. 'Tell me.'

'Something sweet.' She rolled on to her side, watching as he walked down the table, picking his way through the plates and around the candelabras. Finding what he was looking for, he stepped down on to a chair and then to the floor. He picked up a pair of cut-glass bowls, and strode back to her side.

'Fruit,' he announced, putting one of the dishes down, 'for the dancer. And chocolate,' he said, putting the other one on the table, 'for the woman.'

Adele dipped her finger into the sticky brown sauce and sighed loudly as it met her tongue. 'That's heaven.' Two fingers went into the bowl this time, scooping up the molten delight. Spattering its faint warmth over the downward slope of her breast, she smeared it on to her areola. 'Why don't you try some?'

His lips were already there, pursed around her chocolate-coated flesh. She watched the tender skin of her areola being pulled by the suction of his mouth, the dark stain gradually fading to reveal the paler brown beneath. When she was clean she coated the other nipple, and his lips and tongue began their voracious journey again. Watching him, hearing him, his breath quick and hurried, she felt like a Roman empress with her dedicated slave. The sensation of power flooded through her.

'Lick me all over.'

His eyes roamed along her body, deciding where to start. Impatient, Adele dangled the fingertips of one hand into the bowl, and raised her wrist to his face like a queen expecting a kiss on the back of her hand. He grabbed her and sucked each finger with half-closed eyes. Turning her palm upwards, he ran his brown-streaked tongue up the pale inside of her arm, leaning over the table to reach her shoulder. Pushing her on to her back, he softly kissed her neck before his tongue began another trail. Travelling down her cleavage to her belly, he paused to dart into the hollow of her navel, searching for some morsel she might have secreted there. Moving onwards he knelt between her dangling calves, nibbled the tender lips of her pussy and licked her inner thighs, his fingers stroking and tickling wherever his mouth had been, following on behind like the delicate, silvery track of a snail. He sucked each toe in turn, holding her ankles when they jerked at the unexpected pleasure.

'We haven't had any fruit.' Adele sunk her hand into the bowl. Like exotic fish, the cool slivers brushed slimily against her. Grabbing a handful, she dropped the mixture between her breasts and over her taut stomach. It was ice-cold, and goosebumps rippled over her skin. Rafique moved from her feet back to her side. Planting his hands either side of her shoulders, he bent and picked up a crescent of peach with his teeth. Nuzzling between her breasts, he retrieved each piece. Chunks of pear, squares of apple and melon, strawberries and raspberries were gradually cleared from her sticky skin. A mixture of saliva and fruit juice glistened on her body. Watching Rafique's dark eyes, Adele reached for another handful, and trickled its coldness on to her mound.

It was then that Rafique seemed to lose control. He stumbled to the end of the table, and knelt again between her open legs. He dived to her pussy and, as he began to eat from her naked flesh, he nipped her tender skin. Snatching at a long, pink-edged piece of nectarine, he paused to warn her with mischievous eyes, wielding the fruit like the weapons he had tortured her with in the tower. Adele braced herself, but when she felt the chill slithering inside her, radiating shock waves throughout her tingling limbs, her body gave up.

The warmth of his lips quickly followed, sucking the iciness from her vagina and into his mouth. But another small, phallic intrusion was inserted between the gaping lips of her sex, and she was helpless as he pushed its

coldness deep inside her. The walls of her pussy contracted but it was no use; his tongue was there to catch
the fruit and tease her with it, before hooking it out and
eating it. Adele propped herself up on her elbows,
watching in delighted agony as he tormented her with
slices of papaya, mango and orange, their surfaces as
smooth and succulent as her labia.

At last he stood up. Leaning over, he took her wrists
and pulled her up into a sitting position. Dropping his
face to Adele's, he passed a fleshy wedge of peach from
his lips to hers. It tasted vaguely of her.

'Can you taste that? Can you taste yourself?'

'Yes,' she whispered, flinching under the harshness of
his glare. 'It tastes of me.'

He slowly shook his head. 'Why do you have to taste
so good?' His voice was sweet, but the fury in his eyes
was intensifying.

Adele stroked his cheek. 'Is something wrong?'

'No,' he snapped.

'Something's upset you.'

He winced. Blinking, he lowered his eyes. 'Don't
speak. Just don't say a word.'

Bewildered, Adele watched his trousers fall to the
floor. Holding her buttocks, he bowed his head and
inched forward, positioning the plum of his penis
between her open lips. For what seemed like several
long minutes he was still, breathing hard at the sight of
her pussy, helpless and naked as a new-born animal;
breathing hard like a hunter, high on blood and about
to make a kill. Then, with a twisted, muffled grunt of
anger, he rammed himself inside Adele with such force
that, if he hadn't been gripping her, she would have slid
backwards over the polished table.

Adele wrapped her calves around the back of his
juddering thighs. Confusion blurred the sharp edges of
her pleasure. The violence of Rafique's remorseless plun-
dering was nothing new. The way he forced himself so
deeply, skewering her on his hardness, bruising her

inner thighs, banging hard against her engorged clitoris – that much she recognised. But something was different. The vague sense of sorrow she had detected in his eyes had metamorphosed into a rage that held his body in a vice. Every muscle and sinew in his face, arms and legs was straining, lunging frantically for the innermost depths of her sex as if the key to life was in there, and it was just out of reach. His fingers bit into her haunches; his eyes closed tightly as if he was in pain. His breath rose into a groan; he shuddered violently and, with one final, gut-wrenching thrust, it was over.

He collapsed into her arms. His face rested in the slope of her shoulder and his breath mingled warmly with her hair. Adele's hands drifted underneath his shirt and, feeling his sweat, slippery on her fingers, she held him close. His penis throbbed inside her.

'I'm sorry,' he gasped.

'What on earth for?'

An echo of his climax shivered down his spine. 'It wasn't supposed to be like this.'

'What wasn't?'

'Our last night together.' He lifted his head. It was hard to tell in the candlelight, but Adele thought she could see sorrow welling up in his eyes.

'We don't leave until Sunday. What about tomorrow night?'

'Tomorrow's the performance and the party. I'll have to mingle, and so will you. There won't be time for . . . for us.'

'Is that why you're upset?'

His fingers stroked her throat and slowly fell to her breast. 'You're all sticky. Let's run another bath.'

For the third time that evening, Adele wallowed in the warm water. Sitting behind her, Rafique slowly, lovingly soaped her back.

'Rafique, can I ask you something?'

'Anything.'

'Why did you choose me? For the ballet, I mean.'

'That's a long story. It begins when I was a child.'

'Go on,' she urged, intrigued. There was silence for a while, as if he was deciding how to begin. 'Rafique?'

'To explain, I have to tell you about my mother. She was an amazing woman. Half Spanish, half Indian, so you can imagine how beautiful she was. But her real beauty was in her character. She was quiet and gentle but she was a free spirit, always laughing. My father was a businessman, and my mother and I would follow him wherever he went. It was a nomadic lifestyle, but we enjoyed it. We were wealthy, and although my mother didn't believe in sending me to school, she always made sure there were plenty of children around for me to play with. She was very aware of the fact that I was an only child.' Rafique put down the soap and began to rinse Adele's back. 'We were very close. I was a very happy child, up until the age of thirteen.'

'What happened then?'

'My mother died.' His voice and fingers paused. Adele turned in the bath to face him.

'I'm so sorry.'

'My father lost his mind. He refused to grieve. He moved us back to France, where he came from, and threw all his energies into building a business. He raged against the laid-back attitude my mother had had towards my education, and sent me to boarding school in England. He said I needed some discipline in my life. He shut me out, completely.

'School was utter hell. My mother had taught me a lot about people, nature, art and philosphy, but I knew nothing about maths or Latin, or English literature. I was way behind my classmates and they were as cruel as children can be. No matter how much I tried to be accepted, my accent and my dark skin made me stand out. The happy, outgoing, free-spirited little boy got bullied out of me. I left school at eighteen, a bitter, lonely and painfully shy young man.

'By then, my father had built his business into an empire. He wanted me to learn the ropes from the bottom. I wanted to be an artist, to design sets for the theatre, but I was afraid to refuse him. He sent me to India to work for the manager of his factory there.'

His eyelids flickered shyly. 'I fell in love with the manager's daughter. She looked . . .' He paused, his eyes clouding. 'Just like my mother.' He sighed deeply. 'She liked me, but I was so shy, I could barely talk to her. My self-esteem was so low I couldn't believe such a beautiful woman would want me. On top of that, I was terribly ashamed of the way my father was exploiting the workers, using them for cheap labour. I imagined how devastated my mother would have been, to see old women and children slaving away, all for my father's profit. I had a terrible row with him, and ran away. Suraya – the girl I was in love with – begged to come with me. I desperately wanted her to, but something . . . something made me say no.' He looked up at Adele. She nodded, recognising the torment in his eyes. 'I think I was afraid to be happy.'

'I travelled around India for a year, searching for something. My mother's roots perhaps, or peace of mind. I didn't find anything except deeper loneliness and misery. I ran out of money and lost the will to live. I wanted to be with my mother. I used almost all of my last cash to buy some opium, and the last thing I remember was getting into a fight with a beggar who wanted my money. He pulled a knife on me. I tried to fight but I was weak from lack of food and illness, and he knocked me unconscious and took what little I had.'

Leaning forward between his open legs, Adele touched the scar traversing his cheekbone. 'That's where you got this from.'

'Yes.' A tear shone in the corner of his eye. 'I must have been close to death, because I saw my mother.'

Adele gasped. 'What did she say?'

'She didn't speak to me. It wasn't an out-of-body

experience, just a dream. She was dancing in a garden, by a waterfall. She was laughing, and full of life.' He blinked, and the tear began a slow journey down his handsome face. 'That was the moment I realised that she had enjoyed her short life, and that she would have been furious to see me wasting mine.'

Adele didn't know what to say. Words could not take away the pain he was reliving, but she wanted to comfort him. Reaching for the soap, she rolled it between her hands and gently stroked the lather across his darkly haired chest. The faintest hint of a smile lifted his lips in acknowledgement.

'I woke up surrounded by women.' His smile deepened at Adele's surprise. 'At that time, India was a magnet for anyone wanting to escape conventional Western life. I was rescued by some hippies. They took me into their all-female commune, and nursed me back to health.'

'You were very lucky.'

'In more ways than one. Being the only man, I was rather spoilt. And being so shy, the women took it upon themselves to further my education.' This time, the twinkle in his eye was not a tear.

'You mean –'

'They taught me everything; to love life, to love women, to love myself.' Cupping his hands beneath the water, Rafique splashed his face. 'I stayed there for three years. I would probably still be in India now, if I hadn't found out that my father was dying.'

Adele rested her hand on his thigh in sympathy as his tale turned back to tragedy. 'How on earth did you cope?'

'It was very hard. Illness had brought my father back to his senses, and he was punishing himself for neglecting me. On his death-bed, he begged for my forgiveness and made me promise to use my inheritance in the way my mother would have wanted – in the pursuit of pleasure and beauty. He left me a fortune. I came back to England.'

'I thought you would have hated England, after what happened to you at school.'

'I did. But I had made a pledge with myself, to confront all those bad memories. I enrolled at art college in London.'

'And you became an artist, like you'd always wanted.'

'Not exactly,' he laughed. 'I was hopeless. But what I lacked in skill, I made up for in appreciation. I quickly realised that my talent wasn't going to rock the world, but that my money could help. I supported everything I loved, and everything that needed my support. Films, theatres, art galleries, museums, opera companies . . .'

'And ballet companies.'

Rafique nodded. 'I love ballet. Almost as much as I love women.' He looked down at her hand on his thigh, as if he had just noticed it, and laced his fingers with hers. 'I've supported the National Ballet for the last twenty years. When David Renfell took over as director, he encouraged me to become more actively involved. It was a dream come true for me. As well as supporting the company financially, I've become a silent artistic director. David welcomes my input on everything – repertoire, casting, even set design.'

'I still don't understand why you picked me, for the role of the succubus.'

'Come here.' He pulled on her hand, and Adele knelt on her heels between his thighs. Retrieving the soap, he worked up a soft white lather between his dark fingers and, watching his hands, he spread it over her breasts. 'I recognised my younger self in you. I watched you, in class, in rehearsal, on stage, even at those corporate-hosted parties you all hate so much. I could see you had talent, but that something, deep inside, was holding you back. From the day you joined the company, I tried to find a way to help you let go.' His palms smoothed around the sides of her breasts. His thumbs reached inwards to her nipples, circling them until they peered stiffly through the soft curtain of soap. 'When the company lost its funding, I seized the chance. I wanted you to find freedom. The same freedom I found in that commune in India.'

Adele touched his neck and he looked up. 'Thank you.'

'Don't thank me. I wasn't being totally unselfish. I also wanted to fuck you.'

His fingers slid beneath her armpits and pulled her up off her heels. Again, he lubricated his hands with soap. His right hand moved over the smooth mound of her pussy, his left slipped around her back and between her buttocks. 'I wanted to fuck you, Adele. And I wanted you to admit that behind that shield you put up around yourself, you're as dirty and desperate as the rest of us.'

She flinched and gasped as a soapy finger slid inside her anus. 'But it wasn't me doing those things. I wasn't in control. It wasn't me acting like that, it was –'

'What? The succubus?' The first knuckle of his finger poked in and out of her bottom, teasing her. 'You could have stopped me at any time, Adele. If you had said no, or pushed me away ... I didn't want to force you into anything. I was playing a game with you. You knew that, and you played along.'

Was it true? Adele thought back. 'But I saw the succubus in the window, that night in the tower. And Joe saw it, in my eyes.'

He reached between her legs. Roughly, he fingered the tender, bruised lips of her sex. Adele could feel her clitoris stiffening again as the heel of his hand rubbed against it. 'There isn't a succubus in the Manor, Adele. The succubus is in here.' A long finger poked inside her vagina and stroked its ridged walls. 'The demon lives in all of us. Some people, Alexei for instance, allow it to control them. Others, like you, are afraid of it, and try to deny it exists.' Another finger slid easily alongside the first, and his thumb pressed over her bud.

He was right. She had been afraid, but not any more. Like a snake shedding its skin, she wriggled out of her old inhibitions once and for all. Squeezing the muscles of her vagina around his fingers, she pressed down on to Rafique, forcing him further inside her. 'I've changed,' she whispered. 'You've changed me.'

He nodded. 'You're free now. Free to be the woman you are inside. Strong, powerful, sensuous.' He rubbed against a magical place, a place where nerve endings seemed to gather and spark, just beneath the surface of her skin. The sensation drew an involuntary whimper from Adele and he looked down at his hand. 'Your pussy looks incredible like that.' He looked up again. His eyes grew limpid with desire. 'You're incredible, Adele.'

Rafique withdrew his hands. Leaning right back until his hair touched the water, he brought his knees up to his chest, then straightened them again through Adele's open legs. He urged her nearer with a pull on her hips. Dropping his gaze, he eased her over the tip of his erection, which was peering eagerly above the water. Adele heard his breath catch in his throat as she lowered her pelvis and engulfed his hardness within her interminable, insatiable softness.

This time she controlled the pace. Slowly, savouring every detail of his flesh, she slid up and down. The water lapped and swelled around their bodies between each gentle thrust, bathing them in warmth, as if the heat flowing between them wasn't enough. Aware of his gaze on her face, she allowed her fingers to lazily trail over his torso, brushing the dark discs of his nipples, tracing the contours of his chest, enjoying the softness of his black hair. There were silver hairs too, curling around her fingers; faint beginnings of grey at his temples as well – the first time she had noticed them. Her touch roamed all over his face, delighting in finally having the time to linger over his features. There was an ease to his good looks, a smooth, exotic opulence; a mixture of inherited genes and supreme wealth. But his eyes were something else, at once knowing and searching, secretive and honest, childishly innocent and wickedly sinful. Adele would never forget them, she decided, as she threw herself into the unending depth of his gaze.

'You're incredible,' she said.

He squeezed her against him, kissing her throat as she rose and fell. Reaching back for his hand, Adele urged it downwards. 'Touch me there.'

'Where?' He hovered over her buttock.

'You know where.'

'Tell me.' His dark eyes glittered.

Adele sighed in a show of exasperation.

'Tell me what to do.' His lips grabbed at her neck. 'I want to hear you say it, Adele.'

'Put your finger . . . up my arse.'

Immediately, delight speared her anus. It still took her breath away to feel so full, so unbearably complete, as it had the first time. She paused for a moment to allow her body to climb to a higher plane, to dive into an infinitely deeper level of sensation. Somewhere in her head, another delight flickered; the joy of telling a man exactly what she wanted, the joy of letting her thoughts out of the confines of her mind and into the open where they could fizz and crackle.

His forbidden touch ignited a more vehement lust and, craving release, Adele moved into a more fervent pace. She pushed down on Rafique's penis with force, the water slapping, her inner thighs aching with the pain of his earlier, frantic fucking. Holding his shoulders she felt his body tremble, trapped in the throes of the ecstasy she controlled. She fed from his desperation, tensing the muscles of her sex, milking his penis until she felt the pleasure rushing from his body into hers. Her skin was on fire, coated with burning oil and, at the moment of climax, she lowered herself back into the water to extinguish the searing flames.

*

222

'Are you looking forward to tomorrow, to the performance?'

Adele rolled on to her back and looked up into the burnt-orange canopy above the bed. 'I never thought I would say this, but yes, I am.' She turned to look at Rafique. 'How about you?'

'No, not really.' He shifted on to his side and propped his head on his hand. 'Tomorrow's the start of a new chapter in your life. You've every reason to enjoy it. But it's different for me. Tomorrow's just another reminder that I'm getting old.'

'It's your birthday, isn't it? How old will you be?'

His fingertips brushed her cheek. 'Twenty-one years older than you.'

Adele did the addition. 'Forty-five?' She sucked in her breath. 'Ancient,' she laughed.

Rafique smiled, but the sadness was creeping back into his eyes, inexorable as the old age he seemed to fear.

'What's the matter, Rafique? Is something on your mind?'

'No.' He scrambled out of bed.

'What are you doing?' Adele sat up, hugging her knees and admiring his behind as he bent over the cabinet.

'I want to take a photo.' He turned, brandishing his camera. 'You'll be gone soon and I want to remember our last night together. I want to remember the way you look after sex, all flushed and – and lovely.'

Adele winced, more at the pain in his voice than at the flash. 'I think I blinked.'

He took another, and another, moving closer to the bed until the film ran out and the motor whirred it back into its cassette. Putting the camera down on the bedside table, he lit the four candles in their miniature candelabra, and turned out the light. He sat down on the edge of the bed with his back to Adele. She shuffled across the mattress and laid a tentative hand on his back.

'Rafique, are you all right?'

She heard him swallow. He turned to look at her, and rested his gentle hand on her neck. 'I'm fine, thank you.'

'This doesn't have to be our last night together, you know.'

'I told you, there won't be time tomorrow –'

'I don't have to leave on Sunday. I could stay here, with you.'

'No, you couldn't.'

'Why not?'

He pushed his fingers up into her hair. 'You've got a life to lead, Adele. A career about to take off. Did I mention that David Renfell's coming tomorrow? When he sees the way you dance now, he'll offer you a promotion, I'm sure.'

'I don't want a promotion. I don't want to go home.'

'Yes you do. There's nothing for you here.'

She grabbed at his hand, pressing it beneath hers. 'You're here. I don't want to leave you.'

'I'm hardly ever here, Adele. What would you do, give up your career and follow me around, living in my shadow?' He slipped his hand out from underneath her possessive grasp. 'Besides, you're in love with Jamie.'

Adele opened her mouth, but she couldn't deny that the mention of his name triggered something inside her. Something different from the feelings she had for Rafique; a yearning as plaintive as the cry of a baby. Whatever it was she had meant to say, she left it unsaid.

He smiled. 'I think we should get some rest.'

Adele rolled over to allow Rafique back into bed. Lying in his arms, she listened to the sound of his breathing as his fingers trickled down her back, stroking her into sleep.

Dangerous Consequences

Pamela Rochford

This sensual extract from *Dangerous Consequences* by Pamela Rochford takes place in the high-brow world of academic research. Strange events begin to overtake Rachel Kemp, junior lecturer at a London university, as she tries to concentrate her thoughts on the editing of a sexually explicit Victorian diary. While immersed in an increasingly sinister and decadent world, Rachel is invited to a party along with fellow academic Luke.

Dangerous Consequences

'*R*achel. What are you planning to wear at the party tonight?' asked Luke.

'Ah, yes. The party. You didn't tell me anything about that.'

'I forgot.'

'You forgot?' Disbelief made her voice sharp. 'Maggie told me this morning that it's an annual event – and you forgot?'

'It slipped my mind,' Luke said. 'Honestly.' His grey-green eyes were sincere. 'There's nothing ulterior in it, I promise.'

'What do people usually wear to Max's party?'

'The same sort of stuff as last night. Max provides all the masks.'

'That's what Maggie said.' Her lips twitched. 'And Max also said that I could wear trousers if I wanted to.'

Luke chuckled. 'You really must have made an impression on him then. He has very definite ideas about how he likes women to look, and trousers are not included.'

'Yes, well. I think that my black dress will just have to do for another night,' Rachel said.

Luke glanced at his watch. 'We haven't really got time

to drive into Norwich and find you something, even if you were a super-fast shopper.' He kissed her lingeringly. 'So I wondered if you'd like me to wash your back instead?'

Her lips twitched. 'And this is something else without an ulterior motive, is it?'

He grinned. 'No.'

'I thought not.'

He stood up, drawing her to her feet. 'Come on.' He led her into the bathroom and pulled her back into his arms, kissing her hard. Rachel found herself responding, sliding her arms round his neck and kissing him back.

He broke the kiss and lifted her hands, kissing her fingers one by one in a gesture which thrilled her and left her aching for more. Then he bent over, putting the plug into the bath, and ran the water. He added liberal quantities of the aromatherapy bath-foam she'd discovered the night before, then turned back to her, his eyes glittering with desire.

He kissed her lightly on the lips, and Rachel's legs turned to jelly as he took tiny nibbles from her lower lip, soothing the sting by running his tongue over it. As she opened her mouth, he slid his tongue in, kissing her more deeply; she felt her sex begin to pool. She wanted him, so very badly.

She arched against him and he tugged at her shirt, freeing it from her jeans. Then he unbuttoned it very slowly, moving from the lowest button upwards; by the time that he'd finished undoing her shirt, Rachel was shaking. He continued kissing her, sliding the garment from her shoulders and dropping it on the floor; then he deftly unclasped her bra, letting that, too, drop to the floor.

Rachel made a small noise of pleasure as he cupped her breasts, his thumbs rubbing against the hardening nipples. She wanted to feel his mouth there, as well as his hands; she wanted him to lick and suck her, taking the hard peaks of flesh between his teeth and biting them gently, arousing her still further.

Still kissing her, he slid his hands down her sides, moulding her curves in a way that made her shiver; then he undid the button of her jeans and the zip, easing the soft denim over her hips and stroking her buttocks as he did so. He left her jeans at half-mast, nuzzling her throat, and slowly tracked his mouth down her body, licking and nuzzling her skin, until he reached her breasts. He buried his face in them for a moment, inhaling her scent, then turned his attention to one of the hard rosy peaks, sucking gently.

Rachel groaned, and he switched to her other breast, making his tongue into a hard point and teasing her nipple, then taking it into his mouth properly, sucking it and using his teeth just hard enough to make her gasp with pleasure. He dropped to his knees, nuzzling her midriff and pulling her jeans down further, removing her knickers at the same time. She leant on him for balance, lifting first one foot and then the other, so that he could remove her clothes.

He smiled, and traced the outline of her navel with the tip of his nose, finally blowing a raspberry against her skin; she chuckled. 'Luke.'

'Mm.' He got to his feet again, faintly disappointing her; she'd half expected him to touch his mouth to her sex, bring her to a delirious climax with his tongue. Instead, he tested the water, then lifted her up and placed her in the bath.

He rolled up the sleeves of his sweater. 'Lean forward,' he said, kneeling down beside her, then picking up the soap so that he could lather his hands.

Rachel did as he asked and closed her eyes, revelling in the way that he soaped her back and then sluiced the suds from her skin. His hands were very gentle, very sure; by the time that he'd finished her back, she was feeling incredibly relaxed and sensuous.

'How do you feel?' he asked.

She looked up at him and smiled. 'Relaxed, happy – and bloody randy.'

'Good,' he said. He soaped his hands again, this time paying attention to her breasts. 'Mm. You're beautiful and lush and ripe, Rachel. I can barely keep my hands off you.'

The huskiness in his tone thrilled her. 'I'm not complaining.'

'I know.' He continued to soap her, washing her feet carefully and gradually working his way up her legs, massaging her calves and the sensitive spot at the back of her knees.

Rachel closed her eyes and relaxed. She had no idea who'd taught him this but, whoever it was, Rachel sent her a silent thank-you. Luke had a sure touch, gentle and yet firm. She ached to feel him touch her, his fingers sliding over her labia and then finally pushing deep inside her, relieving the nagging ache.

Almost as if he could read her mind, he parted her thighs; she shivered as he washed her sex, his fingers playing lightly over her intimate flesh. She waited for him to touch her more deeply, to slide his fingers into her; instead, he leant over to kiss her lightly on the mouth.

He finished washing the soap from her skin and pulled the plug. As she stood up, he wrapped a towel round her and lifted her out of the bath. He dried her carefully, paying attention to every inch of skin; by the time he'd finished, Rachel was tingling all over and longing for him to finish what he'd started in the bath. 'Luke. Don't tease.'

He grinned. 'I'm not. I just wanted to make sure that you were properly relaxed, first.'

'And?'

'And I think that you're just about ready now.' He stripped swiftly, yet with finesse; Rachel watched him, smiling. His sex was rigid, betraying the fact that he was just as aroused as she was.

'I want you, Rachel,' he said softly. 'Turn round.'

She did so; he came to stand behind her, sliding his hands round her waist and pulling her back against him. His cock pressed hard and hot against the cleft of her buttocks; she shivered, remembering the previous night. Was he intending to take her like that again – or did he have something else in mind?

He rested his chin on her shoulder, so that his lips were by her ear. 'Rachel. One of the nice things about Max's bathrooms is that he has mirrors everywhere. You can see exactly what I'm doing to you.'

Rachel swallowed hard as she looked at the mirrored wall. It was steamy from her bath, but she could still make out their reflections. She could see Luke's hand slide down over her abdomen, as well as feel it; she could see the way he squeezed her breast with his other hand. The sight turned her on almost as much as what he was doing.

'Lean over,' he directed gently. 'Put your hands on the side of the bath.'

She did so; Luke, too, leant over, once he'd picked up the towel he'd dropped on the floor and wiped the steam from the mirror. Then he gently repositioned her, widening her stance and pressing down lightly on her back so that she stuck her bottom up in the air. 'Look up,' he told her, his voice husky.

She did so, and her eyes widened. She looked incredibly lewd, like that.

'No. You look beautiful,' he corrected.

She was mortified to realise that she'd spoken aloud. 'I . . .'

'Hey, it's all right.' He stroked her buttocks. 'A perfect heart-shape. Oh, Rachel, if you had the view that I do . . . Your quim's beautiful. All shades of red, from a rich deep crimson through to a dusky pink. You're glistening, as if someone's painted you with runny honey; and you're irresistible. All I want to do is to sink my cock into you.' He curled his fingers round his shaft, fitting the tip of his cock to the entrance of her sex. Rachel couldn't help pushing backwards slightly, and he sank into her with a groan.

'Christ, you feel so good,' he told her. 'I love the way you feel. Warm and wet and tight. You're delectable, Rachel. Utterly, utterly delectable.' Then he began to move, pumping into her; Rachel couldn't take her eyes from the mirror. When he pulled back so that his cock was almost out of her, she could see his shaft, glistening with her juices; and when he pushed back in, her whole body moved forward, her breasts swinging.

'Ah, Rachel.' He spread his hands over her buttocks. 'And here, you're beautiful. Your skin's so soft, and yet you're firm at the same time. I love the way you feel.' He squeezed her buttocks. 'And here . . .' He rested his thumb lightly against the puckered rosy hole of her anus and she tensed. He leant forward, kissing her shoulder. 'I'm not going to do that,' he said. 'Not right now. Your body needs time to get used to the feeling, and I don't want to spoil the memories of last night.'

She flushed deeply. 'I . . .'

'It was good for me, too,' he said softly. 'But right now, all I want to do is touch you there.' He licked the pad of his thumb and continued to massage her, very gently. Although he didn't penetrate her, Rachel's memories were so strong that it felt almost as if he had. She closed her eyes as his rhythm speeded up; and then her internal muscles contracted sharply round him. It was enough to tip him into his own orgasm; he cried out her name and then she felt his cock throbbing deep inside her.

He waited until the aftershocks of her orgasm had died down, then withdrew. He lifted her into the bath, washing her clean, and then dried her tenderly again, wrapping her in a towel. 'I think I'd better go next door while you get dressed,' he said, rubbing his nose against hers, 'or I don't think either of us will make the party.'

She smiled at him. 'I know.'

'I'll see you later, then.' He kissed her lightly, and left the bathroom.

Rachel dressed slowly. She felt languid and warm and content; she really wasn't in the mood for a party. What she felt like doing was padding down to the kitchen, sneaking a large plateful of canapés, and going back to bed with Luke, alternately sating her hunger for his body and for food. But she knew that it would be selfish and rude to do that. Max had invited them for the weekend; and he'd already said that he wanted to drink champagne with her, to celebrate their new working partnership. She couldn't let him down.

Just as she finished doing her make-up, Luke knocked on their connecting door. In response to her call, he walked in. 'Max asked me to give you this.' He handed her a mask.

'Oh.' She examined it in silence. It was an old-fashioned Venetian mask which was designed to cover only the top half of her face, though it was enough to disguise her completely. She put it on and looked at herself in the mirror. Staring back at her was a woman in a black dress, with full red lips. The top half of her face was adorned with peacock feathers; the porcelain mask almost matched her own skin tone, and there was a domino painted around her eyes: a mask within a mask. There was a tiny diamond which glittered in the place of a beauty spot, just above her mouth.

'You look incredible. If it wasn't for the fact that I don't want to ruin your lipstick,' Luke told her, standing behind her and sliding his hands round her waist, 'I'd kiss you right now.' His lips lightly touched the curve of her neck, and she shivered.

'Luke . . .'

'Later,' he promised, disentangling himself from her with obvious reluctance.

'What's your mask?' she asked.

He smiled and put it on. His mask was full-faced, in the design of a Green Man made of oak leaves; she grinned. 'It matches your waistcoat.' Luke's sober black dinner jacket, white shirt and black silk bow tie were in sharp contrast to the richly patterned green silk waist-coat he wore.

He removed the mask again and held her at arm's length, looking at her. 'Rachel.'

'Mm?'

'Can I ask you something?'

'Of course. What?'

He looked thoughtful. 'I'm not sure how to ask you this.'

She frowned. 'Try asking me straight.'

'Well . . . would you do something for me, tonight?'

'That depends what it is.'

He drew her closer, putting his lips by her ear. He licked her earlobe. 'What I'd like you to do is to take your knickers off.'

'Now?'

'Mm-hm. It'd really turn me on, dancing with you tonight and knowing that you're not wearing any knick-ers. And then maybe I can show you Max's rose garden.'

She digested what he'd just said. 'You want me to go out without any knickers on?'

'Yes.' He stroked her buttocks, then began to bunch up the material of her dress; the lining was slippery, and he found it easy to push the skirt of the dress upwards.

'Luke, I . . .'

'Too outrageous for you, is it?'

There was a slightly taunting note in his voice which annoyed her. She lifted her chin. 'No.'

'Then why not do it?' His eyes glittered. 'No one else at the party will know. Just you and me. Of course, if you'd rather not . . .' What he'd left unsaid was obvious. If she'd rather not, he'd know how much of a coward she was.

She didn't want to lose face with him. 'All right.'

'Good.' He hooked his thumbs into the sides of her knickers, dropping to his knees as he peeled the lacy garment downwards. Rachel leant against him, lifting one foot and then the other so that he could remove her knickers properly. He placed the flat of his palms against her thighs, the gentle pressure forcing her to widen her stance slightly. 'Beautiful,' he said huskily. 'I can't resist you, Rachel.' He bent his head, kissing her inner thighs, and Rachel closed her eyes as she felt his breath against her sex-flesh, cool and inviting.

She felt the long slow stroke of his tongue along the length of her quim; and then he slid his hands upwards, holding her labia apart. She gave a small moan of pleasure as he began to work on her clitoris, his tongue teasing the hard bud of flesh from its hood and then rapidly flicking across it.

Her sex grew wet and puffy; he pushed one finger into her, moving his hand back and forth with slow, teasing movements which made her wriggle and squat slightly, pushing her sex against his hand. Just as she was about to slide her hands into his hair and push his face against her sex, forcing him to please her properly, he stopped abruptly and stood up. Rachel opened her eyes in shock and disappointment as she felt him slide the skirt of her dress down to its normal position. 'Luke?'

'Later.' He gave her a wolfish grin. 'I just thought I'd give you a taste of what I have in mind.'

She flushed. 'That's unfair. You've turned me on, and you know it.'

'Mm, I know it all right.' He brushed his knuckles against her breasts, tracing the outline of her hardened nipples.

'You did that on purpose,' she accused.

'Yep. I think I've worked your clitoris to just the right point.'

Her eyes narrowed. 'Meaning?'

'Meaning that your sex is going to tingle as you walk. You're going to think of what we'll do later tonight ... and by the time we finally make it out to the rose garden, you're going to be so hot and wet. And every man who dances with you will smell just the faintest scent of musk, and they'll know how aroused you are, how hot and ready for a man you are.'

Her colour flared. 'Luke!'

'Of course,' he continued, 'you could always put your knickers on again and pretend it hasn't happened.'

She lifted her chin. 'Why do I get the feeling that you're trying to push me for a reason?'

'Oh, I am,' he agreed. 'Personal reasons. The best kind.' He licked his lips, removing all traces of the glistening musky juices from his mouth. 'So, are you ready?'

'I'm ready.'

'Good.' He replaced his mask and escorted her from the room.

Exactly as Luke had predicted, Rachel's sex tingled as she walked. He'd taken her just far enough for her to need to come – and too far for her to put it out of her mind. She could imagine her juices seeping slowly down her leg, the musky aroma of her arousal obvious to anyone who came near enough; it shocked her but, at the same time, she was conscious of a growing feeling of excitement.

Max met them at the bottom of the stairs, his full-faced Harlequin mask pushed up to the top of his head. Like Luke, he was wearing a formal dinner jacket and bow tie. 'Rachel.' He smiled and gave her a formal bow. 'You look beautiful,' he said, taking her hand and kissing the back of her fingers.

'Thank you.'

He tucked her arm through his. 'Come on. I promised you some champagne, earlier.'

He looked at Luke. 'You don't mind if I spirit Rachel off, do you?'

'Of course not.' Luke smiled back at him. 'I'll see you later, Rachel.' His eyes glittered behind the mask. Rachel licked her lips, knowing that she was being obvious, but unable to help herself.

Max led her through into the dining room. Chairs had been scattered round the room and the table pushed against the wall. Maggie had excelled herself with the buffet: there were tiny delicate smoked salmon canapés, little parcels of Brie in filo pastry, and a large selection of dips, satay and small savoury nibbles, as well as the more usual party food of cocktail sausages, nuts and crisps.

'Help yourself, whenever you fancy,' Max said. He handed her a glass of champagne. 'Well – cheers. And here's to a good working relationship.'

Rachel echoed the toast and clinked her glass against his before taking a sip. She quickly realised that although it was a party, Max hadn't bought cheap champagne. The wine had a sharp lemony tang, mixed with the delightful creaminess of top-class fizz. Perfect. She savoured the taste and took another sip. 'This is lovely, Max.'

She could hear the sound of soft bluesy jazz from one of the other rooms and realised that Max hadn't used piped music. He'd hired a proper band.

The room was already filling with men dressed in dinner jackets and women in little black cocktail dresses or brightly coloured taffeta ballgowns; all wore masks.

'When did you decide to start holding a masked ball?' she asked.

'A long time ago.' He smiled. 'It's more fun. People are more likely to mix and stop being shy, if they're wearing a mask and nobody knows who they really are.'

'Except you.'

He grinned. 'That's the host's privilege. You can be who you like, behind your mask.' He glanced over her shoulder and frowned slightly, before putting his mask into place. 'If you'll excuse me, Rachel, there's someone I need to talk to. You'll be all right on your own, won't you?'

'Sure. I'll find Luke; or maybe I'll just mingle with the other guests and pretend to be a high-born Venetian lady.'

He nodded in approval. 'Yes, I don't think that you'll be on your own for very long.'

As he left, Rachel wandered over to the table, taking a plate and helping herself to a selection of nibbles. She ate slowly, savouring the rich tastes and textures of the food; then helped herself to a second glass of champagne and went in search of Luke. Max's words kept echoing in her head: *you can be who you like, behind your mask.* Given the amount of champagne that everyone was likely to consume, she imagined that this was going to be one hell of a party.

She wandered into the sitting room where the band was playing, and stayed to watch them for a while. Even they wore masks: the singer, the pianist and the bass player. Obviously this wasn't the first time that they'd entertained at one of Max's parties, she thought, sipping her wine.

A hand descended on her shoulder and she whirled round, startled. Even without his mask, she wouldn't have recognised the man who stood beside her. He was slightly too broad-shouldered to be Euan or Michael, Max's guests of the previous evening, and he wasn't Luke – he wasn't wearing the Green Man mask or the bright waistcoat.

'Would you like to dance?' he asked.

His voice was quiet, cultured, rather than the braying City type Rachel had dreaded; it was enough to tip the balance. She nodded. 'Why not?'

She placed her empty glass on one of the small occasional tables and allowed herself to be led round the room by the stranger. He was a good dancer and Rachel found herself relaxing, enjoying herself. He moved well, and although Rachel had never learnt any formal dances, she didn't need to: he guided her effortlessly.

When the song finished, he bowed slightly and kissed the back of her hand. 'Thank you.'

'My turn, I think,' a voice said behind her.

Again, Rachel didn't know who he was; she didn't recognise his voice. But what the hell. It was a party; and, as Max had said, she was free to be whoever she chose, behind her mask. She smiled at him. 'Fine.' She danced with him to the next two songs, then changed partners twice more; finally, she protested laughingly that she needed a break.

She wandered back into the dining room, collected another glass of champagne and went in search of Luke. The fact that she'd been dancing with all those men and not one of them had known that she was wearing no underwear ... she wasn't sure whether it excited her, frightened her or shocked her. All the same, she was aware of how warm and puffy her sex felt.

She flexed the muscles of her quim, feeling her clitoris throb dully. God, if only Luke were there with her. Maybe he'd take her into the garden, as he'd promised, and give her the satisfaction she needed. She drained her champagne. Or maybe he'd dance with her, teasing her and rubbing his body against hers, knowing that he was driving her slowly mad with longing and desire, before taking pity on her and taking her back to one of their rooms.

At that precise moment, she felt a hand touch her shoulder, and spun round. 'Luke!' She recognised him instantly. He was still wearing his mask; but he was the right height, the right build, and wore that beautiful green silk waistcoat. So even if someone had had the same mask, she knew that this was definitely Luke.

He didn't respond to her greeting; he merely took the empty glass from her hand and began dancing with her. He moved fluidly; obviously he'd been formally taught. She wondered how: whether he'd taken classes when he'd been younger, or whether a woman had taught him. An older woman, perhaps; a lover, who had taught him all kinds of other things as well.

She shrugged the thought away; the next thing she knew, Luke had waltzed her out through the French doors to the patio. Although it was a warm and pleasant night, no one else was outside. She smiled. 'Don't tell me – you're going to show me Max's rose garden?'

He inclined his head; she smiled to herself. Obviously he was playing a part behind his mask: the silent Green Man. The pagan British representation of fertility. If this was the way he wanted to play it ... She remembered again how he'd persuaded her to go without her knickers, and a thrill shot through her at the memory.

She let him slide his arm round her shoulders and guide her over towards the wall at the side of the garden. She hadn't explored the outside of the house, having been captivated by Max's library, but there was a formal garden at the back, with low lavender bushes, clipped box, fragrant herbs and large marble statues on pedestals.

There was a small green door in the wall. 'Don't tell me – this leads to the walled garden?'

He nodded and opened the door, ushering her through. To her delight, she discovered that the walled garden was actually a rose garden. She could imagine how beautiful the place would be on Midsummer Eve, filled with fragrant old-English roses spilling their scent into the night, moonlight glistening on the flowers. Because it was late spring, the roses were merely in bud, but she could still appreciate the beauty of the place.

She was about to turn to him, tell him what she'd been thinking, but he took the initiative, pulling her back against his body and moulding her to him so that she could feel the heat and hardness of his cock against the cleft of her buttocks. His hands spanned her waist; he let one hand drift up to curve over her breast, squeezing the soft globe gently. Her nipple hardened almost immediately in reaction, and he made a small soft sound of pleasure in the back of his throat. He let his other hand drift down over her abdomen, stroking her; she arched against him, willing him to go further. They were alone. No one knew where they were, and no one could see them. She wanted to make love, oh, so badly.

She felt him bunch the material of her dress between his fingers, hoisting her skirt up. She closed her eyes and tipped her head back against him, luxuriating in the feeling. He was going to do it. He was going to bare her to the night and take her.

When her quim and her buttocks were bare, he slid one hand along the inside of her thighs, finally letting his hand come to rest on her delta; the heel of his palm pressed against her and his fingers touched her warm, wet quim. She willed him to touch her more intimately; he waited for a moment, tantalising her, and then at last she felt his finger part her labia.

She moaned softly as his finger slid up and down her satiny cleft, dabbling in her musky juices. He drew his hand up to her mouth, smearing the glistening juices against her lower lip; still with her eyes closed, she opened her mouth and sucked gently on his finger. She could feel his cock starting to pulse, and she knew that he was as excited as she was. She turned to face him. 'Luke. Finish what you started earlier.' Her tone was a mixture of pleading and command; he remained silent and she knew what he was waiting for. 'I want you to fuck me,' she said. 'I want you to fuck me, right here and right now. I want to feel your cock deep inside me, filling me and stretching me. I want you.'

She undid the button of his dark formal trousers, sliding the zip down. He was wearing silk boxer shorts and the rigid outline of his cock was clearly visible through them. She curled her fingers round his shaft, squeezing gently, and then pushed his trousers down, taking his boxer shorts with them.

He groaned and lifted her up, balancing her against the wall. She didn't care that ivy was ruffling her hair into wild disarray, that the wall was slightly crumbling; all she wanted was to feel him inside her. She slid her arms round his neck, resting against him for balance, and crossed her legs round his waist. He tilted his hips forward and she could feel his cock butting against the entrance of her sex. She moaned as he slid into her. God, it felt so good, the way he filled her and stretched her.

He began to thrust, all the time balancing her weight against his and keeping her still so that the bricks at her back wouldn't scratch her or ruin her dress. She threw her head back, ignoring the ivy as he thrust into her. If only he'd remove that damned mask, so that she could kiss him properly. But then, what the hell? The rhythm between their bodies was more important than anything else, right at that moment.

She felt her orgasm building, flowing through her body. It was as though she were at one with the night, and it made her want to howl, almost wail her desires at the moon. She couldn't help crying out his name as her climax suddenly ripped through her. Her internal muscles contracted sharply, tipping him over the edge into his own orgasm. She felt him pulse inside her; then, gently, he withdrew, letting her slide down his body until she was on her feet again. He steadied her, putting her dress to rights, and then straightened his own dress. She noticed that he still hadn't kissed her, that he still kept his mask in place; it irritated her mildly, but she decided not to push it. Besides, she was still wearing her own mask.

Without another word, he traced the curve of her lower lip; then he led her back out of the rose garden. As he closed the green door behind them, she suddenly noticed another couple standing in the formal garden, behind one of the statues, hidden from the rest of the party. She flushed deeply. Christ. They must have heard her cry out in orgasm, and known exactly what she was doing. But then again, she thought, maybe they were too engrossed in what they were doing to have noticed.

The man was leaning back against the statue, his hands gripping the top of the fluted marble column; the woman was on her knees in front of him. The top of her black dress was pushed down to expose her breasts. Her skin was creamy in the moonlight and her nipples were large and dark, erect and elongated where he'd obviously been touching and kissing them earlier. His trousers were halfway down his thighs, as were his underpants; the woman was fellating him, her head bobbing back and forth rapidly.

Rachel's eyes widened. This was something that she hadn't been expecting. To her shock and surprise, Luke didn't lead her straight back to the house. Instead, he guided her towards the couple. She opened her mouth to protest, but he anticipated her move, putting a finger to her lips to warn her to stay silent.

As they neared the lovers, Rachel realised that the man wasn't wearing a mask. There was a harlequin mask lying in the middle of the lawn – obviously the one that he'd discarded. She looked at his face and realised with shock that the man groaning in pure bliss as his cock was being sucked was none other than Luke himself. Rachel didn't know the woman who worked him; she was about to turn to her companion and demand to know who the hell he was, who the woman was and what they were playing at, but he was too quick for her. He slipped his hand over her mouth. 'Sh,' he breathed in her ear. 'All in good time.'

He held her close to him. Rachel watched, fascinated and appalled, as the woman continued to work Luke to orgasm, taking him deep into her mouth. She heard Luke's cries and moans as though through some kind of fog; sounds which were so familiar to her from their own love-making, and yet he was like a stranger to her at that moment. She had no part in his pleasure.

Shaken, Rachel allowed the stranger – the man she'd just made love with – to lead her back to the party. She still couldn't quite take it in. Luke was the one being fellated by the woman in the garden – and he knew that the woman wasn't her. She was wearing a different mask, a different dress – she even had different-coloured hair. How could he do that to her?

She'd just made love with a complete stranger – not only a man whose name she didn't know, but a man whose face she'd never seen. As they reached the patio, she stopped. 'I want to see your face.'

He nodded and removed the mask. Rachel stared at him, surprised. She didn't recognise him; she'd never met him. Part of her had begun thinking that her incognito lover had been Max, that the harlequin mask on the lawn had belonged to their host; now she realised that he wasn't. 'Who are you?' she asked.

'My name's Edmund.'

'And you're a friend of Max?'

'And Luke.'

'I thought that you were Luke.'

He raised a disbelieving eyebrow. 'Luke was, shall we say, otherwise engaged. As you've just seen.'

'But you're wearing his mask, his waistcoat.'

Edmund nodded.

'So Luke knew that I'd think you were him?'

Edmund's eyes glittered. 'Yes.'

Rachel frowned. 'But – why?'

'Why not?' was the annoying answer. 'Rachel, it's a party.'

'So you know my name. How?'

'Max pointed you out to me.'

She sighed. 'Christ. I'm beginning to think that I'm out of my depth here.'

He smiled, stroking her face. 'Rachel. Don't be angry. Max believes in pleasure – he believes in giving people what they want. And you wanted to come, didn't you?'

She flushed dully. Of course she had. He'd known that, the minute he'd touched her sex and found how aroused she was. 'Did you know that I was . . . dressed like that?'

He nodded. 'Luke told me.'

'Luke planned this?'

'No. I think he'd genuinely intended to do it himself. But . . . circumstances changed.'

'I see.'

Edmund replaced his mask. 'Look, if you want to have a fight with him, do it later. Right now, I feel like drinking champagne and dancing. It's a party. Either you can sulk on your own – or you can join me. The choice is yours.'

A choice, a decision: it was almost as though Max enjoyed playing games with people, enjoyed putting them in circumstances where they had to choose. Choose something unfamiliar, something unsettling – but something that they really wanted, at the same time. She nodded. 'All right.'

He slid his arm round her shoulders, squeezing her to show his approval. 'Come on. I think we both need a drink.' He stooped slightly so that his lips were next to her ear. 'Because the more I think of what you're not wearing beneath that demure dress of yours, the harder it's going to be not to take you into some dark secluded corner and make love with you again. At least champagne will help to take my mind off it.'

His words were so outrageous, so deliberately chosen, that it made her smile. 'Mm. Let's go inside.'

Circles

Gillian Martin

The setting for this short story is rural England. A chance encounter with a lusty Scotsman makes Louise's weekend more interesting than she'd bargained for.

Circles

*L*ouise reached the top of the rise and paused to draw breath. Her efforts paid off, though; the view from the hill was stupendous. The Dorset coast undulated against a sparkling sea in late-summer sunshine and birds wheeled above her head as if dancing for the joy of living. She had decided to take a long weekend to explore the area's ancient archaeological sites. The countryside was littered with barrows, the burial mounds of ancient chiefs placed on high ridges to emphasise their importance to their peoples. There were a few stone circles, too – their significance was lost to the modern world but in their time they would have seen ceremony and mystical ritual. Louise had been searching for one such circle and found it in a field of cows that had eyed her nervously as she approached. The circle was small with the stones now fallen or half buried, but the atmosphere of the place was unmistakable. She took some photographs of her find, but the clicking of her camera seemed intrusive: a mechanised modern sound that had no business in an ancient place.

The peace of the country around her was balm to Louise and she sat down on a stone outside the circle to catch her breath. It was bliss to be away from telephones, faxes and the endless demands on her time. The new job was tremendously exciting but she knew this long week-end break would prepare her for the public inquiry that began on Monday. She would need all her wits about her if her company was to get the approval it needed. Arriving early would give her time to gather her thoughts. As public relations officer for her organisation, she would face a barrage of antagonistic questions from angry villagers.

Sitting on her sarsen stone, Louise felt her shoulders relax and her lungs fill with clear, clean air. She dragged out her lunch and Ordnance Survey map and struggled to orientate herself. It was all very well being kitted out with the requisite gear but she was no seasoned walker and the whole business of footpaths, survey points and map references was still confusing. As she munched on her sandwich she tried to find her next intended site. Much to her dismay, the group of barrows she wanted to visit seemed to be across three more hills. A hot bath was going to be very welcome when she got back to her hotel. Her limbs were already starting to ache and were a nagging reminder of the many missed visits to the gym. Oh well, by the time she returned to work she would be fitter and have colour in her cheeks.

Across the field a tall, rangy male figure was making its way towards her. Oh blast, just as I was beginning to enjoy the solitude, she thought. Unsure of the etiquette among walkers Louise decided to stride towards the man; he was, after all, on the path she needed to take next. She could just acknowledge him and be on her way – that should deal with the niceties. They met only a few hundred yards from the circle of stones and paused to exchange a few words. He was very tall; at least six foot with dark straight hair and a trimmed beard and moustache. Very handsome, thought Louise and then mentally kicked herself for such a thought. It was ridiculous how the months alone had started to put such startling images into her head when she was near a fanciable male.

'Hi, I've been looking for this circle all morning,' he said, 'but you beat me to it. Quite impressive to still be so complete, isn't it?' He was a Scot, the warm tones of a Highlander colouring his voice. He had an easy smile and a very direct gaze. Louise felt herself a bit flustered – he was gorgeous!

'Well, yes, I guess it is quite a sight,' she said. 'I'm a bit new to this so I haven't seen other places to compare with this one.' Louise smiled back at him hoping her interest in him wasn't too obvious. Good grief, brown eyes like that could put a woman on heat. He was fit, too; the steep climb had not left him short of breath.

'These old sites are a passion with me. I'll tell you more about them if you like,' he offered. She could have sworn his eyes ran over her body as he spoke. Louise thought for a minute; his knowledge would improve her appreciation of her walks and the company of a good-looking man was a treat she had not expected.

'All right, I would enjoy that. Are you sure I'm not spoiling your walk?' she asked.

'Not at all, I'm working here for a week or so and don't know anybody. I needed the exercise but it is lonely on my own,' he replied. They turned and went back to the stones and sat on the same sarsen.

'My name's Rory Galbraith by the way,' he said.

'Louise Dunn. Pleased to meet you,' she replied, smiling inwardly. The weekend might turn out to be more interesting than she had expected.

Rory pulled his rucksack off his shoulders and rummaged inside for his map. His copy was well used, creased and annotated; Louise felt a real town girl with her pristine map neatly folded in her chain-store backpack.

The stone they sat on was not very large and, of necessity, their thighs touched. Louise felt agitated at the close proximity of the man beside her. He had incredibly long legs and strong thighs. The breeze stirred his dark fringe and gave Louise the crazy impulse to run her fingers through his hair. She had heard of instant attraction but never thought it would be an experience she would come across. Rory turned towards her and spread out his map across their laps.

'Could you hold that side for me?' he asked her. She took the corner and hoped her shaking hand would not betray her. He proceeded to tell her all about the Neolithic peoples who had built the stone circle, and what had been discovered on similar sites. His knowledge was comprehensive and she found herself lost in stories of long-dead cultures and tribes. Then his manner changed completely.

'Can you believe it, some money-grabbing bunch of heathens is wanting to open a countryside theme park just outside the village, in the valley down there?' Rory's voice shook with outrage as he pointed to the site.

'Really,' murmured Louise, 'but is that all bad? Surely the local people will be glad of the employment, and it will bring in lots of money to the area?'

'Don't you believe it,' came the retort. 'Hordes of tourists paying some conglomerate exorbitant prices to see what they can have for free if they'd just step outside their cars. Can you imagine the traffic, the litter, the noise? The company have already said they expect to employ most of their staff from Desborough, 10 miles away. It will destroy this community. Not much money will come into the village. With an all-inclusive ticket, who's going to go outside the complex for anything? A few teashops and B&Bs might see some extra cash, but the way of life will be wrecked. All I can say is thank heaven it won't rip up any of the archaeology; there's precious little left these days.'

Louise let Rory vent his feelings; he obviously felt very strongly about the subject to rant on about it to a near stranger. After a while he calmed down and the two of them set out for the next site with Louise struggling to keep up with Rory's long strides. The afternoon sped by and reluctantly Louise said she ought to get back to her hotel for a bath and dinner.

'Where are you staying?' Rory asked.

'At the Master's Arms, in Summerbourne. Do you know it?' she said.

'I should think so. I'm staying there too. My work will keep me here until next weekend at least,' came his reply. 'Would you like to share a dinner table? We seem to have got along very well today.'

Trying to hide her pleasure, Louise agreed, and they hiked back to the hotel, chatting all the way. She had found him more attractive by the hour; so intelligent and with a lean strong body that she could just imagine in the throes of passion – with her preferably.

In her room Louise quickly removed her clothes and ran a steaming bath, adding a foaming oil. Relaxing into the water with a sigh she lay her head back and let the aches ease away from her tired muscles. The soft bubbles slid over her skin and she raised her hand to trickle more over her breasts. Her mind ran back over the day and, as Rory's face swam into her memory, her nipples tightened. He had such a sensuous mouth framed by his beard and moustache. What would it feel like to have them brush over her skin? The thought gave her a well-remembered frisson of pleasure between her legs. It had been some time since a man had caressed her and she felt it time to return to the fray. Perhaps she would throw caution to the wind and actively flirt with Rory over dinner. She smiled and soaped herself all over.

Louise dressed with care – not too much make-up and a dress that made the most of an ample cleavage and skimmed over her rounded hips. She was proud of her hair that was fairly short but lustrous and thick. It was a honey-gold colour that had been lightened by the sun. The fresh air had brought a glow to her cheeks and the whole effect was one of a healthy, sensuous woman. A

dab of her favourite musk perfume and she was ready.
Rory was already in the restaurant and looked appreciatively at her as she crossed the room towards him.

'I hadn't realised I was in the company of such a sexy
lady all day,' he said. 'You look gorgeous.'

'Thank you, sir, but I am ravenous. Where's the
menu?' Louise was pleased at his reaction and boldly let
her eyes rove over him. He had changed into a sea-green
cotton shirt and black chinos that made the most of his
dark colouring. He too looked very sexy with his hair
damp from his shower.

The restaurant was well-known for its excellence and
they ordered the most exotic items on the menu. The red
wine was a good choice, too, and they had killed off two
bottles before the end of the meal. The conversation
never faltered. Louise found she could make Rory laugh
with her quick wit, and he had fascinating tales of his
world travels. All through the evening Louise felt her
pulse race at the proximity of this man who so obviously
liked her. Rory had frequently touched her hand to
emphasise a point and she expected to see fire on her
skin the feeling was so erotic. His fingertips lingered and
stroked her. They had held each other's gaze often
during the evening and the message was clear to both.

Coffee arrived with liqueurs and the mood of the
evening moved up a few gears. Rory was sitting next to
Louise and, as he leant across her to reach the cream for
his coffee, his arm brushed her breast and she could
hardly hold back a groan of lust. His hand, hidden by
the tablecloth, made its way to her thigh and purposefully stroked its way up her leg. The hem of her dress
rose as his questing fingers lightly brushed the soft flesh
of her inner thigh before moving upwards to her private
place. Louise tried to keep the thread of her conversation
but her breathing became faster and all she wanted to
do was drag him to the floor and let him finish what he
had started.

She said in a low, breathless voice, 'I think I've had enough to eat. What about you?'

He gave a wicked smirk as his fingers explored inside her now damp panties. 'Oh surely not. Can't I tempt you with anything else? I like a woman with an appetite.'

Louise smiled at him and let her fingertip trace that sensual mouth. Who cared about the lingering waiters. With his dark eyes locked on hers Rory took her finger between his lips and sucked it gently. The sensation was heavenly.

'Well, I suppose I could be persuaded but they are closing the restaurant now. Any ideas?' she asked, trying not to moan from the pleasure he was giving her with his caresses under the table.

His eyes narrowed a little and he said, 'I have some excellent whisky in my room I'd like to share with you. You're the kind of woman that appreciates good things.'

Louise needed no second invitation. His touch was driving her mad and all caution was thrown to the winds. 'Let's go then,' she said as she rose and smoothed her dress down. His arm slid round her waist as he guided her to the door. As they climbed the stairs he was one tread behind her, stroking her bottom as it moved under his hand.

They reached his room and, once inside, he swept his bed clear of newspapers, laptop and other clutter. She was pleased he obviously hadn't planned to seduce her as it made the whole experience far more erotic for her. He stood in front of her and wrapped her in his arms and kissed her soundly, she returning the passion – each running their hands over the other's body, discovering and exploring. He pushed her on to the bed and pulled off her shoes, then his own. He lay beside her and covered her face with light kisses as his hand stroked her hair. He ran his tongue very delicately around her mouth and dropped butterfly kisses on to her lips. His fingers traced down her throat, his mouth following. The imagined feeling of his beard was now real, its roughness contrasting deliciously with the moist flesh of his lips. He moved lower, unbuttoned her dress and slipped his hand inside to cup her breast.

'Oh, such a lot of woman,' he breathed. 'I adore women like you – curvy and soft and warm.' Louise squirmed under him. She moaned as his mouth reached her nipple. His tongue flicked the taut bud and then his mouth roamed over the soft mound of her breast. He moved one leg between hers and she wriggled against his powerful thigh, rubbing herself on him until she almost brought herself to climax. She could feel a huge erection against her; her hand flew to it and rubbed the hard cock through the fabric. He laughed gently, sat up and drew her upright. Her dress was whisked off over her head and her bra was expertly undone. Both his hands moved forward and he held her breasts, his thumbs playing with her nipples that tightened so much they hurt. She fumbled with his shirt and, in the end, dragged it over his head. His shoulders and chest were broad and finely muscled. She let out sighs of pleasure as she ran her hands over him, then her fingers slipped into his waistband in an attempt to reach the engorged manhood inside.

Again he pushed her back on to the bed and stood towering over her, his eyes sweeping over her body as he loosened his belt and stepped out of his trousers. Her eyes must have given away her surprise; his boxer shorts could barely contain his massive erection. Louise spread her legs and raised her arms to welcome him. Rory knelt between her thighs and ran both his hands up over her torso to her breasts as her hands caressed his broad shoulders. Louise by now was whimpering in delight and allowing herself to be lost in the pleasure of his skilful touch. Now he flattened his body on hers and moved her hands above her head, one hand holding them fast as he nuzzled each breast in turn. His other hand moved down to her panties and his fingers slipped under the elastic. He was very strong. She liked the feeling of being restrained but there was no threat or danger. He simply revelled in her and she was drunk with the sensations he was arousing in her. She was doing her best to hold her mounting excitement and prolong the pleasures sweeping over her. With a low growl, Rory rose to his knees and dragged her panties off her, diving between her thighs to lick and suck and flick his tongue around her clitoris. Louise let out a yell of pleasure – how could anything feel so good? As his tongue worked its magic, his hands played with her breasts and she writhed against his face, holding his head, feeling his silky hair under her fingers. He moved his tongue along her inner thigh, kissing her so gently and then returning to taste her again. His tongue darted in and out of her, then twirled around the entrance before moving again to her throbbing clitoris. It was all too much and, despite wanting to wait until he had entered her, Louise just had to let her orgasm rush over her. It started in her toes and raged upwards to explode in her brain. Her cries were loud and her body bucked against him. All the time, Rory kept on devouring her until she begged him to stop.

Louise raised his head from between her shaking legs and sat up to kiss him, her scent lingering on his moustache, her own wetness glistening on his skin. She coaxed him to lie back and began to kiss her way down his chest. Her tongue flickered over the firm flesh and she felt the muscles ripple as she moved lower to the softer dip of his waist and stomach. She reached for the band of his shorts, then pulled them off him. His cock leapt from the fabric, standing proud and hard. She moved to kneel between his legs and, bending over, she let her breasts envelop his balls. His penis was so large and stiff she was easily able to put her mouth around the head while the shaft was buried in her cleavage. As her velvet mouth closed around him she raised her eyes to find him gazing right at her – his mouth slightly open and his brown eyes locked on to hers. Louise ran her tongue around his wonderful manhood, teasing and probing, making him gasp with pleasure. She opened her mouth wider and took more of him inside. Now she could suck him hard while she ran her fingers very lightly behind his balls and into the crease between his legs. She could hear him breathing faster and she made sure he could see what she was doing to him. Her tongue lingered around the tiny opening of his prick; she could taste the slight saltiness as a drop of fluid appeared. She pursed her lips and blew very gently over the exposed delicate tip.

At this, Rory cried out and pulled her up to smother her face with passionate kisses, kneading her breasts with one hand, the other clasping her buttocks to him. He rolled her over and pushed her legs apart with his knee. His long body loomed over hers as he guided his pulsing cock between her thighs. He gently started to enter her – mindful of his size – but she was so wet by now that his prick glided in and Louise could feel the glorious sensation of a man completely filling her.

He was very skilful, moving in and out of her while never actually leaving her body. His dark eyes moved from watching her face to watching himself slide deep into her. The two of them moved in time, as if to a rhythm only they could hear.

Louise felt another climax rising within her and clawed at his back as she drew her legs up around his waist and thrust her hips. The deep penetration was so stimulating she urged him on as her fingers dug into his back. Rory too was beyond restraint, his long muscled thighs and slim hips moving rhythmically to bury himself into her softness, his face contorting with the ecstasy building in him. Louise broke first; never a quiet lover, she buried her face in his shoulder as her orgasm crashed over her. The cries were muted by his body. A second later, Rory reached his limit and his powerful body shuddered as his climax raced through him, his bottom pumping against her thighs.

He was breathing heavily and, although spent, still rocked gently above her, making her whimper as faint echoes of that incredible passion went through her like aftershocks of an earthquake. Seeing his exhaustion, Louise unravelled her legs and drew him down to lay on her – his head resting below her breasts. He kissed her stomach so sweetly as she stroked his hair and she felt complete contentment. After a while, Rory drew himself up and looked down at her, smiling with genuine affection.

'Where's my camera?' he said. 'I just have to have a photo of this sexy woman on my bed. I just won't believe this was real tomorrow.'

Louise threw a pillow at him. 'You'll do no such thing, you pervert. And where's that promised whisky? You've got me in here on false pretences.' She laughed and rolled swiftly away from him as he made a grab for her. 'No more until I get something to drink,' she said, almost covering her body with the quilt.

'You're a hard woman, Louise Dunn.' Rory did his best to look mournful. He stood up and stretched, then padded over to the dressing table to retrieve a bottle of Island malt – one with an unpronounceable name. He poured the golden liquid into two glasses and added a splash of bottled Highland water.

'Here you are, madam, your drink.' Rory sat on the side of the bed and handed Louise a glass as she sat propped up against the pillows. She took a tentative sip. The smoky smooth flavour rolled over her tongue leaving a taste like a perfumed fire. It was very good and seemed to finish off the evening's exertions beautifully. Louise took another drink and snuggled down on the bed.

'That was beautiful, Rory,' she said, stroking his arm.

'The whisky or the sex?' he asked, eyes dancing with mirth.

'Both, if you must know,' she replied.

'It was my pleasure,' he said, more serious now. He drew the quilt down to reveal her body and tipped his glass slowly so a few splashes of whisky landed on her stomach. Placing his glass on the side table, he bent his head and very carefully lapped the spirit from her body, his tongue a tiny point of flesh that gave a world of pleasure. Louise sighed ecstatically and lay back with eyes closed as he roamed over her curves.

After a little while Rory raised his head, his moustache damp with whisky. He smiled at her. 'How about a shower?' he asked. Louise opened her eyes and looked at him sleepily.

'That sounds lovely, but I was so enjoying myself.'

'Me too,' he grinned, 'but I think you'll enjoy this as well.' He hauled her upright and they went into the tiny bathroom.

'Why are hotel showers always so cramped?' Louise commented as Rory adjusted the water temperature.

'Get in here with me and you'll see why they are so small,' he said. The two of them stepped into the cubicle and the water sluiced over their bodies. Rory reached for his shower gel and squeezed some into his hands. Louise had her eyes closed as she raised her face to the water; she kept them shut as she felt his hands glide over her skin. The soap slid smoothly over her breasts and she was lost in the sensation as Rory's hands covered her body, massaging her shoulders and stroking her stomach.

'Turn around, Louise,' he said in a husky voice. She did as she was asked, her hips rubbing against him as she moved in the confined space. Again he soaped her all over, but now his hands ran down over her flanks to bury themselves between her legs. He moved closer behind her and his burgeoning erection grew harder against her buttocks. Louise raised her arms to the wall and laid her forehead on them. Rory began to rub himself against her. His strong arms held her to him and he nuzzled her neck, making her go weak as he touched her erogenous zones. The warm water cascaded over them as he moved her legs further apart. He bent his knees slightly and guided his once-more-stiff cock into her velvet channel. Louise let out a gasp of pleasure as Rory clasped her to him, one hand around her hips, the other kneading her soap-covered breasts. She braced herself against the wall of the shower as his movements became more urgent. It was a wonderful feeling – the sensation of love-making enhanced by the erotic passage of water streaming over her body and stimulating the parts of her not currently being enjoyed by Rory.

The steady rhythm of Rory's strong thighs pushing against her made Louise moan as yet another climax began to rise in her veins. His lower hand was by now caressing her forest of soft pubic hair and his fingers found the hard little nub of flesh buried there. Her hips undulated and rolled as his prick slid smoothly inside her. Once more her orgasm caught her off guard with its intensity, and she cried out as her blood turned to fire and the conflagration swept over her. Feeling her shaking with passion, Rory gave vent to his own climax, holding her slippery body hard to him as he came, his thighs shaking with effort, and his every muscle seemingly carved of stone. Exhausted, they held on to each other, the water still falling over them. Slowly, it revived them.

'Now you see why these hotel showers are so small,' Rory said as he kissed her softly. 'Just enough room for horseplay like that.'

Louise could only smile and, turning around, she buried her face in his chest. They finished washing each other and emerged from the steamy bathroom to dry each other off. They climbed back into bed and cuddled together, the passion spent now, and tender kisses were exchanged.

'I want to know you better, Louise. Can we see each other again?' His words came in between kisses.

'I'd like that very much,' she murmured sleepily and snuggled closer into his embrace.

The next morning, Louise managed to reach her own room without being spotted by the other guests. She showered and dressed, taking care with her appearance; she needed to look efficient but approachable today. Rory was not in the dining-room at breakfast. Getting more sleep, she thought to herself, wishing she had that luxury as she poured more coffee.

After breakfast, Louise gathered her briefcase and presentation material, jumped in her car and drove off to find the venue for the inquiry. It was being held in the village hall, not far from the Master's Arms. In the car park, she drew a deep breath, and with head held high walked into the hall. Already the seats were filling up with local residents; a journalist and photographer from the regional paper were fussing around, trying to take pictures of the members of the parish council.

There was a long table set out on the stage, and Louise made her way to the steps at the side. The chairman of the inquiry saw her and came to greet her as she climbed up.

'Ah, Miss Dunn, welcome.' He shook Louise's hand. 'Let me introduce you to your opposite number, hired by the residents' action committee: Mr Rory Galbraith – an environmental-impact specialist, so he tells me.'

At the mention of his name, Rory appeared from behind the projector screen. 'Well, hello, Miss Dunn,' he said. 'I hope this will be a good, clean fight. I hear you can be a formidable opponent.' His voice was cool, giving no hint of the glorious hours they had spent on his rumpled bed, but his eyes glinted mischievously.

'I think I can promise you a run for your money, Mr Galbraith,' replied Louise smoothly. 'We may both find this a long and tiring week, but I am sure we can find common ground between us.'

'That's the spirit,' boomed the chairman. 'Now let's

get this show on the road – a lot of ground to cover, you know.' He laughed at his own bad joke and bustled around getting everyone seated. As he called the meeting to order, Louise had to work hard to keep a straight face. Fraternising with the enemy had not been in her job description.

Jasmine Blossoms

Sylvie Ouellette

This extract is from a recent Black Lace novel, *Jasmine Blossoms*, by the popular French-Canadian author Sylvie Ouellette. Joanne, a businesswoman working in Japan, has been receiving a series of mysterious, anonymous messages. In this extract, she has agreed to meet her unknown admirer, so that she can discover the truth. The stranger begins to draw her into the exotic and sensual underworld of Japan.

Sylvie Ouellette has written two other Black Lace books: *Healing Passion*, in which an inexperienced nurse finds work at an exclusive clinic; and *The King's Girl*, where a young Frenchwoman, Laura, experiences decadence and sensuality in a 1660s North American colony.

Jasmine Blossoms

❧❧❧

She checked her watch for the fourth time, cursing herself. Why had she come? Once again, temptation and curiosity had been stronger than plain common sense, and now Joanna found herself alone on an empty road, with no means of getting back to the city. If only she had asked the taxi to wait!

The person she was supposed to meet was now more than fifteen minutes late. She should have stuck to her first resolution and stayed at the hotel. She had nothing planned that evening and she probably would have ended up being bored to tears, but at least she would have been safe.

She took a first step along the road, hoping she wouldn't have to go very far before meeting someone from whom she could hitch a ride. The thought of bumping into some lunatic entered her mind. But she couldn't let that worry her. She was in enough trouble already.

She waved frantically as a car appeared from around the bend in the road. It stopped in front of her and the back door opened. It was a big car, much bigger than the average Japanese one; more like a limousine. The dark tinted windows wouldn't allow her to see much of what was inside, but she could see there was at least one passenger in the back seat, a man.

'Do you speak English?' she asked as she bent forward to speak to him.

'Yes, Miss Parsons,' said the man. 'I humbly apologise for being late. Please do get in.'

Joanna was stunned. She had given up on anyone appearing, but now it seemed she hadn't been stood up after all. She hesitated. Accepting the invitation would perhaps bring her one step closer to solving the mystery, but could she really get in a car with a stranger, a man whose face she couldn't even see?

The passenger gave an order to the driver, who turned off the engine. Slowly, the man got out and walked towards Joanna.

Her heart jumped when she saw his suit: a pale shade of green, just like the one worn by the man from the bar. But it wasn't him. Yet there was no mistake to be made: even the pink shirt was identical, not to mention the tie. The face had changed, but this man was just as handsome as the stranger from the bar, albeit a few years older. And his eyes were smaller, more mysterious. Another thing both men had in common was unusually thick hair, coarse and unruly, like a wig.

He walked towards Joanna with tremendous self-assurance and class. He was the same height as she was, although his broad shoulders made him look taller, more impressive. As he approached, the cool air blew in her direction and carried his fragrance which she recognised: jasmine.

The scent stirred her memories and the effect on her was overwhelming. Suddenly, she was there again: sitting at the bar, with the stranger next to her casually slipping his hand between her legs to pleasure her.

'I can see you are still not convinced we are really those you have asked to meet,' the man said. 'Let me assure you, there is no reason for you to hesitate.'

Joanna didn't reply. What on earth was he talking

about? She couldn't even surmise he was talking to the wrong person. Although he had addressed her by another name, she knew he was indeed the man she had come here to meet.

'Who are you?' she said loudly in a defiant tone. What do you want from me?'

The man laughed softly. 'You may call me Torima. Of course, it is not my real name. And, really, you should know better than to pretend you don't know what this is all about. Come. What you've been waiting for is within your reach.'

Joanna didn't budge as he turned and started to walk back towards the car. When he saw she hadn't followed him, the stranger came back towards her.

'You know you will not regret this,' he continued. He edged towards her, coming closer than before. As his hand reached up, Joanna knew he was going to touch her, but she didn't move. Her instincts were telling her to let him have his way, just like the man at the bar.

And, as she had guessed, his fingertips slowly brushed her, breasts. Her nipples stiffened readily. His other hand followed the curve of her waist and lightly fondled her buttocks. As he pulled her towards him, Joanna gasped. Under his clothes, she could feel his body, hard and trim. Her hips instinctively pushed against his. Immediately, Joanna realised she wanted him. She wanted to be taken by a real man, something that hadn't happened for a long time.

'Pleasure, Miss Parsons,' he whispered as his lips caressed her earlobe. 'That's all we want from you, for you. To give and receive pleasure. You have nothing to fear. You won't be hurt.' He paused for a moment and pulled away before finishing his sentence. 'Unless that is what you desire.'

She resisted the urge to tell him her name wasn't Parsons but Wilson. What difference would it make, anyway? The mistake had been made so often she had

stopped correcting it and couldn't be bothered to do s
now.

The man stood so close to her she could still feel th
heat of his body. She gave up trying to rationalise. N
matter how disconcerted she was by this mystery, he
instincts were telling her that the man wasn't lying: sh
had nothing to lose, and much to gain – pleasur
Without a word, she got in the car. The man got in afte
her and closed the door behind him.

'We hope you understand the need for this,' he sai
as he pulled out a piece of black fabric.

Joanna remained idle as he blindfolded her. Sh
wasn't afraid any more. Having accepted that fightin
her instincts was pointless, she was filled with trus
And, more than anything, she was incredibly aroused.

They drove for quite a long time. Not a single wor
was exchanged. Joanna felt hot but calm. Eventually
they stopped and she was helped out of the car, sti
blindfolded. Both the stranger and his driver helped he
along what seemed like a narrow path made of cobble
stones. She could hear music, and occasionally her nos
caught whiffs of cooking, but there was nothing else t
tell her where they had taken her. There were practicall
no noises, except for a lone cricket and the very distan
rumble of traffic. The cool air was slightly humid an
gave her the impression that they were in the country
but those were the only clues.

Once inside, the blindfold was removed. Joanna wa
overwhelmed by the light assaulting her eyes. The roon
in which she found herself was enclosed by rice-pape
panels, and was not unlike several places she had beer
before: the bath house, the inn near Tokyo, one of th
hotels where she had stayed.

She wasn't even surprised when a panel slid open
Torima left and two geishas came in. The scene was s
familiar that Joanna's heart began pounding in antici
pation. Now, for the first time, she knew what wa

270

coming next. They undressed her and she felt herself melt.

When she saw the kimono one of the geishas held out for her – pale pink and adorned by wispy green sprigs of jasmine – she realised it was exactly like the one she had received as a present a few days earlier. Finally, the puzzle in her head was coming together. Now there could be no mistake: whoever these people were, they had made jasmine blossoms their emblem.

To her surprise, another panel slid open, this time on her right. Joanna turned sideways and watched, hypnotised, as it opened on to another room. It was a large banqueting hall, almost completely empty, and with a very high ceiling. Alongside the wall on the left-hand side, about a dozen people were kneeling in a single row behind a low table arranged in a crescent.

It was as if they were expecting something to happen in front of them, in the middle of all this empty space. In front of them, at the other end of the banqueting hall, an enormous door was closed. It was massive, made of dark lacquered wood and adorned by big metal studs.

As Joanna peered in, the people behind the table looked towards her and bowed in unison. Mechanically, she bowed back.

Behind her, Torima reappeared. He too had changed into a kimono, entirely black and embroidered with gold threads in the jasmine sprigs pattern that was now so familiar. He looked like a samurai, something out of an old film. Only then did Joanna realise she had been right when she had guessed he was wearing a wig. Now that it had been removed, she could see his real hair, which was long and tied into a bun on top of his head.

He placed his hand on the small of her back and gently ushered her into the room. Everyone smiled at her and bowed again. The men in attendance were all Japanese and were dressed in the same fashion as Torima. Joanna recognised one of them as the stranger from the bar. He, too, had removed his wig and his own hair was skilfully arranged. He smiled and bowed at her.

The women, however, were Westerners. Although they all wore kimonos like Joanna's, they weren't made up to look like geishas for they didn't wear any white make-up or black wigs.

Not a single sound was made as Joanna entered the room. The table was lavishly set with elaborate dishes which hadn't been touched. They had been waiting for her. She was invited to sit at the centre of the table. She was the only one who didn't have to kneel. Rather, she was provided with some sort of legless chair, made entirely of cushions and slightly reclining. As she sat, Torima encouraged her to stretch out her legs. This way, she couldn't reach the table, but she didn't really mind. Food was the last thing she was thinking of at that moment. Everyone was still staring at her, but not a word was exchanged. Joanna's mind raced with dozens of questions, but she sensed now wasn't the right time to ask them.

Torima knelt next to her. He clapped his hands, and suddenly the party began. The music started and all the guests helped themselves to the food on the table. Two young men appeared on either side of Joanna. One after the other, they picked up the dishes on the table and brought them within Joanna's reach.

She ate without really thinking about what she was putting in her mouth. Several of the dishes were served in the traditional Japanese fashion, brought to her in a square shallow lacquered box. There was a lot of raw fish, small servings of oddly shaped mushrooms, and the usual noodle soup which everyone slurped loudly. The flavours and textures mixed in Joanna's mouth as she savoured each bite, every morsel awakening her senses.

The two attendants never left her side. They brought the dishes for her to sample with pointy chopsticks, but at times they even fed her themselves and joyfully

Joanna let them. To drink, she had a choice of tea, sake, plum wine and liqueur. All she had to do was point and the cup was brought to her lips.

She let herself relax, intoxicated by such an overwhelming display of delicacies. On either side of her, the other guests were also gorging themselves, using both chopsticks and bare fingers to pick up their food, sometimes directly from the serving trays.

Although the guests casually chatted among themselves, no one talked to Joanna. Even Torima, who now and again turned to smile at her, never uttered a word. She observed the scene for a while, soon noticing one constant: the guests kept glancing towards the empty space in front of them. Only then did Joanna notice the lights along the ceiling were aimed directly for that spot. Obviously, everyone was expecting a floor show at some point. By then, her surroundings seemed so familiar to Joanna that she even expected her musician friends Keiko and Atsuko to show up at any moment, to entertain them with songs and dances.

The atmosphere had changed drastically from when she had entered the room: from rather cold and formal to totally uninhibited. Now it was exactly like any other dinner party: mostly cheerful and at times even rowdy. The food was plentiful, varied and exquisite. The amount of sake Joanna had drunk was also a contributing factor to the state of blissful relaxation in which she now found herself.

Although she had been here for well over an hour, still no one had said anything to her. Torima was very attentive and constantly smiling, but beyond informing Joanna about the dishes presented to her, he didn't try to engage her in conversation. Yet it was obvious that Joanna was the focus of silent attention, being made to feel like a queen and waited on by two lovely young men.

She could sense she was the topic of conversation, yet she felt no malice. Rather, everyone seemed pleased by her presence among them, as if she were a guest of honour, a trophy on a shelf to be admired. And, for once, she didn't even have to work at it.

At some point, the music stopped. The lights above them were dimmed, making the empty space in front of them only more obvious. The guests stopped eating and straightened up.

Two young Japanese women appeared through the side door and came towards Joanna. The other guests moved away slightly to allow them more space. The women were both dressed in white and carried towels and small bottles. At first glance, they looked like beauticians, and Joanna guessed she would be entitled to yet another treat.

One of them knelt next to Joanna's legs and proceeded to massage her feet. The other young woman delicately opened Joanna's kimono and pulled away the sides to expose her naked body.

Joanna felt the hair of the back on her neck rise on end. At first, she was horrified to be exposed in such an unceremonious way. As her skin was uncovered, the cool air in the room made her shiver. But she didn't dare stop the women. She looked around, rather worried, but a moment later she was pleased by the other guests' reaction. Ohs and ahs of admiration reached her as they all stared at her, stretching their necks to see her better.

Such a display of appreciation was indeed flattering, and the alcohol flowing in her veins had left her hot and uninhibited. When tiny hands began spreading jasmine-scented lotion on her thighs, her stomach and her breasts, she simply took a deep breath, let out a long sigh, and decided to relax and enjoy it. The massages were sensuous but not so daring as to be unduly arousing. Above all else, they were mostly pleasant and soothing.

Joanna was beginning to think she might fall asleep when suddenly, from outside the room, a gong resonated loudly. She was startled, stirred, and in a fraction of a second found herself wide awake. The other guests also became more attentive, intently staring at the large door in front of them. Only a moment later, it opened.

A man stepped in hesitantly, escorted by the two young men who had waited on Joanna earlier. He stared at everyone in turn and appeared uneasy, even somewhat feverish. Joanna couldn't help but think of how he looked like he didn't belong in such a place. He was dressed in a dark smart suit, with his tie properly done and his hair neatly combed. Immediately, Joanna understood he was a *salary-man*, just an average Japanese bloke working in an anonymous office, in an anonymous building.

One of the women stood up and went to him, bidding him stand in the middle of the empty space. Next to him, she also looked out of place. Joanna hadn't paid much attention to her before, but now she couldn't help but notice how strikingly beautiful she was. Her skin was the colour of coffee, and her vaguely Hispanic features made her look South American, perhaps Brazilian. The pink kimono definitely didn't suit her; she would have looked better in a pareo or sarong, in bold colours.

The man looked at her, then glanced towards the people still at the table. His eyes paused on Joanna and he gasped. His eyes opened wide and he licked his lips nervously. Joanna writhed with satisfaction. It was extremely gratifying to be reminded once again of how beautiful she was. In the semi-darkness, her skin glowed softly and looked even more velvet-like. Her nipples had grown stiff and dark and pointed insolently towards the man. If he wanted to look, she would let him. Obviously, what he saw pleased him.

Torima pushed away the bottles and the dishes in front of Joanna, clearing the space to afford the beholder a better view. Everyone around the table smiled, but no one said anything. In the man's eyes, Joanna could read both fear and excitement. She guessed the fear was motivated by the unknown, for he looked like he didn't quite know what to expect. But his excitement was obvious in the bulge stretching the front of his trousers.

Joanna wasn't surprised by the latter, but she was amused by the expression on his face. By now she had grown accustomed to solemn glares and polite smiles, and his bewilderment was a welcome change.

The gong resonated once again, and it was Joanna's turn to gasp when the woman standing next to the man suddenly dropped her kimono. Underneath, she was half-naked and simply wore a sheer corset made entirely of fine white lace. Joanna immediately recognised the garment as French and admired its quality. It was beautifully crafted, just strong enough to emphasise nicely the slender figure of the woman by cinching the waist and lifting her bare breasts without cupping them. Yet it seemed delicate enough to make it a delight to wear, and made her skin look even darker. Although the woman was probably in her early forties, she was impressive to behold; rather short and stout, but neatly sculpted and amazingly firm.

Joanna's eyes wandered all over her body, along with those of the man, and stopped at the same place as his: the junction of the legs. Under the frilly lace, an enormous luxuriant thatch of thick black hair was plainly visible. Along its edge, on the right-hand side, a thin sprig of jasmine had been tattooed, the vine clinging to her bush and following its contour to curve at the top.

Joanna saw the man lick his lips at the sight of such abundance. She remembered how she had once heard that in Japan pubic hair was considered the ultimate taboo. Even in the most risqué pornographic magazines, the hair was hidden or mechanically erased from the photos. As a result, Japanese men often developed a fetish, a fixation that could only be appeased by the sight of an unusually well-furnished mound.

The woman's other assets were her gorgeous breasts, adorned by large dark-brown nipples so stiff and erect they were practically begging to be suckled. As she admired them, Joanna also noticed two abundant forests tucked under the woman's armpits. They added something primitive to her, a raunchy and feline aura. Silently, she walked around the man, moving about as lithely and graciously as a dancer. The man followed her every move by turning his head, never letting her out of his sight, but obviously unaware of what he was supposed to do.

Joanna shifted in her seat, trying to fight the surge of arousal now invading her. She was eagerly anticipating what would happen next. The woman waved her hand towards one of the attendants still flanking the *salary-man*. Without uttering a single word, he obediently brought her a riding crop which he passed to her with a deep bow. Joanna was impressed. Obviously, he knew the drill.

The Spaniard said only a few words and, although her Japanese was atrocious, their meaning was unequivocal: undress and kneel. The *salary-man* didn't need to be told twice. He obeyed promptly and shed his clothes at record speed. Soon he knelt, completely naked, in front of the woman who exercised such a fascination over him. His body was average, not very tall but nicely shaped. His organ, already erect, was just as unremarkable.

But Joanna wasn't too disappointed: the man himself wasn't the focus of her interest at that moment. She was much more curious about what her dinner companion would do with him.

The woman walked around the prostrate figure a few times without so much as brushing him; either to examine him or to test his patience, Joanna thought. Nonchalantly, she then let the flexible tip of the riding crop run up along the ridge of his spine. The man twitched faintly, but didn't try to move away or reach out to her.

She stopped in front of him and, standing precariously on one leg, offered him the other, putting her pointed toes on his lap and pressing her knee towards his mouth. Without wasting any time, the man eagerly kissed and licked the whole length of her calf and shin. His eagerness was matched only by the speed of execution. His tongue moved swiftly and didn't miss a single spot.

His mistress seemed pleased, but when his hands came to grab her leg to pull it closer to his wet lips, she directed the riding crop in a precise blow on his forearm. The man squealed in pain.

'Don't touch,' she ordered.

Sitting back on his heels, he looked at her defiantly for a moment. But as soon as his eyes resumed their journey over her appealing body, he once again bowed his head in submission. Hesitantly, he kissed her leg again, curbing his enthusiasm for a while but soon letting his passion resurface.

Yet, although he seemed to enjoy his humiliating position, now and again it became obvious that he couldn't restrain himself. Often his hands came forward in an attempt to touch the woman, but pulled away just in time to avoid another strike. When his mouth strayed above the mistress's knee, she pushed his head down forcefully and intimated that he should wait for her instructions.

As she watched from the other side of the table, Joanna felt more and more excited. She was impressed by the way the woman toyed with her slave, allowing him to touch her only as she pleased, never hesitating to strike with the crop when he strayed.

The other guests also watched silently, mesmerised by this performance, never flinching or betraying the way they felt. Only Joanna showed signs of agitation. Voyeurism was something she had never experienced before, and she found it tremendously arousing. Her blood coursed through her veins to converge in her breasts and her pelvis, making her hot and wanton. Every time the *salary-man* dared to do something forbidden, Joanna shifted in her seat in anticipation of the forthcoming strike, which made her feel even more wicked.

The woman set her foot back on the floor and stood in front of her slave, legs parted. The man remained still, as if hypnotised by the enormous mound of hair now just inches from his face. She grabbed him by his hair and pulled his head towards her waiting flesh. His eyes closed in fervour as he stuck out his tongue readily. Without further ado, he frantically rubbed his face over her silken mound, grunting loudly as he let his tongue trail all over it. He bent down even further, setting his hands on the floor for balance as he lapped endlessly.

At first, the woman didn't react, but soon her slave's eager caresses began to affect her visibly. Her pelvis slowly swayed and ground against his face. Her face betrayed the pleasure that swelled within her as he grew more enthusiastic with each passing second. When his hands finally came up to grab her thighs and pull her even closer to his mouth, she didn't try to stop him.

Yet that was all she would let him do. When his hand strayed and he grabbed his own stiff phallus, the woman noticed immediately and mercilessly lashed him until he let go. He remained docile for a while, but she once again had to stop him a little later when he tried to reach up and touch her generous breasts.

Although the woman seemed keenly aware of the possibility that her slave might try to stray again, that didn't stop her from enjoying herself. Her breath soon grew shallow and she whined repeatedly. Her hips swayed majestically, her round buttocks contracting as she thrust towards her slave's mouth, her thighs trembling under the strength of the pleasure gathering within her.

Joanna's throat was dry but she was unable to take her eyes away from them, too enthralled even to think about taking a sip of sake. In just a few seconds, she knew the woman would climax right in front of them, and she couldn't wait for that moment.

The woman's head jerked back and forth a few times, forcing her hair to come undone and fall all over her shoulders and breasts. At the same time, she began hitting her slave's bottom with the riding crop, each blow making him grunt both in pleasure and in pain. Even as her orgasm came, she didn't stop the thrashing. Down on all fours, his dick straight and engorged, the *salary-man* climaxed under the blows. He didn't have much time to recover, however.

The woman stepped back unexpectedly. The two attendants rushed forward to help the man on to his feet and lead him hurriedly out of the room. Staggering, the man needed considerable coaxing. As he walked away reluctantly, he kept his head turned, looking behind him as if unwilling to leave just yet, perhaps even hoping for more. But already the Spaniard had donned her kimono and returned to sit at the table. As she took her place and the door of the room closed shut behind the *salary-man*, everyone round the table broke into a round of applause. She blushed and bowed modestly.

Joanna was flabbergasted. Thousands of thoughts flashed through her head, and she was dying to ask what that was all about. Was it real or just a cleverly constructed play? She didn't have time to ask, however. The gong resonated again and another man, looking just as scared but excited as the first, appeared in the doorway. This time another woman, tall, blond and vaguely Swedish-looking, stood up and went to him. This one was younger, probably in her late twenties, but she exuded a calm and a coolness that led Joanna to believe that she had just as much experience in the field of domination as the Spaniard did.

Somehow, Joanna expected a repeat performance of what she had just witnessed, but when the kimono fell around the woman's ankles, she knew she was wrong. Underneath, the girl was dressed in leather from head to toe. Her body was just as slender as it was tall. The *salary-man*, shorter than the previous one, barely reached her armpits.

As he stared, his eyes bulging and unblinking, the girl pulled on two zippers circling her breasts. To Joanna's amazement, the leather cups fell to the floor and revealed small but perfectly rounded breasts, each adorned by a pale, erect and pierced nipple. The girl wriggled her shoulders, making her breasts wobble and the rings dangle insolently in front of the man's face.

Only then did Joanna notice his hands were tied behind his back. Obediently, he stuck out his tongue. He knew what to do and not a word was exchanged. The woman continued twisting her shoulders, and guided the tip of her breasts over his mouth. She swayed in a slow, lascivious motion, using his lips and tongue to caress herself.

Unwittingly, Joanna echoed the motion, moving her shoulders in tempo with the girl's, as if she also had a man's mouth to abuse. She realised what she was doing and suddenly stopped. A bit embarrassed, she looked at Torima. He was looking at her and had plainly seen what she was doing, but he didn't say anything. He smiled, nodded, then turned his head to enjoy the show once again.

By now the girl had undone the *salary-man*'s trousers and pulled them down round his ankles. Under the hem of his white shirt his dick sprang out proudly, brushing against the tip of his tie.

An attendant brought a long slim chain. The woman wound it round her slave's prick, then slowly pulled on it so that it enveloped its length and rolled around it. The man shivered but didn't make any effort to pull away. The mistress and the slave held each other's gaze as she cruelly pulled on the chain. It unrolled from around his shaft at considerable speed, gliding along his skin seemingly without any friction.

Next, the girl passed the chain between the man's legs and tugged on it to make it glide back and forth. The man trembled at the knees and his erection seemed only the more prominent. Still standing in front of him, the girl undid a long zip between her legs and swiftly displayed all her flesh. Her mound was bare, closely shaven, and Joanna felt her mouth go dry at the sight of it. It also bore a tattoo of jasmine blossoms, but this one was a full bush instead of a lone sprig.

With wickedly slow movements of her hands and hips, the girl inserted the chain inside her tunnel, link by link. Joanna shuddered at the thought, as if she could feel it herself. Once the chain was almost completely in, the girl twirled the few links that were still protruding and writhed as the chain inside her moved in reply.

She moaned as she slowly pulled it out again. The metal links reappeared, glistening and covered with her dew. The girl let the chain bunch up in her hand and used it to rub her slit, panting incessantly as she pleasured herself.

The *salary-man* was sweating profusely, licking his lips constantly as he watched. The girl's back arched as she climaxed with a loud cry that echoed round the room. Grabbing the chain, still slick with her juices, she rubbed it against the man's mouth, smiling naughtily as she watched the expression of bliss which instantly appeared on his face.

As she was taller, she had to look down at him. The expression on her face was one of sheer contempt. Without a word, she let the chain drop to the floor, grabbed his buttocks in both hands and brought his hips towards hers.

Throwing her leg around his waist, she impaled herself upon his dick and encouraged him to thrust. Holding on to him for support, she cried again and again as pleasure swept her. She held him firmly, never allowing him to stop thrusting. The man was exhausted. At times he nearly lost his balance as he had to support the woman, who was standing on one leg. But obviously he had no desire to stop. At one point, however, the girl decided she had had enough. She pulled away, quickly donned her kimono and returned to the table. Just as before, two attendants appeared who pulled up the *salary-man*'s trousers and ushered him out of the room. And, just as before, the man kept looking behind him in silent protest, unwilling to leave having received so little satisfaction.

This man's exit was also followed by a round of applause. The session had been shorter than the previous one but just as intense. Joanna's palms were moist, and she could feel sweat trickling down her back. Her senses were ablaze, her heart pounding with excitement and her head spinning. Both scenes had been surreal, like a dream, yet there was no mistaking the effect they had on her.

After the applause died down, the lights were switched back on and more food was brought in. Conversations resumed as if nothing had happened. Still, no one deemed it necessary to talk to Joanna about what they had just witnessed.

As she settled back in her seat and tried to calm down, it took Joanna some time to realise that the new dishes were all phallic representations. There were mushrooms which had unmistakably been chosen for their shape, as well as long fat asparagus, whole cucumbers artistically carved and carrots whose rounded tips made them resemble a man's erect penis. The vegetables were arranged to stand upright, each accompanied by a couple of hard-boiled eggs at the base, and laid on a bed of parsley to mimic pubic hair.

Even the sake cups had been taken away and replaced by another set. These cups were shaped like a phallic mushroom with a hole pierced in the glans, allowing the liquid to be sucked. Joanna remembered having seen these in a souvenir shop, but she thought they were meant as a joke and never would have believed anyone actually used them. But, as she glanced round the table, she realised they were in fact *de rigueur* with her dining companions who thought nothing of sipping their drink in such a lewd fashion.

As they were brought in, the dishes were first presented to Joanna, who didn't quite know what was expected of her. The vast array of vegetables didn't look like a dish to eat, but rather an implement for her to put to other use. Looking round, she saw that the other guests were not paying much attention to her, so she refrained from taking anything. She wasn't hungry any more. Her stomach was comfortably full and the new dishes being brought in weren't all that appetising, so she didn't wish to sample them.

Her dinner companions, who had initially been so enthralled by the sight of her, wouldn't even glance in her direction any more, let alone talk to her. But Joanna no longer cared. In fact, she was quickly getting bored. After the excitement of the show, she was now in a lull, her heart having returned to its regular pace and her body numb after such a rush.

The only thing she was conscious of was the skilful massage still being administered by the two geishas. By now Joanna's body glowed with a faint sheen from the lotion applied everywhere. The girls' touch had turned into a more daring caress, their fingertips gently rubbing the inside of her legs and expertly flickering over her nipples to keep them erect. Joanna was aroused as a result. But rather than a violent hungry eagerness, what she felt was a mellow gently simmering heat.

Just as she settled back to continue relaxing, the lights went out and the gong resonated a third time. The door opened again and a large contraption was rolled in. Simultaneously, all eyes turned to look at Joanna.

She gasped in amazement as she watched a man being pushed forward on a mobile platform. Hanging by his wrists from some sort of rack, he was completely naked from the neck down. The only thing he wore was a leather mask which entirely covered his head save for his nose. There were zippers over his eyes and mouth.

Those over his eyes were fastened, whereas the one over his mouth had been pulled open. There, an enormous rubber ball, held in place by a chain fastened behind his head, gagged him.

Despite his precarious position, the man was already erect. Joanna didn't need to see his face to know he was yet another *salary-man*, brought into this temple of lust to serve as a willing slave. There was no way of knowing how he must have felt. Only his heaving chest betrayed his fear. For there was no way for him to know what would be coming next, but it was indeed very easy for Joanna to guess.

Torima turned to Joanna. 'Come,' he said as he held out his hand towards her. 'The time has come for you to show us what you are capable of.'

Joanna stood obediently, and silently let him lead her to the middle of the room. Her heart pounded. Now she understood why everyone was staring at her: it was her turn to supply the entertainment. The thought both excited and horrified her. She would never know what to do. Yet the prospect was so enticing that she was willing to go along with anything they would ask of her.

Torima took her kimono and went back to the table. Now Joanna stood naked in front of her audience. Curiously, she didn't feel shame but pride, and she was wickedly pleased by the notion of providing the entertainment. Between her legs, her juices had collected and were now bathing the inside of her thighs. Her blood rushed to her abdomen and rekindled the heat of her arousal. She held the power.

Again she stared at the man, only now noticing his ankles were in shackles. At his feet, a whole panoply of torture devices had been left for her: nipple clamps, a whip, a riding crop, a large leather dildo, a vibrator, a chain and even a few contraptions she had never seen before. Instruments of pain and pleasure. The pleasure would be hers, naturally, and the pain for this faceless slave obediently waiting for her to have her way with him.

What was she to do? Anything she fancied, obviously. Judging from what the two other women had done earlier, Joanna guessed she had to torture her slave, leave him wanting more, never give him satisfaction. In the process, she was allowed – even expected – to take as much pleasure as she could. The thought was overwhelmingly alluring.

Stepping on to the platform, she came closer to the man but didn't touch him. All the hair on his body had been removed, from his neck to his ankles. He was very muscular, trim and fit, and covered with jasmine-scented oil. Under his skin she could see his muscles play as he pulled in vain on his restraints. She set her hands flat on his chest and slowly let them glide down towards his abdomen. Surprised, the man fidgeted but didn't try to move away. Not that he could, even if he wanted to.

Joanna felt elated. Not only could he not see what was happening, but she realised he probably couldn't hear anything either. Several of his senses had been numbed. He couldn't see, hear, touch or taste her. All he had left was the possibility of feeling what she was going to do to him, but there would be no way for him to see it coming. Every caress, no matter how rough or gentle, would be a surprise.

He was all hers, to tease, to torture, to toy with. This was better than anything she'd ever experienced. There would be no need for naughty conversation or elaborate seduction schemes. This one was already hers. He was at her mercy.

She felt his skin, amazingly soft, break into goose bumps under her fingertips as they approached his hairless pubis. At that moment she would have liked to see his eyes, know that he wanted her, read the fear and desire on his face. Yet she knew that her treatment would be more efficient, both frightening and arousing, if he couldn't see her.

Her hand ran upwards again and settled on his chest. Underneath, she could feel his heart pounding prodigiously hard and fast. In contrast, Joanna was now strangely calm, even amused. Swiftly, she reached down and picked up the two small metal clamps. Using only her tongue, she worried his nipples until they stood stiff and swollen. The man moaned under her caresses but a second later he cried out in pain as Joanna fastened the clamps in place. She stood back, silently watching him reel from the surprise.

His dick throbbed in the air, the shaft shaken by small spasms and the purplish head shedding tiny tears of excitement. Joanna was disappointed by its smallness, but she quickly dismissed it. Tonight her pleasure would come mostly out of domination.

Picking up a rod made of thick braided straw, she briskly slapped his thighs, concentrating mostly on the inside and gradually moving dangerously close to his sac which hung limp. Soon the man's skin rose in welts and Joanna had mercy on him. There would be time for more later.

Slowly, she crept up behind him, treading carefully so he wouldn't know she was there. His legs were parted wide, causing his buttocks to spread, making the puckered ring of his anus plainly visible. As quietly as she could, Joanna grabbed the whip and gauged the girth of its handle. As her fingers closed round it, a naughty thought rose in her mind and she couldn't resist it. Parting her legs wide, she pushed the handle deep inside herself, letting it stretch her mercilessly, wetting it with her own juices.

Although at first she had only meant to lubricate it, its rough caress was so pleasant that for a moment she almost forgot the task at hand. She pushed it in and out a few times, attempting to quell the hunger of her flesh. She sighed loudly, but soon grew weary. Besides, she didn't want to keep her slave waiting any longer.

Without any warning, she inserted the handle deep

inside the man's arsehole. He bucked under the attack, letting out a strangled yelp, and thrust forward in a vain attempt to escape. The restraints held him back.

Joanna pushed the handle as deep as possible, then waited a moment to let her prey recover from the shock. Never letting go of the whip, she twirled it to tease the man's anus. She watched, mesmerised by the sight of his thighs tensing as she continued assaulting him.

Before long the man stopped reacting. No matter what Joanna did, his moans grew feeble and his body lethargic. Joanna was disappointed. She figured he probably needed constant, renewed and varied stimulation. Slowly, she pulled the handle out and let the whip fall to the floor. She stared at it as it lay limply, now no more threatening than the other implements, no longer of any use to her.

Her eyes paused on something unusual, a contraption made of several leather straps. As she picked it up, she realised it was a dildo with a harness, something for her to wear so she could pretend to be male, albeit from her slave's point of view.

She managed to put it on in a flash, amazed by how quickly she had worked out the proper way to wear it. Two large leather straps were worn over the shoulders, like braces, pressing against her swollen breasts and gently tickling her nipples. There was another strap, fastening round the waist and holding the large leather dildo right on top of her pubis. Finally, the last strap had to be slipped between her legs and fastened at the back. This was the part Joanna found by far the best feature of this weird contraption. Her flesh, now wet, swollen and unbelievably sensitive, was unceremoniously attacked by this last strap, providing her with exquisite torture every time she moved.

Her slave couldn't see what she was doing but, judging by the amount of sweat pearling on his back, he knew she would soon continue what she had started.

She positioned herself behind him, legs apart and

solidly planted on the ground. Parting his arse-cheeks with her thumbs, she penetrated him with a swift movement of the hips, just as roughly as she had inserted the handle of the whip.

And, just as before, the man bucked under the attack. His reaction only served to fuel Joanna's excitement. She began thrusting immediately, powerfully, taking him like a man, her hands forcefully holding on to his hips.

Soon, she forgot her surroundings. The strap between her legs rubbed sharply with every jab she gave and brought her closer to orgasm. The treatment she was inflicting on her willing slave, be it humiliating, painful, frightening or even pleasurable, brought her an immense high. She increased her momentum until she came, no longer willing to wait. She was the mistress, she was owed pleasure and she wanted it now.

Her belly was slick with the sweat trickling down the man's back. In her grasp, he was now as limp as a rag doll, having ceased to resist and simply given in to her desire. Yet now and again she could feel him twitch as she withdrew, pulling out until the tip of the dildo almost fell out of its target. But every time she pushed in again there was a certain point at which her slave's arousal seemed to be enhanced. Despite the cavalier treatment he had endured at her hands, he was still fully erect, perhaps even more excited than before.

But, as her orgasm swept her and subsided, Joanna was exhausted. Her position was not comfortable; her knees had grown weak and wobbly. She pulled out completely, got rid of the cumbersome gear and knelt on the platform.

Her flesh clenched faintly and, although her climax had been quite powerful, Joanna knew this would not be enough for her. She wanted more, as soon as possible. But she wouldn't allow the man any satisfaction.

Down on all fours, she slowly made her way around the platform until she came to kneel in front of him. Inches from her face, his stiff prick was offered to her contemplation. Although fully erect, it hadn't grown much bigger than its resting state. His balls had hardened and his sac was tighter. It wouldn't take much to make him come.

Just as she pondered what to do next, one of the attendants came up to her and handed her a velvet pouch. Joanna opened it and fished out something that was perhaps the most appropriate answer.

It was a penile sheath carved out of ivory: a latticed, hollow tube topped with a glans. Joanna immediately recognised its potential and couldn't wait to try it. Her exhaustion quickly vanished as she found herself fretfully excited.

She picked up one of the rings that lay amongst the panoply of torture devices and slipped it round the man's stiff rod. This way, she could be sure he would maintain his erection. The hollow tube fitted perfectly over the man's shaft, tight enough to stay in place but loose enough not to afford him any unwanted stimulation. She stared at it for a moment, admiring the contrast between the ivory lattice and the dark, purplish skin visible through the small, carved-out holes.

She rose to her feet and, just like the tall girl before her, threw her leg around her slave's waist. Her fingers quickly guided his covered phallus towards her eager flesh and she impaled herself upon it. Its intricate pattern tickled delightfully and she moaned loudly as it filled her.

The man didn't move. His face was just an inch from her chest, for she was much taller than him. However, blindfolded and gagged, there was nothing he could do to her. Holding on to his shoulders for balance, Joanna bounced on one leg, letting out a small cry each time the ivory-covered member penetrated and stretched her tunnel. She held on for as long as she could, feeling the muscles in her legs burn as a result of exhaustion and extreme arousal. For it was there, deep inside her thighs, that pleasure was born before it rose to her pelvis.

Her arousal peaked and she came again. This time there was no reaction from her slave. Pleasure was hers, and hers alone. It pierced her like a bolt, sending shock waves through her abdomen, rampaging through her entire body, making her toes curl and her hands clench violently around the man's shoulders.

Even more exhilarating was the notion that the man took absolutely no satisfaction. He was a faceless stranger and would remain so; a body offered for her sole benefit. She kept on going for a while, wanting more, much more. When she grew tired, she pulled away, changed legs, repositioned herself and resumed her bouncing. Pleasure rose and subsided, then gathered again in an endless series of orgasms. For the first time in many months, if not years, Joanna Wilson finally felt entirely satisfied.

She was hot, sore, out of breath, but filled with such contentment that she couldn't even believe it herself. Now the man held absolutely no interest for her. She had taken what she wanted; she had no need for him. She moved away, turned her back on him, and slowly walked back towards the table. She knew the attendants would take care of him. Her dinner companions broke into a loud round of applause. Just like the women who had performed before her, Joanna couldn't help blushing modestly.

'You did very well,' Torima finally said as he threw the kimono over her shoulders.

Joanna knelt at the table, next to him. To her surprise, most of the guests stood up and left the room. Dinner was over, and Joanna found herself alone with her host and two other Japanese men, one of whom was the stranger from the bar.

'We are very pleased with you,' Torima continued. Whereas up till now he had hardly said anything to her, now he seemed unwilling to remain silent. 'The men who come to us are looking for a very special woman, very domineering, very cruel. It's not always easy for us to recruit candidates who will so perfectly fulfil their fantasies of submission.'

So, this is what the place is all about, Joanna realised. Not that it was much of a surprise. The men who had been brought into the room tonight were looking for a kick. She knew that the average *salary-man* was used to his woman – be it girlfriend or wife – being docile and submissive. For them, the ultimate thrill lay in the exchange of roles.

'I never thought I had it in me,' she confessed in an exhausted voice. Now that her host seemed much more talkative, Joanna felt relief that she could finally pour her heart out. Whether she would tell Torima that she wasn't Stacey Parsons was another matter.

BLACK LACE NEW BOOKS

Published in July

THE BARBARIAN GEISHA
Charlotte Royal
£5.99

It's the 17th century and Annabel Smith is shipwrecked and washed up on the shores of feudal Japan. However, she is taken into the hands of the brutal warlord, Lord Nakano who is enchanted by her beauty. He takes her to his fortress home where the Mamma San is to teach Annabel the art of giving pleasure. Will she ever be accepted as a barbarian geisha?

ISBN 0 352 33267 0

DRAWN TOGETHER
Robyn Russell
£5.99

When Tanya Trevino, graphic artist, creates a sexy alter-ego in the form of Katrina Cortez, private investigator, she begins to wish her life were more like that of her comic-strip character's. Tanya's bank-manager boyfriend expects her to play the part of the executive girlfriend but she's not so keen. Especially as the gorgeous Stephen Sinclair with whom she works is giving her the green light. If only Tanya could be more like Katrina – a voluptuous wild woman!

ISBN 0 352 33269 7

Published in August

DRAMATIC AFFAIRS
Fredrica Alleyn
£5.99

Esther Reid is relaunching her career as a stage actress after being publicly dumped by her famous actor boyfriend. As the acting troupe she is with begins a national tour, she realises that she's harbouring powerful passions for more than one man in the company. Her admirers have hidden agendas, however, and she will have to keep her wits about her if she is to steal the show and satisfy her desires.

ISBN 0 352 33289 1

PANDORA'S BOX 3
ed. Kerri Sharp
£5.99

Anthologies of erotic writing are very popular. To coincide with the fifth anniversary of Black Lace, we're bringing out the third collection of extracts from the best of this revolutionary imprint. The diversity of the material, including four previously unpublished short stories, is a celebration of the female erotic imagination. This is unashamed sensual indulgence for women.

ISBN 0 352 33274 3

To be published in September

DARKER THAN LOVE
Kristina Lloyd
£5.99

It's 1875 and the morals of Queen Victoria have no hold over London's debauched elite. Young and naive Clarissa is eager to meet Lord Marldon, the man to whom she is betrothed. She knows he is handsome, dark and sophisticated. He is, in fact, depraved and louche with a taste for sexual excess.

ISBN 0 352 33279 4

RISKY BUSINESS
Lisette Allen
£5.99

Liam is a hard-working journalist fighting a battle against injustice. Rebecca is a spoilt rich girl used to having her own way. Their lives collide when they are thrown into a dangerous intimacy with each other. His rugged charm is about to turn her world upside down.

ISBN 0 352 33280 8

DARK OBSESSION
Fredrica Alleyn
£7.99

Ambitious young interior designer Annabel Moss is delighted when a new assignment takes her to the country estate of Lord and Lady Corbett-Wynne. The grandeur of the house and the impeccable family credentials are a façade for shockingly salacious practices. Lord James, Lady Marina, their family and their subservient staff maintain a veneer of respectability over some highly esoteric sexual practices and Annabel is drawn into a world of decadence where anything is allowed as long as a respectable appearance prevails.

ISBN 0 352 33281 6

If you would like a complete list of plot summaries of Black Lace titles, please fill out the questionnaire overleaf or send a stamped addressed envelope to:-

Black Lace, Thames Wharf Studios, Rainville Road, London W6 9HT

BLACK LACE

BLACK LACE BOOKLIST

All books are priced £4.99 unless another price is given.

Black Lace books with a contemporary setting

ODALISQUE	Fleur Reynolds ISBN 0 352 32887 8	☐
VIRTUOSO	Katrina Vincenzi ISBN 0 352 32907 6	☐
THE SILKEN CAGE	Sophie Danson ISBN 0 352 32928 9	☐
RIVER OF SECRETS	Saskia Hope & Georgia Angelis ISBN 0 352 32925 4	☐
SUMMER OF ENLIGHTENMENT	Cheryl Mildenhall ISBN 0 352 32937 8	☐
MOON OF DESIRE	Sophie Danson ISBN 0 352 32911 4	☐
A BOUQUET OF BLACK ORCHIDS	Roxanne Carr ISBN 0 352 32939 4	☐
THE TUTOR	Portia Da Costa ISBN 0 352 32946 7	☐
THE HOUSE IN NEW ORLEANS	Fleur Reynolds ISBN 0 352 32951 3	☐
WICKED WORK	Pamela Kyle ISBN 0 352 32958 0	☐
DREAM LOVER	Katrina Vincenzi ISBN 0 352 32956 4	☐
UNFINISHED BUSINESS	Sarah Hope-Walker ISBN 0 352 32983 1	☐
THE DEVIL INSIDE	Portia Da Costa ISBN 0 352 32993 9	☐
HEALING PASSION	Sylvie Ouellette ISBN 0 352 32998 X	☐
THE STALLION	Georgina Brown ISBN 0 352 33005 8	☐

------ ✂ ------------------

Please send me the books I have ticked above.

Name   ....

Address   ....

  ....

  ....

  .... Post Code ....

Send to: **Cash Sales, Thames Wharf Studios, Rainville Road, London W6 9HT**

US customers: for prices and details of how to order books for delivery by mail, call 1-800-805-1083.

Please enclose a cheque or postal order, made payable to **Virgin Publishing Ltd**, to the value of the books you have ordered plus postage and packing costs as follows:

UK and BFPO – £1.00 for the first book, 50p for each subsequent book.

Overseas (including Republic of Ireland) – £2.00 for the first book, £1.00 each subsequent book.

If you would prefer to pay by VISA or ACCESS/MASTERCARD, please write your card number and expiry date here:

....

Please allow up to 28 days for delivery.

Signature   ....

------ ✂ ------------------

WE NEED YOUR HELP . . .
to plan the future of women's erotic fiction –

– and no stamp required!

Yours are the only opinions that matter.

Black Lace is the first series of books devoted to erotic fiction by women for women.

We intend to keep providing the best-written, sexiest books you can buy. And we'd appreciate your help and valued opinion of the books so far. Tell us what you want to read.

THE BLACK LACE QUESTIONNAIRE

SECTION ONE: ABOUT YOU

1.1 Sex (*we presume you are female, but so as not to discriminate*)
    Are you?
    Male   ☐
    Female   ☐

1.2 Age
    under 21   ☐   21–30   ☐
    31–40   ☐   41–50   ☐
    51–60   ☐   over 60   ☐

1.3 At what age did you leave full-time education?
    still in education   ☐   16 or younger   ☐
    17–19   ☐   20 or older   ☐

1.4 Occupation _____

1.5 Annual household income _____

1.6 We are perfectly happy for you to remain anonymous;
but if you would like to receive information on other
publications available, please insert your name and
address

_____

_____

_____

_____

SECTION TWO: ABOUT BUYING BLACK LACE BOOKS

2.1 Where did you get this copy of *Pandora's Box 3*?
    Bought at chain book shop ☐
    Bought at independent book shop ☐
    Bought at supermarket ☐
    Bought at book exchange or used book shop ☐
    I borrowed it/found it ☐
    My partner bought it ☐

2.2 How did you find out about Black Lace books?
    I saw them in a shop ☐
    I saw them advertised in a magazine ☐
    I read about them in _____
    Other _____

2.3 Please tick the following statements you agree with:
    I would be less embarrassed about buying Black
    Lace books if the cover pictures were less explicit ☐
    I think that in general the pictures on Black
    Lace books are about right ☐
    I think Black Lace cover pictures should be as
    explicit as possible ☐

2.4 Would you read a Black Lace book in a public place – on
a train for instance?
    Yes ☐   No ☐

SECTION THREE: ABOUT THIS BLACK LACE BOOK

3.1 Do you think the sex content in this book is:
    Too much   ☐   About right   ☐
    Not enough   ☐

3.2 Do you think the writing style in this book is:
    Too unreal/escapist   ☐   About right   ☐
    Too down to earth   ☐

3.3 Do you think the story in this book is:
    Too complicated   ☐   About right   ☐
    Too boring/simple   ☐

3.4 Do you think the cover of this book is:
    Too explicit   ☐   About right   ☐
    Not explicit enough   ☐

Here's a space for any other comments:

SECTION FOUR: ABOUT OTHER BLACK LACE BOOKS

4.1 How many Black Lace books have you read?   ☐

4.2 If more than one, which one did you prefer?

4.3 Why?

SECTION FIVE: ABOUT YOUR IDEAL EROTIC NOVEL

We want to publish the books you want to read – so this is your chance to tell us exactly what your ideal erotic novel would be like.

5.1 Using a scale of 1 to 5 (1 = no interest at all, 5 = your ideal), please rate the following possible settings for an erotic novel:

Medieval/barbarian/sword 'n' sorcery ☐
Renaissance/Elizabethan/Restoration ☐
Victorian/Edwardian ☐
1920s & 1930s – the Jazz Age ☐
Present day ☐
Future/Science Fiction ☐

5.2 Using the same scale of 1 to 5, please rate the following themes you may find in an erotic novel:

Submissive male/dominant female ☐
Submissive female/dominant male ☐
Lesbianism ☐
Bondage/fetishism ☐
Romantic love ☐
Experimental sex e.g. anal/watersports/sex toys ☐
Gay male sex ☐
Group sex ☐

5.3 Using the same scale of 1 to 5, please rate the following styles in which an erotic novel could be written:

Realistic, down to earth, set in real life ☐
Escapist fantasy, but just about believable ☐
Completely unreal, impressionistic, dreamlike ☐

5.4 Would you prefer your ideal erotic novel to be written from the viewpoint of the main male characters or the main female characters?

Male ☐ Female ☐
Both ☐

5.5 What would your ideal Black Lace heroine be like? Tick
as many as you like:

Dominant	☐	Glamorous	☐
Extroverted	☐	Contemporary	☐
Independent	☐	Bisexual	☐
Adventurous	☐	Naïve	☐
Intellectual	☐	Introverted	☐
Professional	☐	Kinky	☐
Submissive	☐	Anything else?	☐
Ordinary	☐	_____	

5.6 What would your ideal male lead character be like?
Again, tick as many as you like:

Rugged	☐		
Athletic	☐	Caring	☐
Sophisticated	☐	Cruel	☐
Retiring	☐	Debonair	☐
Outdoor-type	☐	Naïve	☐
Executive-type	☐	Intellectual	☐
Ordinary	☐	Professional	☐
Kinky	☐	Romantic	☐
Hunky	☐		
Sexually dominant	☐	Anything else?	☐
Sexually submissive	☐	_____	

5.7 Is there one particular setting or subject matter that your
ideal erotic novel would contain?

_____

SECTION SIX: LAST WORDS

6.1 What do you like best about Black Lace books?

_____

6.2 What do you most dislike about Black Lace books?

_____

6.3 In what way, if any, would you like to change Black Lace
covers?

_____

6.4 Here's a space for any other comments:

_____

_____

_____

_____

_____

Thank you for completing this questionnaire. Now tear it out of the book – carefully! – put it in an envelope and send it to:

> **Black Lace**
> **FREEPOST**
> **London**
> **W10 5BR**

No stamp is required if you are resident in the U.K.